JACARA

THE ANNIVERSARY EDITION OF
HERMAN CHARLES BOSMAN

*Planning began in late 1997 – the
fiftieth anniversary of Bosman's first
collection in book form,* Mafeking Road *–
to re-edit his works in their original,
unabridged and uncensored texts.
The project should be completed by
2005 – the centenary of his birth.*

GENERAL EDITORS:
STEPHEN GRAY AND CRAIG MACKENZIE

Already published in this edition:
MAFEKING ROAD AND OTHER STORIES
WILLEMSDORP
COLD STONE JUG
IDLE TALK: VOORKAMER STORIES (I)
OLD TRANSVAAL STORIES

Herman Charles Bosman

JACARANDA IN THE NIGHT

The Anniversary Edition

Edited by Stephen Gray

HUMAN & ROUSSEAU
Cape Town Pretoria Johannesburg

Copyright © 2000 by The estate of Herman Charles Bosman
First published by Human & Rousseau in 1980
Anniversary edition published in 2000 by Human & Rousseau (Pty) Ltd
Design Centre, 179 Loop Street, Cape Town

Back cover photograph of Herman Charles Bosman in Johannesburg,
by an unknown street photographer, courtesy of the Harry Ransom Humanities Research Center.
Design and typeset in 11 on 13 pt Times by ALINEA STUDIO, Cape Town
Printed and bound by NBD
Drukkery Street, Goodwood, Western Cape

ISBN 0 7981 4084 4

No part of this book may be reproduced or transmitted in any form or by any means,
electronic or mechanical or by photocopying, recording or microfilming, or stored in any
retrieval system, without the written permission of the publisher

JACARANDA IN THE NIGHT, the novel, is the first book by Herman Charles Bosman (1905-51), issued by his publisher, the APB Bookstore, in early 1947. As Bosman was then resident in Johannesburg, we may assume that he had a full hand in preparing and proofing the text, so that it appeared entirely as he intended it to be. It was greeted as a major contribution from the post-war school of writers who were creating a new South African literature in the hard realist mode.

As the introduction here shows in a wealth of new detail, *Jacaranda in the Night* is based on Bosman's 1943 experience as the editor of *The Zoutpansberg Review and Mining Journal* in Pietersburg, from which the setting of his typical Northern Transvaal dorp is drawn, and substantially from his earlier career as a teacher in the Transvaal Education Department. This material he would revisit in his final masterpiece, *Willemsdorp*.

The last sequence set in the Pretoria prison-yard leads into his next work for APB, his classic *Cold Stone Jug* of two years later.

Contents

Introduction 9
Jacaranda in the Night 23
Notes on the Text 213

Introduction

THE essential soul of a culture is that it must be indigenous. Its roots must be deeply entangled with the dark purple of the raw tissue of the life that is at hand. It must start off with depth. And it can't go deep enough. Afterwards it can be enriched with the opulent splendours of other cultures. But it must start off alone, like every individual thing is born into the world alone... The place for South African literature to take root is here...

Thus Herman Charles Bosman (in "An Indigenous South African Culture is Unfolding" in *The South African Opinion* in April, 1944), nailing his colours to the mast at the time he was preparing to write this work.

Here is another example (from "The Dorps of South Africa" in *The South African Opinion* in July, 1945):

And a dorp is unquestionably the best place in which to study [this] life at close hand. Because it is all in slow motion, you don't miss the significant details. And you get a complete picture, circumscribed by that frame which cuts off the village from the rest of the world.

Then again (in the same piece):

There was the veld and there was John Calvin. And the Voortrekkers assumed, without enquiry, that the truths that the veld taught them of life were one with the rigidities of sectarian doctrine, as embodied in the more starless conceptions of predestination and original sin. The spirit of the veld was large. Calvin's, not quite so large.

Hence his setting of 'Kalvyn' in this, his first attempt to produce a work focusing exclusively on South Africa's own platteland.

The work in question was to be *Jacaranda in the Night*, the first of three novels written and completed over 1947-51, the last, very productive half-decade of Bosman's life. It was followed two years later by *Cold Stone Jug* and by *Willemsdorp* (first published posthumously in 1977), both of which have already appeared in this anniversary edition of his works.

Three times previously he had commenced work in the novel form: in the early 1930s with *Johannesburg Christmas Eve* and with *Louis Wassenaar* (both first published only in 1986), and then while in London mid-decade with *Leader of Gunmen* (the flavour of which is given in excerpts in the introduction to *Cold Stone Jug*). For various reasons none of these opening attempts was ever completed. A possible incentive for Bosman now to change the locale of his work was that his brother, Pierre, had already made an attempt on *Jacaranda*-type material in his serial written for *The Touleier* which, in the first issue of December, 1930, began with the immortal words: "Mara is a small village stuck somewhere in the Northern Transvaal stretches of sand-hills and mimosas..."

So *Jacaranda in the Night* turns out to be his first published book-length work. This was rapidly followed by his second – the collection of short stories which he put together later in the same year as *Mafeking Road* for the CNA's Dassie Books. In his lifetime he would see only one further book into print – the *Cold Stone Jug* of 1949, produced by APB, the same publisher which had courageously launched him with this text.

The years of Bosman's life leading up to the publication of *Jacaranda in the Night* are worth tracing in some detail for the light they shed on his first major text. Finding more than freelance work as a journalist in South Africa after his repatriation from Europe early in the Second World War could not have been easy; while the Springboks fought for liberty up north, it was petrol- and paper-rationing on the home front. By January, 1943, Bosman was resident in Pietersburg in the Northern Transvaal (living rather scandalously together with his second wife, Ella, and his wife-to-be, Helena); in March that year he became employed as the editor of the town's venerable *Zoutpansberg Review and Mining Journal* – presumably the original of the newspaper referred to only in passing as the "rather obscure" weekly here.

Highlights of his stint on *The Zoutpansberg Review* were the mid-year South African general election, which saw General Smuts ("that sincere friend of the people and one of the great statesmen of the age", to quote an editorial of his on 8 June) returned to power with a landslide victory – although the United Party candidate for the Pietersburg whites, Frederik van Zyl Slabbert, was in fact narrowly defeated by the Nationalist one, the longstanding Tom Naudé – and the campaign visits of his old classmate from Jeppe High School days, the Communist lawyer and Senator, Hyman Basner, who represented the surrounding constituency of some 3½ million black people. Bosman records the fall of Mussolini, expressing his detestation of Fascism and all dictatorships; deplores rising food prices and the Native Trust policy which he sees reduces tribal smallholders to starvation; decries the rise in university fees which he predicts will make tertiary education more elitist; advocates that narrow language allegiances be broken down through introducing dual-language schools in favour of a larger South African cosmopolitanism; welcomes another spring and the opening of the new luxury Astra Cinema showing *Mrs Miniver*; encourages 'Anne' of the Women's Page in Town and Country; advertises not only for immunised mules, but for new railway schedules and Wood's Great Peppermint Cure, while condemning the measled cattle in the abattoir.

Pietersburg itself was not exactly a backwater. Founded by the burghers who first colonised the Schoemansdal area under Hendrik Potgieter in 1847, it had been the last seat of Boer government during the Second Anglo-Boer War. Thereafter extensively occupied by Britishers, by 1929 with the opening of Beit Bridge over into Southern Rhodesia it became a welcome stopover on the Great North Road. In his paper's Social and Personal column, Bosman routinely listed all the particulars of the register at the Grand Hotel (here clearly Mrs Manning's brandy drinking Northern Hotel). The mining of corundum, that adamantine spar or aluminium oxide second only to the diamond in hardness, flourished there during the war and in 1943 Hans Merensky discovered the world's largest chrome deposit nearby.

The Bosmans moved from 29, Hans van Rensburg Street, down the road from the Pietersburg Club, to 68, Plein Street, where to this day the garden of their modest bungalow, with its fine stoep and pressed steel ceilings, is sheltered by the jacarandas the present owners swear Bosman planted himself personally. (Two of them – the third was cut down by a previous householder, the academic Michael Rice.) Picnics out at the precipitous Wondergat near Princess Alice's lands, listening to H. G. Wells and J. B. Priestley on the radio, selling his proprietor, Mr Marcus's famous dahlia seeds (large, miniature and pompom) in the *Review* shop in aid of War Funds, burying the remains of the fallen,

Bosman's home, Pietersburg, 1976 (photo: S. Gray)

warding off Helena's boss, Willie Snyman, headmaster of the Pietersburg Afrikaans-medium Laerskool and for no less than five terms in succession the local mayor (whom Louis Changuion in his 1986 history of Pietersburg is convinced is the inspiration for the notorious Sybrand van Aswegen here)... such were the daily events on which Bosman was able to draw.

Pietersburg even provided a rival local colourist, Mrs Nancy Courtney Acutt, who followed C. R. Prance in contributing what she called kaleidoscopic portraits of the descendants of Voortrekker and Settler alike, of Native life and Mission folk, to Johannesburg's *The Forum* and *The Star*; indeed, later Bosman would swipe one of her bright ideas for organising life out in 'the Bush' about a distant postmaster when he devised his own Voorkamer stories about Jurie Steyn's Post Office. Sarah Gertrude Millin would also set her 1950 masterpiece here – *King of the Bastards*, the story told by the coloured Buysvolk of their rouseabout founder.

Of the cultural loss caused by the war Bosman wrote in one of his frank pieces ("The Soul of the People" on 2 April):

In the tragic tale of human suffering forming the background of this war, there is another victim, whose voice is but seldom heard in protest.

From one point of view, of course, it is only to be expected that amid the horrors that are perpetrated almost daily (and with a foulness unparalleled in the history of mankind), not much commiseration can be spared for the fate that has overtaken the culture of the nations.

Yet it is, after all, by the things of the spirit that we live... We need the gentleness of peace in which to paint our pictures and to write our poems... Where there is no vision the people perish...

It was to counter that holocaust-born "rotting of inner values" that *Jacaranda in the Night* would be written.

The next year Bosman and his entourage moved to Johannesburg, where he found sympathetic employment on Bernard Sachs's revived *South African Opinion*, variously as its literary editor, columnist and reviewer. Together with many short stories, almost all the essays and cultural commentary included by Lionel Abrahams in *A Cask of Jerepigo* (1957) date from here. Two examples are quoted above, but in many other pieces he also showed himself to be a staunch promoter of what willy-nilly became the post-war revival of South African literature. In *South African Opinion* and in the pages of *Trek*, to which Bosman moved when they combined in 1947, the message was clear: write local, build anew.

In 1946, to give an example, he was involved as an adjudicator for Sarel Marais, the publisher of Johannesburg's APB Bookstore, of a Prize Novel Competition which Bosman went out of his way to publicise. As he reported in the July number of *The S. A. Opinion*,

I regard this local development in the book-publishing trade as an essential preliminary to the creation of an authentic South African (English) literature. And for their pioneering work in this field I feel that APB must be given the fullest possible credit.

Daphne Rooke was a winner with *The Sea Hath Bounds*, soon published by APB. The co-winner was one Elizabeth Daggerleaves (actually Elizabeth Charlotte Webster, the late sister of Mary Morison Webster and once a contributor to the old *Sjambok*) with *Expiring Frog*, a merry burble about the seduction of a miracle-working Anglo-Catholic nun at the Schreiner Street Refuge for Fallen Women, which partly thanks to Bosman's logrolling became a runaway bestseller; repackaged as *Ceremony of Innocence* it did well in the United States thereafter. One of the contestants was Bosman's first wife, Vera Sawyer, with a novel called *Frustration*. The winners were soon joined by the likes of Victor Pohl (who later became a Faber and Faber author) and C. M. van den Heever in a translation by T. J. Haarhoff of his idyll, *Somer*, as *Harvest Home*, the subject matter of which is containing the convict in our midst. Other authors published by APB included Eugène Marais (Afrikaans short stories) and the perennial Iris Vaughan. Nonfiction titles emanating from 75, Loveday Street, included ones like *Fundamentals of Reconstruction* and the early annuals of *The S. A. Bloodstock Breeders' Review*. Thus was the programme launched; in October, 1947, Bosman wrote an admiring profile of Marais for *Trek*, in which he noted:

> We are at this late date in the history of this country beginning with the creation, through the medium of the English language, of a literature that is fundamentally and intrinsically our own.

Such activities obviously motivated Bosman, for on 15 October, 1946, he wrote to his cousin Zita, "I'm having a novel coming out shortly and am in a hell of a state. I've had to wait a quarter of a century for this. I can't stand the strain of waiting."

If Bosman's *Jacaranda in the Night* was not APB's Johannesburg novel the critics of the new generation were calling for –

> In Johannesburg the garish tempo of living does not provide enough time to stand and stare. The big novel which this city deserves and demands has not yet been written. We have a roaring, husky a-moral panorama. And it shouts to high heaven for satire

(thus Oliver Walker in *Trek*, in September, 1947) – at least its last pages closed in on the big city of post-war drifters. Helena (by now the third and last Mrs H. C. Bosman) and Herman threw a party in celebration of its publication, taking pleasure in inviting friends to their

Cover of the first edition, 1947

residence at 16, Sovereign Street, Kensington – a property surrounded by a dairy farm on the rocky eastern boundary of the Johannesburg municipal area – for the afternoon of Saturday 18th January, 1947.

The love story of Hannah Theron and Herklaas Huysmans, by no less than one Herman C. Bosman, was presented like the sinful Hollywood film it so resembled. The poster-like cover featured the suggestive face of a dreamy, shiny-lipped starlet with huge eyebrows in a bouquet of blossoms turning into stars. The rather cursory blurb read as follows:

> Herman C. Bosman has written a large number of stories with a South African setting over a period of more than a dozen years, and several of these stories have been translated and published locally under various titles.
> *Jacaranda in the Night* is a study of the stress and emotional compulsions pervading the inner lives of the inhabitants of a small Transvaal town, in striking contrast to the air of tranquillity that dorp life wears on the outside.
> It is a strong story, with the lusts and conflicts of the characters

closely woven into the dark fabric of nature's seasonal changes. The book is described as representing a significant contribution to contemporary South African literature.

But the reception accorded *Jacaranda* in the press expressed no such opinion: in a word, the launch was disappointing. The Johannesburg *Sunday Express* (on which Bosman was soon to work as a subeditor) had recently appointed to the book-page a 'British Writer Resident in South Africa' (presumably Francis Brett Young) who, as 'Gustator', chose to lavish fulsome praise on new lives of Frederick the Great and the Duke of Wellington, while refusing to review any indigenous work. If there was a local boy making good (on 30 March), it was Durban-born Noël Langley in London, author of the screenplay *Deep End*, written for Trevor Howard, with the new play *Edward their Son*, a new novel *Music of the Heart* and a revival of the stage version of his *Cage Me a Peacock* (and always with the *Wizard of Oz* movie to fall back on).

The *Cape Argus* acknowledged receipt of a review copy of *Jacaranda in the Night* on Saturday 8th February, while reporting on the activities of the Government Board of Censors during the previous year – of 2 377 films viewed, 2 101 were allowed to be released (150 of those not to be shown to Natives), with *Tiger Woman* being banned for its scenes of criminality and street fighting, *The Mummy's Curse* for its treatment of death and religious convictions and *Joe Louis's Greatest Fights* for including a pugilistic encounter between a European and a non-European. Cape author Uys Krige received favourable coverage for his fine prisoner-of-war memoir, *The Way Out*. If there was another South African making good, it was the novelist David Rame (David Divine), despatched from London by the Kemsley group of newspapers to cover the Royal Visit from the White Train itself, filing delectable accounts of how Princess Elizabeth and her sister took time off from what became their Triumphal Tour to trot at dawn on horseback across the wide-open Free State, accompanied by their craggy father, King George VI. The *Cape Times* received its copy on Saturday 8th March, but also passed up the opportunity to review it, carrying rather in its Weekend Magazine a three-page spread by Brett Young again on "The True Meaning of Monarchy." Their only item devoted to South African writing over the next months would be a notice of the passing of the much respected Dr C. Louis Leipoldt (in April).

In Johannesburg both *Die Transvaler* and *Die Vaderland* overlooked

Bosman's debut (but then they utterly ignored the presence of any prancing British royals as well). Only *The Rand Daily Mail* had a go at *Jacaranda*, in the person of its book-page editor, Mary Morison Webster herself. Despite being a dear friend of Bosman, she was to make no less than *three* attempts (such was the scarcity of reviewers!) to sink the work without trace. Her first was in the *Mail* of 8 February:

> There is some fine writing in *Jacaranda in the Night*, though the author finally fails to make the most of his gifts and material... Over his heroine, Hannah Theron, Mr Bosman tends at times to become sentimental and even lachrymose... His villain, Bert Parsons, builder and rake, is, in contrast, magnificently drawn...

Then in *The Sunday Times* (on 16 March, 1947):

> Unfortunately he too often drops the reins and allows the steed of his imagination to run amok in prairies of metaphors and lush-sounding phrases.
> The chief criticism which will be aimed at this book is that it presents sordidness almost unrelieved. Too many books published in this country (and out of it) emphasise drinking, crime and passion without the antidote of some goodness. Life is not an unrelieved licentiousness, and not every person is neurotic. The censor will have to be more alert...

(The same page carries an article by Roy Campbell about the success rate of South African writers who "Gravitate Oversea": Langley and William Plomer, Stuart Cloete, F. T. Prince and Charles Madge, in the spoor of Olive Schreiner, Pauline Smith and Millin who had all achieved distinction in London first. But Campbell conceded that he would now through the BBC support the growth of an indigenous school, which he proceeded to do by broadcasting several Bosman stories.)

The Webster wipe-out of *Jacaranda* concluded some years later in Volume 14 of the *Standard Encyclopedia* where it is described by her as both "crude" and "shrewd"; yet in her final view all it amounts to is an exposure of the "anomalies in the procedures of the Education Department" (p. 353).

On the side of the affronted was also C. W. Hudson (in the bilingual *Noord en Suid* of 15 March, 1947):

An unusual novel... A good deal of intellectual reflection and psychological insight is pleasing to the more profound reader whilst the story itself is certainly told very easily and interestingly, although one cannot be called prude for objecting against certain motifs in the plot, one may even go so far as to call some of the incidents described as verging on the border of pornography.

A pro-*Jacaranda* faction was gathering, however. In *The South African Jewish Times* Edgar Bernstein kept out of the rumpus by ducking reviewing *Jacaranda* itself, possibly out of squeamishness, but none the less praising Bosman's Jewish-friendly writing in general to the skies (in "H. C. Bosman and his Work" on 21 March, 1947). In *The South African Opinion* of April, 1947, Edward Davis, the UNISA lecturer, weighed in with a lengthy review which he obviously hoped would turn the tide. It began: "Let me say at once that this is a good book, the product of a rich spirit. And now to demonstrate... " His colleague, the Scottish poet F. D. Sinclair, followed up in *Trek* in a pair of articles devoted to 'Post-War Literature in South Africa' (over June-July, 1950), placing Bosman centrally in the new grouping, which now had expanded to include young Doris Lessing, Nadine Gordimer, Ezekiel Mphahlele, Peter Abrahams and so on, all notably publishing in those very same pages. Charles Eglington (in the *Trek* of October, 1951), refusing to be patronised by tired old has-beens, slammed his case home when he reported:

> It is, of course, true that our writers have no local audience [as yet]. They must compete with the constant flow of English and American books, and their market is overseas. They do reach South Africa via England or America. It is true, too, that the standard of criticism here is very low... But from a very small number of English-speaking people – a million at most, probably – a not discreditable number of poets, prose-writers and even critics are emerging. They know the prospect before them and are applying themselves to their work...

In the long term, however, the indigenous South African literature of the 1940s and 50s did not become very entrenched. In Martin Tucker's survey of 1967, *Africa in Modern Literature*, due attention was paid to the emerging alignment of white and black writers against early apartheid but, although it would have been of interest to trace satires of segregation back to Union days, Bosman's pioneering work is not mentioned. Likewise in John Povey's chapter on South African literature in Bruce King's *Literatures of the World in English* of 1974. In the same year the Johannesburg scholar based in Canada, Rowland Smith, in his influential paper on the "Johannesburg 'Genre'", continued to leave Bosman and that entire post-war formative group out, preferring to give space to newer writers (like Dan Jacobson and Jillian Becker) who, by passing the old test of overseas recognition, were making themselves eligible to enter the ranks. Partly to redress this snobbish imbalance the Canadian researcher C. J. Fox answered back with his "The Smile that Stings: Herman Bosman of South Africa" (in *The Antigonish Review* of Summer, 1984), advocating the view that Bosman should not be erased, but that indeed he did hold a special interest, particularly for readers familiar with post-colonial bilingual societies (nevertheless he rated *Jacaranda* as early and "disastrous").

By 1980, when Bosman's new publisher, Cape Town-based Human & Rousseau, relaunched *Jacaranda in the Night* as their ninth title of his, bringing their uniform edition of his work to completion on the seventy-fifth anniversary of his birth, the time was ripe for reassessment. This "story of a South African dorp and its people with their idiosyncracies", as it was now described, began to draw some serious consideration.

The tribute of the American-based Johannesburger, Rose Moss (in *World Literature Today* in the Winter number of 1981) is a good example, where the work's stridencies and overwriting are taken in her stride as typically Lawrentian. On 6 March, 1980, on *Die Burger*'s book-page, edited by Kerneels Breytenbach, Hennie Aucamp astutely set the tone of the revaluation:

> In retrospect *Jacaranda* acquires something which it could never have had in its own day, 'a sense of period.' The 1940s strike you on every page, even from the name of that brown 'pegamoid' covering on those chairs in the Northern Hotel. One is even sorely tempted to go back for the source of some of his melodramatic effects to the films of the period, those moral movies starring 'tainted' women (Joan Crawford, Bette Davis) which were so wildly popular... [My translation]

André Brink helped by claiming Bosman as an early dissident figure (in his *Mapmakers: Writing in a State of Siege* of 1983), doubtless thanks to scathing passages like his Baas/Boy comments here, although Brink's description of Bosman as "an Afrikaner writing exclusively in English" was inaccurate on two counts (he was English-speaking, as *Jacaranda* clearly shows in its almost total lack of borrowings from Afrikaans, and he did write in both languages).

In 1985 the American scholar, Emily Buchanan, made the first in-depth critical study of *Jacaranda*, using the resources of the Bosman collection at the Harry Ransom Humanities Research Center at the University of Texas at Austin (where the *Willemsdorp* typescripts had long been held), for ever redeeming the work from obscurity and neglect. From the American tradition of novel-writing Buchanan knew exactly how important it had always been, especially for Southern writers, to use the *Jacaranda*-type formula: unattached city folk drift into hick, backwater town, interact, fail to adjust themselves to seasonal rhythms, yet find one another...

Inevitably, with *Jacaranda* reappearing in 1980 – by which time Bosman had at last become South Africa's topselling English-language author – speculation was going to run rife as to how revealingly 'autobiographical' it all really was. By then Valerie Rosenberg's scandalous biography was well known, his *Cold Stone Jug* with its blurred line between fact and fiction was firmly established and even the censored *Willemsdorp*, with its obvious author-surrogate – the UP-supporting, drunken and dissolute Charlie Hendricks, editor of that *Northern Transvaal News* – was available for illuminating comparison.

Certainly the hints Bosman left in his texts were tantalising. For example, the bony and cadaverous *Her*klaas Huys*mans* looks teasingly like being the repressed intellectual version of *Her*man Charles Bosman. Indeed, Bosman would use him again – in "My Eerste Liefde" (in *On Parade* on 26 November, 1948) as the lone schoolmaster at Heimweeberg Farm School in the 1920s who spoils the maiden with whom Oom Schalk Lourens's son is so hopefully in love; and also in 1949 Three-Stroke-Seven-Eight-Huysmans recurs in *Cold Stone Jug*, no longer as a lawyer or a teacher, but as the unregenerate travelling salesman who specialises in seducing under-age farm girls with sweeties.

A further clue is that Bosman married his first wife, Vera, under another of his heteronyms: Herbert Charles Boswell, and for years she knew him as no other than her 'Bertie.' Is brawny Bert Parsons, the swaggering, earthy ladykiller of Kalvyn (or more correctly, Calvyn), then not an alternative version of the author, so that the triangular rivalry between him and Herklaas, with Hannah Theron as trophy, illustrates the classic Freudian id/ego/superego tussle for dominance?

Then there is Hannah herself, replayed as Lena Cordier in *Willemsdorp* – who does (or does not) become pregnant out of wedlock, is forced to seek refuge in Johannesburg as a supply teacher (at Damelin College cram school, like the third Mrs Bosman)... Obviously the prime suspect as her original was Bosman's surviving widow, by then living in retirement as Mrs Helena Lake. The book critic Madeleine van Biljon tracked her down for the occasion (see *The Sunday Times* of 6 April, 1980), hoping perhaps for some revelatory indiscretion. With great dignity Mrs Lake proceeded to fend off any suggestion that real-life gossip-stories would offer a magic key to unlock Bosman's genius. As keeper of his flame, while stressing how loving their eight years of domestic cosiness had proved to be, she tactfully referred her investigator back to the works themselves, works which must speak for themselves.

Surely *Jacaranda in the Night* was Bosman's attempt to write a particular kind of novel in which a chain reaction of unreleased sexual passions and wounded masculinities would lead to the bad-taste farce of no less than murder with a milk bottle. In this respect the literary reference in the Huysmans link should not be overlooked: Joris-Karl Huysmans was of course the Parisian author who cherished the Dutch name of his ancestors. He wrote in reaction to the dominant Naturalist movement of authors like Emile Zola, whom he felt kept portraying average characters in precisely described settings, endlessly repeated and predestined always to be moving on the same spot. With *Against Nature* of 1884, Huysmans made his reply with the so-called 'decadent' novel – almost plotless, over-descriptive, relishing obscure detail, narcissistic, often sadistic and always deeply sensual. His topic was the decay of literature as such and the enervation of old ideals as they collapsed into the scandals of the nineteenth-century fin-de-siecle. The correlation with the mood of Bosman's post-war Johannesburg world is striking.

But in his portrait of Hannah Theron, it should also be mentioned, he was for the first time in the world of South African letters attempting to depict an independent spirited woman, quite capable of making her own life-decisions. Hannah is, in effect, the Villon-loving, Poe-imitating Bosman's Salome, the one who releases all of the morbid psychology of his strange soul. 'Decadent' writing also meant capturing not the surface of life, but its essence, after all. At least *Jacaranda in the Night* should be seen as a noble experiment with interesting antecedents, conducted pressingly in the last days of General Smuts's disintegrating state.

To be sure, it must also be admitted that *Jacaranda in the Night* was hurried in composition, its neat four-part, twelve-chapter scheme abandoned halfway and its ending scamped. The pages needed thorough tweaking into consecutive paragraphs, with commas sprinkled in on some reliable system. Instead of taking the opportunity of drawing earlier themes like that of inter-class violence, of corruption in the Town Hall and on building sites, of sex for favours and of the abuse of power in the schoolroom all into one concluding trial scene, Bosman seems to have just left all that on hold while he made his quick escape from Kalvyn. Perhaps at the time he grasped the potential of such material only "smokily" – the last word of the novel, singly placed (and inexplicably gone missing in the 1980 printing).

But at all events, he would soon return down Voortrekker Street to face Kalvyn once more, only to find the much more comprehensive Willemsdorp there, for the novel *Willemsdorp* is a rare instance of a major writer taking stock of an earlier work in order to get it right once and for all. While *Willemsdorp* turned out to be his masterpiece, *Jacaranda in the Night* was the depth-sample without which the panorama would not have cleared.

Stephen Gray
Johannesburg, 2000

Chapter One

1

KALVYN is a small town in the Northern Transvaal. You can speak of it either as a town or village. There is only one made street. There is a hotel and a couple of stores and a bioscope. There is a mill for the extraction of base minerals, mined at various spots in the surrounding bush. A post office, a couple of banks and administrative buildings, including a recently erected town hall. The social and recreative amenities of the town include a golf course, a bowling green, a swimming bath and a football field. There is also the exclusive Kalvyn Club. And in the town hall, dances are held almost every Saturday – organised by local bodies ranging from the Women's Agricultural Union to the Voortrekkers and Boy Scouts.

Kalvyn is also by way of being an agricultural centre. And in accordance with the Transvaal Education Department's new policy of centralisation children from the farms in the district come to Kalvyn for their education, and are accommodated as boarders in a number of school hostels.

The above list constitutes practically the sum of the commercial and cultural and industrial enterprises centred around Kalvyn. There is a garage, of course, and for a place of its size Kalvyn is well provided with churches, including two Dutch Reformed churches and an Anglican and a Methodist church. There are also two cafés and a small printing works, whence a rather obscure newspaper is issued weekly.

For as many miles as you like to think of, and on all sides, Kalvyn is surrounded by veld. To the north and east and west are the shrubbery and low woods of the Bushveld. Southwards extends the flat open country that is the Transvaal Highveld. Kalvyn is peculiarly situated, in a kind of midway position, near the meeting place of the Bushveld and the Highveld.

Life in Kalvyn flows smoothly and evenly, like the water in the Wilgespruit, which cuts off the lower end of the town from the golf course. On the surface, the lives of the people of Kalvyn are disturbed only by the ripplings of a sudden wind, which always dies down towards the sunset. On the surface their lives are as placid as the waters of the Wilgespruit when it has passed under the North Bridge and flows smoothly and gently in the shade of the overhanging willows. But there are undercurrents to the life of Kalvyn's inhabitants that are not present in Wilgespruit's depths and shallows.

Behind the facade of a small town with regular if unmade streets, with houses set far apart and with a number of old-fashioned, weather-beaten Government buildings existing side by side with a modern Town Hall and an up-to-date hotel; behind the slow pace that everyday life pursues, a restfulness verging almost on somnolence, there is a strong and gusty state of being, like another kind of existence altogether. It is a dark, strong life, heavily interwoven with earthy feeling. It is a life that is thick with the tides surging turgidly within the flesh.

The people who live in Kalvyn are but one step removed from the black soil. If the roots fastening them to the damp earth are not visible to the naked eye, it is only that all roots are like that, thrusting their sightless way into the deep underground, deaf and inward, in serfdom's obedience to an unknown will and unquestioned urge.

The Voortrekkers, when they founded their settlement on the Wilgespruit, the wheels of their wagons coming to rest at that place where the rolling plains of the open Highveld began to yield to the bush country that stretched infinitely far to the north, named the beginnings of this new hamlet after John Calvin, the Reformation leader, in whose sombre spirit they found that hard and unrelenting thing which they took to be the way of life. In their stubborn faith, heavily brooding on the naked reality of mating and giving birth, and on the stark fact of death, they assumed, without thinking, that the truths that the veld taught them of life were one with Calvin's starless doctrines.

Their ponderings were on the Bible. In their spirits was a dark mysticism that was yet (although they would never know it) not far removed from romance. If their thoughts moved heavily in the laws of the Old Testament, slowly, with a lumbering ungainliness, in the way that their ox-wagons made passage through the gramadoelas, there were nevertheless times when their ruminations would be massively illuminated, as though by strange fires. And the results would be equally strange.

And so in the souls of those people who lived in Kalvyn, whether they were descendants of the Voortrekkers or they had come to that place afterwards, there was that conflict that was a deep part of their heritage. And it was a conflict that had not been created entirely out of extrovert stress, out of wars and a struggling against the elemental forces. There was that frustration, also, born of the eternal strife within.

It was almost as though there had been some reason for that queer mischance whereby the settlement of Kalvyn had not been spelt in accordance with correct orthography, almost as though it had come about through some inner understanding of the fact that the lore of the veld was not quite the same thing as Calvin's teachings.

The religious faith of the Voortrekkers was as narrow as the veld was large. And if in their minds they accepted the rigidities of sectarian truths as embodied in the gloomier conceptions of predestination and original sin, in their blood there was the other teaching of the veld, which they could not reject easily. The beginning of a dark inward conflict.

2

And still, in Kalvyn, town or village, whichever you choose to call it, the people are not far removed from the soil. If the changes that take place in the seasons – the spring succeeding the winter and the summer thickening into a heavy ripeness – do not lay overt demands of the soil on the inhabitants of Kalvyn in terms of seed-times and harvests, at the same time there is a sullen conforming on the part of the people to those dark tides at whose flow the jacarandas purple overhead and at whose ebb the yellowed fields fall silent.

3

Sybrand van Aswegen was the principal of one of Kalvyn's primary schools. He was a man of medium height and of undistinguished appearance, inclined to premature baldness. He was rather on the young side to be occupying the much sought after position of principal. He had achieved this distinction through those processes that are an eternal mystery to the outsider, who is unable to fathom the hidden labyrinths through which promotion takes place in apparently lifeless organisations like the various branches of the administrative services.

How do you impress your boss when he is the Government or the Provincial Council? The outsider doesn't know these things. He accepts it that, unless you have influence, progress in a job of this nature must be a matter of the dullest form of plodding, a waiting for dead man's shoes. So that when Sybrand van Aswegen gets promoted over the heads of senior school-teachers, and is appointed principal of a primary school when he is still comparatively young, a person who is not in the Education Department is mystified. But Sybrand van Aswegen's former colleagues were not mystified. When mention was made of Sybrand van Aswegen's advancement, there were those who sneered.

Sybrand van Aswegen did not have much background. His parents were of ordinary peasant stock, and when he was orphaned at an early age there were no relatives who were willing to take care of his elder sister and himself. The result was that these two children spent a great deal of their childhood in the orphanage at Langlaagte. Sometimes, latterly, in Kalvyn, Sybrand van Aswegen would flaunt his humble beginnings. With none of the regular opportunities offered him by life, he had nevertheless succeeded by his own efforts in winning for himself a senior position in the Transvaal Education Department. It was only in the company of one or two intimates, however, that he would allow himself to push out his chest and declaim, and each time, after he had allowed himself to blossom out in this fashion, he was left with a sense of dissatisfaction, with the feeling that his from log-cabin-to-President talk had failed to impress. In places like the Kalvyn Club he never made mention of his origins.

The bare circumstance of his having been orphaned at an early age was further complicated by the manner in which he had lost his parents. For there was a regrettably ludicrous side to what was, for the rest, a simple tragedy of the veld. One day Sybrand van Aswegen's father had failed to return from a visit he had made to the far end of the farm, where there was dense bush. And his mother never recovered from the shock she received when the news was imparted to her, a few days later, that her husband had been overpowered and swallowed by a python. She died shortly afterwards.

Consequently, Sybrand and his sister, Alie, were taken in by the Langlaagte Orphanage, where minedumps on the skyline replaced the wooded koppies of the farm. And whenever Sybrand saw his sister Alie weep, it was with a sense of shame, in the realisation that her sorrow was deep-seated and her tears genuine. Whereas his own grief was not so much on account of his parents' death but because of the fact of his being without parents meant that he had to live in the orphanage. This knowledge convicted him in his mind of a secret unworthiness.

The manner of their father's sudden dying remained to haunt the two children for a considerable while. They never spoke about it among themselves, and when other children, in the cruelty of youthful inquisitiveness, tried to elicit some of the lurid details from Sybrand, he would reply that he didn't know (which was true). He had even to put up with a certain amount of mockery from his fellow orphans, who saw no incongruity in ridiculing a child because his father had died in a ludicrous fashion, when they had themselves been orphaned. To die of pneumonia was all right, apparently. To be swallowed by a python put your children outside of some sort of a pale.

When Sybrand and his sister were admitted to the orphanage the person in charge of the registration, who had an inclination towards the sensational, wrote in the column 'Cause of Father's death' the words 'Swallowed by Python.' In the original Afrikaans it sounded even more startling, 'Ingesluk deur Luislang.' Afterwards the superintendent of the institution changed the entry to 'Accidental Death.'

The superintendent also gave instructions that in the evenings, after the hour of study, when the children in the orphanage were allowed a period of relaxation, Sybrand and his sister had to be supplied with a set of ludo or a draughts board when they sat to play at the long table. The superintendent was a well-intentioned man with a strong religious sense, and he felt that it would be wrong for Sybrand and Alie van Aswegen to take part in the games of snakes and ladders, which were then very popular with the inmates of the orphanage.

Now a married man with four children, and principal of the Afrikaans-medium Primary School in Kalvyn, Sybrand van Aswegen, slightly bald and approaching middle age, sat behind his desk to interview the new school-teacher for Standard Two, who had been sent to Kalvyn from the head office in Pretoria.

"So you don't think I should go on staying at the Northern Hotel?" Hannah Theron asked. "You see, I was sent here without much notice. I shall have to make enquiries first. I might get accommodation with private people – "

"Or there may be a vacancy in one of our Afrikaner boarding-houses," Sybrand van Aswegen answered. "There are several that I can recommend you to. But you will understand that it has nothing to do with me as to where you choose to stay. I never presume to interfere in the lives of my teachers. Only, it is not quite in accordance with the traditions of our school that a lady teacher should live in the hotel."

"I see," Hannah Theron replied.

So that was that. As it happened, Hannah Theron did find other accommodation in Kalvyn after a while. As a matter of fact, she moved about quite a lot. And when she did, at one period, stay with private people, it was hardly under the conditions which Sybrand van Aswegen had envisaged.

The interview was at an end. Sybrand van Aswegen felt drawn to the new school-teacher in a way that was at once pleasant and disturbing. He saw her as a girl and as a woman. This was a new experience for him. Hitherto a member of his staff had had for him little of the ordinary kind of human significance. His teachers carried out their duties with a certain degree of efficiency. When he got hold of new ideas, new teaching methods, his staff would conform to his requirements. His school got good reports from the inspectors.

Sybrand van Aswegen knew in detail what was going on in each classroom at each hour of the day. He would sit in his office, or he would be teaching the Standard Six class, and he would know what was going on in the other classrooms. He knew in what lesson Japie Kruger would give his class writing work to do, so that he could take a surreptitious glance at the sports page of the newspaper folded up under his register. He knew at what intervals Herklaas Huysmans would slip out of the classroom for a cigarette. And how many days Lettie van der Walt was in arrears with her record of work book. And that the elderly Miss Reinecke had sadistic tendencies which she tried to conceal. And so with each member of his staff.

And while they were acquainted with the fact that he had extensive knowledge of what went on in their daily lives, the members of his staff also felt there were certain things about them of which Sybrand van Aswegen couldn't know for sure. And in this uncertainty there was created between the principal and the members of his staff a relationship that had about it a number of peculiar features. His teachers were never comfortable in his presence. And those of them who had worldly wisdom applied Sybrand van Aswegen's methods towards securing discipline in their class. Psychological stuff.

For many minutes after Hannah Theron had gone out of his office, Sybrand van Aswegen remained seated in his chair, gazing straight in front of him, with eyes that took in nothing. He looked past the silver cups and dusty school trophies. Past the framed photographs of pupils and staffs of other days. Past the sterile stacks of files and papers and index cards.

4

Hannah Theron sat in the lounge of the Northern Hotel after supper. It was her second day in Kalvyn. She would start at the school on the morrow. There were other guests in the lounge, with its settees and armchairs covered in brown pegamoid; with its half-dozen tables whose tops were cracked and stained with old circles, that were deeply engrained in the wood, as though the trees from which the tables were made had in them, as annual rings, while they were still growing, the rings of wine and beer and brandy glasses.

Those two men in the corner looked like commercial travellers. Hannah Theron caught a few snatches of their conversation. One of them looked in Hannah's direction. She knew that look. She averted her gaze, coldly. The man understood. She was after other game, that dark, thin girl sitting there by herself. Not that she would object to him personally, he felt. He could see by the way she had turned her face aside that she knew men. The manner of a woman's looking away was more revealing than anything she could convey in words.

She had, no doubt, had experience of commercial travellers. She now wanted more than a casual acquaintanceship, to be broken off in a few days and to be resumed at desultory intervals. The man believed that if he put himself out to make further advances the girl would not rebuff him. Only, what each had to offer was not quite what the other wanted. And the commercial traveller had not much time to waste in Kalvyn.

5

Hans Korf, the barman in the pub adjoining the lounge, dropped in to see if there were customers. Hans Korf was tall and thin and somewhat deaf. There was that new school-teacher sitting alone, her features cold and her gaze directed at nothing in particular. Hans Korf liked her profile. Not exactly pretty, of course, but classy. If she wasn't quite so thin she would perhaps even be a dame he could take a fancy to. But he didn't like them thin. You had to have something you could get a hold of. He had often thought that why he didn't like thin girls much was because he was so bony himself. It must be true what people said about persons falling for their opposites. Another thing about this Miss Theron that put a man off, Hans Korf reflected, was the fact that she was a school-teacher. A man who didn't have too much education didn't like to feel that he was going around with a girl who knew more than he did.

Hans Korf went up to Hannah Theron's table. "Anything for you, miss?" he asked.

Hannah Theron shook her head. "I'm going to bed soon," she explained. "I'm whiling away a few minutes."

She spoke softly. Hans Korf heard not vowels and consonants cut up into syllables, but a blur of sound, a rise and fall of an utterance that was not unmusical. And there was something not unpleasing about the way her lips moved. Afterwards she would find out that he was a bit deaf and she would talk more loudly. And then her voice would, perhaps, not sound so musical.

"It must be quiet for you here," Hans Korf said, "after Pretoria. But you'll soon make friends."

"Oh yes," Hannah Theron answered, "I am sure."

Hans Korf was getting ready to say some more. He had scarcely begun to speak, however, when his name was called in the pub next door, which was separated from the lounge by only a wood and iron partition.

"Korf!" the voice came again, more loudly. "Cut out the women and come and mix us a man's drink!"

Hans Korf chuckled. "That's Bert Parsons," he informed Hannah Theron. "Always having his bit of fun. You'll meet him one of these days. Shouldn't be surprised if you like him, too, in spite of everything."

Hannah Theron would have liked to know more about what the barman meant by 'everything', but there was that voice again, calling on him to hurry, and Hans Korf vanished into the pub.

Hannah Theron went on sitting in the lounge for a few minutes. Men's voices from the pub. An incessant drone. Voices rising and falling, the words only faintly distinguishable, filtered through the partition; the words sounded about the same to Hannah Theron in the lounge as they did to Hans Korf in the bar room. And occasionally there came that other voice, deep and heavy, with more force in it than resonance, which she recognised as belonging to the man whom Hans Korf had designated as Bert Parsons.

Hannah Theron got up from the table and began walking across the lounge towards the passage leading to her bedroom. The voices got very loud suddenly. The side door of the pub had been opened. Without meaning to look in, Hannah Theron had obtained a glimpse of the interior of the pub. And in that moment she had viewed Bert Parsons.

She was left with a vivid impression of a young man with a very red face and his mouth wide open. A blue suit and a flaming tie. In his hand a raised glass. She also noticed, in that swift glance, that he had an abnormally large hand.

Hannah Theron was sure that that young man was Bert Parsons. And she didn't know whether he had seen her. And she knew she would see more of him.

6

There was a hitch in the building of the new stores in Voortrekker Street.

This emporium was to be a three-storey affair, planned on modern lines, and when completed it would be the most impressive looking building in Kalvyn's high street. They had reached the stage where the roof was going up. The wooden principals had been hoisted into position and nailed to the wall-plates, to the accompaniment of the shouting and bad language and ill temper that is inseparable from this feat. There was prolonged, if ungrammatical, talk among the workmen about things like hip-rafters and joists and purlines, and eventually there was erected against the skyline a timbered skeleton, vast and gaunt and appearing to sway in the blue void, on which the galvanised iron of the roof would be nailed. The framework was strong and slender and open, and so suggestive of infinite space that it seemed as though the roof was to be fastened not on to two by three timber but on to a cloud.

"Where's your purlines for the front here, Andrews?" the carpenter's foreman asked of one of his men. "Where are you going to put your iron – on a sky hook?"

"We can't go on with this, Bert," Lionel Andrews said to Bert Parsons, who was the carpenter's foreman. "The clerk of works was round here when you was away from the job. The contractor was here also. He looked like he thought you had ducked round to the pub for a quick one."

"I went to order four-inch nails," Bert Parsons answered sullenly. "What's the bleeding idea, expecting us to work without nails?"

"Search me," Lionel Andrews answered, "but that ain't what the clerk of the works was talking about."

Bert Parsons, of whose red face Hannah Theron had caught a brief glimpse in the bar of the Northern Hotel on the previous evening, affected unconcern at the information Lionel Andrews had to impart. Bert Parsons was, after all, carpenter's foreman. He had his prestige to maintain. He couldn't allow himself to look rattled about some squeal or other that the bosses were putting up. They were always raising all sorts of bleats – contractors, architects, clients, clerks of works. That was part of every job. The hardest part, in any way. A lot of squeals that usually, in the end, turned out to have been unnecessary. And he certainly wasn't going to let this young Lionel Andrews think that he was upset, or that he cared even. But for God's sake what was the bleat about, anyway? He had to know. But he just couldn't go and ask Lionel Andrews directly.

" — the clerk of the works," Bert Parsons announced, "and that goes for the contractor as well. And for you also, leaving out them bloody purlines."

That would make Lionel Andrews come his guts, all right. Picking on him first. He would have to talk now.

"Purlines can't go up," Lionel Andrews replied. "Pitch is too high. Principals got to be shifted back. You got to cut a new lot of rafters."

"Not me," Bert Parsons responded indignantly. "I followed them blueprints, ain't I? Correct to a bloody half inch. Let that bloody architect go and saw a new set of rafters. And I'll tell him where he can go and stick his blueprints. And his new lot of rafters. That job stays put."

Lionel Andrews sniggered.

Bert Parsons had climbed as high as the first-floor scaffolding planks before the argument had started. He now laid his saw and hammer on a trestle, divested himself of his bulging nail-bag and climbed down on to the ground. Without a word he made his way over the uneven ground in the direction of the temporary wood and iron lean-to that was used as a business and pay office on the building job.

"I've measured that wall-plate and you can go and see for yourself," Bert Parsons said, striding into the lean-to. "I don't know what Andrews is talking about. He ought to get his backside kicked for not nailing up them purlines. He's getting lousier every day."

Bert Parsons had come into the lean-to out of the sunlight. Rage and the gloom inside had made it difficult for him to see clearly. It was only when he was halfway through his little speech that he awoke to the fact that there were two men present in the office.

At first he had seen only the timekeeper. But he quickly realised that he was also talking to Gerrit Neser, the contractor. That was a different matter. The timekeeper was only an employee, like himself. But Gerrit Neser was the boss. Accordingly, in the same breath of denouncing the architect and the boss and the clerk of works to the timekeeper, Bert Parsons had switched to a general tirade directed against Lionel Andrews.

"It's not Andrews," Gerrit Neser replied, "it's you that's cock-eyed. How the hell did you get a pitch at that angle? If you bring it over another couple of inches, you'll have a roof and a veranda. Yes. All in one. You better go and get that fixed up. That's half a day wasted. How the hell can I make a profit with all this extra wages for doing a job over twice?"

"It is all correct, sir," Bert Parsons persisted. "It's all like it's on the blueprint. I got every measurement in."

"What did you measure with, a blooming shovel?" the contractor demanded. "If I wasn't stuck for a carpenter's foreman I'd have fired you the day this job started. I got a good mind to fire you in any case, and to give the job to that chap Andrews."

Bert Parsons said that he would check the measurements again, which would prove that the mistake had been made by the architect.

"I can't waste any more time," Gerrit Neser said. "I've got to go and see about another tender. Pull yourself together, Parsons. You're a good man and I wouldn't like to lose you, but you know what it is. You've done a bit of contracting yourself. You know how the wages bill runs away with a job. You're bankrupt in this game before you know where you are."

The tone Gerrit Neser adopted was, in a rough way, conciliatory. Bert Parsons wasn't a bad workman, as workmen went, and Gerrit Neser felt that he would probably get more out of him if he didn't make him feel too small over this mistake.

"I felt like telling him what he could do with his bleeding job," Bert Parsons informed the timekeeper, when Gerrit Neser had left. "Him having the cheek to talk to me about being a contractor. I been my own boss before, and I'll be my own boss again. It's just there's no buildings being put up in this lousy dorp this time of the year. That's why I got to work here as foreman carpenter. But wait until the real building starts. Then I'll be sticking in some tenders. And I'll have Neser working for me. And not as foreman, neither. I'll give him the lousiest kaffir job that's going. He can be the tea-boy. 'Come on, Neser, you bastard,' I'll say, 'up with that tea. And don't use them new cleats for the fire. Where's your brains? Make the fire with your tender papers and your cost books. You won't need them no more.' That's what I'll say to Neser. Just you watch out, that's all."

"You're right there," the timekeeper answered.

The timekeeper was a peace-loving man. He didn't want to be drawn into other people's quarrels. What the hell. He had a wife and five children to support. And he had to get on with the boss and the workmen. On a building job there was a new argument going on every day, and he had got to side with each person in turn. The rights or the wrongs of a dispute didn't matter a cuss to him. It was none of his business. All he wanted was his pay at the end of every week.

So when there was a row he would agree with everybody in turn. Anybody that walked into his office would find he was on his side. There was a lousy job for you, if you liked. You had to say yes to everybody. Everybody except the labourers and the kaffirs, that was. You could treat them like dirt, of course. In fact, you had to. But these tradesmen, these so-called skilled workmen – not that he could see where their skill came in – they made him sick. Carrying on like a lot of women. Each one picking on the other. And then, when the going got too rough, running to him for sympathy.

And all he got for it was that they called him Ou Ja-Broer. That was his nickname with the workmen. He bet none of them knew what his real name was. 'Ou Ja-Broer' was good enough for them. Imagine the cheek of calling him that to his face. Ah well, he had got over that long ago. He was used to being addressed by a nickname that was an insult. He didn't bother about it any more. Only, now and again, when he thought about it, it rankled. This was sure a hell of a way to make a living. And just a bare living, too, no more.

"Yes," the timekeeper said, "it must be hard on you. We all know that you are just unlucky today. Look at some of those contracts you have had in your time. And just because they didn't take your tender, and there's no other building going up now, you got to work for a boss. Yes, it must be hard."

But not as hard as it is for me, the timekeeper thought. And what does Bert Parsons do when he gets a contract anyway? Lives like a lord, he does. Spends all the dough he makes on booze and low women. Wait till he's got responsibilities like what I got. A wife and five children. He won't have a chance to look at any more women. The timekeeper thought of this period in Bert Parsons's life with a good deal of satisfaction.

"Who got the contract for the Sanitary Board disposal building, five miles out of town?" Bert Parsons demanded. "I ask you, who?"

"You did, of course, Bert," the timekeeper answered. "And a swell little job you made of it, too. And you had to cart all the materials over half a koppie, where there was no road."

The timekeeper knew the story: he had had to listen to it so often.

"And finished on time," Bert Parsons concluded. "Right to the very day."

Talking thus of a triumph out of the near past, Bert Parsons began to feel better over what happened between himself and Gerrit Neser. He would talk to Lionel Andrews about the measurements for those principals, he thought, as he strode back to the job. He would consult with Lionel Andrews. He knew that Lionel Andrews, in spite of being the lousiest tradesman he had ever come across, was quick at following a blueprint. He would talk to him, and they would work together, and before they knocked off for the evening the first sheets of galvanised iron would be nailed on to the roof.

The timekeeper watched Bert Parsons's huge body undulating over the uneven ground, becoming part of the stacks of blue and red bricks and blending with the wooden scaffolding reared towards the sky. The timekeeper envied Bert Parsons his height and girth and the sway of his body, that was youthful in spite of his bulk. You could see the steel springs of his muscles, the life in his shoulders and hips and thighs right through that yellow overall. It was because of his magnificent body that the women all fell for Bert Parsons, the timekeeper reflected. He thought of his own wizened frame with an inward shrinking, as though he was trying to draw away from his body that had no strength in it, and to hide away, somewhere, where people wouldn't have to see him.

Chapter Two

1

Hannah Theron liked her new job. She was glad to get away from Pretoria. It was not for the reason of Pretoria being a city that she felt she wanted rest. You can live in the din and tumult of a city for years, and even for ever, and no storms will come and shake your branches and toss your torn leaves to the night. But you can stay on a lonely farm, enveloped in the dun-coloured isolation of the veld and under the remorselessness of a flat sky, and life will come to you, and out of the thickness of breath you will be left with a grey wound.

And why Hannah Theron was glad to get away from Pretoria was because it meant that she would be two hundred miles away from Willem Retief. In Kalvyn she found calm, in which she drenched herself; a peace on which she floated like on water.

Hannah Theron found that her Standard Two class was easy to handle. Her colleagues, the men and women teachers at the school, seemed ordinary enough people, and so their influence on her was at least restful. She hoped to remain long immersed in the coolness of this tranquillity.

Although she was quite alone in this dorp, and had as yet met nobody for whom she felt anything more than the most impersonal kind of friendliness, Hannah Theron knew that she was slowly beginning to discover anew the essentials of a happiness that went deep because it was devoid of ecstasy.

Every day, when school ended, she would walk back to the hotel, her way at first leading through that part of the village where the houses were far apart and scattered and the roads ill defined, and then for a short distance she walked over the paved sidewalks of the high street where the shops were, and the bioscope and a café, and the bank and a few blocks of business offices. And then she would go in through the front door of the Northern Hotel.

She liked these walks, daily, in the morning and in the afternoons, in the early spring. The first part of the walk was through the grass and past thorn-trees and the kaffir-boom, whose bursting into flower was like the breaking of sudden red flesh, and under the jacarandas that were purple overhead for a little while and were thereafter purple in the grass and on the pavements and by the roadside for a little longer. The second part of the walk, that was the clicking of her heels on the cement, was brief but was also pleasant, but in a different way.

After a few days Hannah Theron found that there was no need for her to walk down the main street, and to enter the hotel by the front door. There was a shorter way through the back gate, a path leading through a stretch of veld that had not been built on. But by that time she had grown used to the other way, although it was longer. And so she invariably came into and walked out of the hotel through the front entrance.

And because Kalvyn is a small town, people noticed this habit of Hannah Theron's and commented on it. "Why can't she go out through the back door and over the veld?" people said. "It's only half the distance. Does she want to flaunt herself on the main street? Does she want to make sure that she is seen?"

That was how people spoke. Hannah Theron knew nothing about what they said, of course. She had none of those intuitions that you develop through living in a dorp, so that your unconscious mind catches up the thinking that is going on around you and you pattern your life in accordance with what the community demands of you, and you do all sorts of set things without knowing why.

The time was to come when Hannah Theron no longer walked down the main street unnecessarily. When she tried to avoid the main street as much as possible. But that time was not yet.

2

Japie Kruger was one of the first members of the staff of the school with whom Hannah Theron became acquainted. Japie Kruger was in his early twenties, a few years younger than Hannah Theron, and his after school activities consisted in organising the junior and senior football teams. He was a cheerful young man, careful about his dress, but somewhat on the heavy side.

In conversation with Herklaas Huysmans, who had been a schoolteacher for fifteen years, and had hated the job during all that time, Japie Kruger always tried to keep to everyday subjects, like the fact that there was a new waitress at the Elite Café, or that the Town Council was thinking of extending the sewerage scheme. He would also talk politics and, of course, sport. But whenever it came to something abstract, Japie Kruger used to get distressed and bothered, with Herklaas Huysmans doing most of the talking and Japie Kruger the listening.

Tall and cadaverous, Herklaas Huysmans – who had been a schoolmaster for a decade and a half, and who had consequently lived in the atmosphere of chalk dust since he had first gone to school at the age of seven – had had ambitions of leaving the Education Department from before he got his first teaching post. Teaching was to have been only a stepping stone in his life, a means of enabling him to realise his childhood ambition of practising at the bar.

So he had become a school-teacher. He had taught during the five hour day in a school on the Rand where the teacher was not expected to undertake much in the way of extra duties, and he had studied law in his spare time and during the school holidays. It was heavy going. But he stuck it.

There was a time when he was transferred to a country school. He was kept there from one term to the next. It seemed as though his hopes were destined to be shattered for ever. Miles away from the law library of the Witwatersrand Division of the Supreme Court, Herklaas Huysmans was hopelessly handicapped in the pursuit of his studies. There were evenings, in the loneliness of the vlaktes, when he thought of the dismal little whitewashed schoolhouse to which his future was now being doomed, and his mind would be occupied with a dark resolve. Life seemed, then, too much for him.

Nevertheless, Herklaas Huysmans kept on. He grew grim in his determination... And then, one day, he qualified. It was near the end of a period of long school leave that he ultimately got the LL. B. degree.

And he never practised. When it came to the point where he had to give up teaching and rent an office in a building in Pretoria or Johannesburg, where he would have his fellow advocates as neighbours, and he had to sit behind his desk and wait for clients – it was at this point that Herklaas Huysmans's nerve failed him. He knew he couldn't do it. He didn't have it in him. It was all a dream. Golden froth. The crazily swaying edifices of a drunkenness. He was a schoolmaster. The LL. B. degree meant nothing. He dared not try to sneak through the purple hangings of those brave portals. It was all a vision, a snare, a gaudy beckoning that had lured him down the years – but only thus far. That magnificence was not for him. And he knew it. In front of the open door he turned back. If the door had been barred against him for ever he would have been all right. He would have kept on knocking. Opened, the door announced to him his defeat.

Herklaas Huysmans had gone so far as to buy an office desk out of his slender savings. It was an imposing looking desk, heavy and ponderous and charged with legal atmosphere. He was afraid even of that desk at first. But afterwards he got used to it. And he carted it around with him wherever he went. When the Education Department once more transferred him – this time to Kalvyn Primary School – he took that desk with him.

Herklaas Huysmans was convinced that his defeat had been brought about by the Transvaal Education Department. That time when they sent him to the school on the veld, that farm school with its whitewashed walls. That period, he told himself, had broken him. The struggle after that was too severe. The struggle had broken him. So that when he passed his final examination he had no more guts left with which to face life. The Education Department had done that to him. Beyond a point you broke. After that you couldn't go on.

The result was that Herklaas Huysmans had grown embittered. He saw himself in self-dramatisation as a man who was disillusioned with life. He couldn't take to women. At least, they couldn't take to him. Nor did drink appeal to him. So he contented himself with making saturnine observations about life in general and successful people in particular. In this way he obtained a reputation among his colleagues for intellectuality and philosophical profundity. For this reason, of course, they avoided him. They did not dislike him so much as that they felt uncomfortable in his company. And the person who felt most nervous of him was Japie Kruger.

"I read something in the *Vaderland* this morning," Japie Kruger remarked at tea-time in the teachers' common room. "It's about that school-teacher Labuschagne. I don't know whether you have heard of him. He seems to have been quite notorious. He was had up in court for assaulting a child and he has just been remanded to a mental hospital for observation."

The members of the staff, who were congregated around the table in the staff room, drinking tea, suddenly began taking a measure of interest in the conversation, which was usually of a desultory nature, the teachers being, in general, bored with each other and not particularly anxious to conceal their boredom.

"Is he in trouble for caning a child?" Miss Reinecke, the elderly spinster who taught Standard Four, enquired.

"And how he caned that boy," Japie Kruger answered. "According to the evidence, he lashed him all over the place, over his arms and legs and body, and when the child climbed in under the desk, screaming in terror, this Labuschagne kicked him out from under it, and started walloping him all over again."

"How terrible," Lettie van der Walt said. "That is a man, now, that I call a disgrace to the teaching profession."

"On the contrary," Herklaas Huysmans ejaculated, shifting his long body into a more comfortable position in the chair which he occupied at the head of the table, as vice-principal, in the absence of Sybrand van Aswegen, who usually had his tea alone in his office. "I think that man, Labuschagne, whoever he is, is a credit to the teaching profession. He is an ornament to a profession that has lost all its status since the Education Department, years ago, brought in those regulations about caning. We belong to a profession whose hands are tied. Only the principal can cane a child, and then the cane must not be more than four feet long, and he is not allowed to swing his arm backwards over his shoulder. You didn't know those were the regulations, did you? And do you know that only the headmaster is permitted to inflict a caning?"

He asked these questions of Japie Kruger, who did not quite know how he was expected to answer.

"Well," Japie Kruger said, "of course, we never stick to the regulations. I don't think it is necessary to have these regulations. I mean, we are sensible men and women. And in every school the teacher is allowed to use his discretion in this matter. I only wanted to say that I had heard of this fellow Labuschagne before. And this morning I read about him in the newspaper. I think he must have been drunk to have carried on like that."

"I still say he's a beast," Lettie van der Walt said, her pale cheeks flushing in anger. "I say he's a bully and a coward. Imagine his kicking a child out from under his desk, and then caning him some more. I am sure he's mad."

"But you don't know the circumstances," Herklaas Huysmans persisted. "*Audi alterem partem.* That's a very sound principle of law. Hear the other side, even if the other side hasn't got a case at all. You don't know whether the accused used a light cane or a bamboo cane or a length of hippopotamus hide. You don't know whether he kicked the child in the face with his booted foot, or whether he merely prodded him in order to get him out from under the desk. You don't even know what he caned him for. Labuschagne might have had serious provocation. The child might have helped himself to the bottle of gin Labuschagne kept in the school cupboard, hidden behind the boxes of coloured chalk. That would constitute very serious provocation. Just think how this teacher must have felt, going to his cupboard at the lunch interval, after three hours of boredom, and finding that there is nothing left in the bottle, because one of his pupils has guzzled the lot. So he has to do without his well-earned tot of gin and lime. Do you mean to say he wouldn't slosh into that pupil if he caught him?"

"I have never heard of a school-teacher keeping gin in his cupboard in the classroom," Miss Reinecke answered. "Except, perhaps, for medicinal purposes. And I don't know why you are suddenly so sympathetic towards that awful man on these grounds. We all know you don't drink."

"Anyway, I think we ought to get up a subscription for Labuschagne," Herklaas Huysmans said, "to show our appreciation. He's helping to maintain the prestige of our profession. Because we are not allowed to cane the children just when and how we like, they have no respect for us. The upshot of it all is that their parents have no respect for us, either. And this feeling of contempt for school-teachers communicates itself to the whole community. Now, then, who will contribute to this fund? I'll start it off. The Labuschagne Defence Fund. Will you give something towards it, Kruger?"

"Not on your life, I won't," Japie Kruger replied. "I only wish I was the warder who has got to look after him – he won't be so quick to knock a school kid about again – "

"Not a warder," Herklaas Huysmans answered, "he's not in prison. You said he was sent for observation. That's under Section 5, sub-section 2 of the amended – "

"Perhaps we should contribute something, not because we approve of what he did," Hannah Theron said, "but because he is a human being in misfortune, and perhaps what he has to go through now will change him."

"That won't do," Herklaas Huysmans cried. "That won't do at all. I'm not going to have my defence fund corrupted into a sentimental church bazaar sort of affair. The fund is to register our downright satisfaction with Labuschagne's mode of conduct. More power to his right arm. I'd sooner have no fund for him at all than to have to organise it on the milk-and-water basis that Miss Theron suggests."

In the lull that followed his last remark, Herklaas Huysmans rose to his feet and sauntered towards the door. He paused on the threshold.

"I'm going," he said. "I'm going to see if anybody has tampered with the bottle of gin in my cupboard, behind the chalk boxes."

"It seems as though there are other mad school-teachers besides Labuschagne," Miss Reinecke said, significantly, after Herklaas Huysmans's departure. "And imagine a man like Huysmans being vice-principal."

"But they say he's very clever," Lettie van der Walt said.

Miss Reinecke sniffed. "If he is so clever, why didn't he go and practise as a lawyer after he had qualified?" she demanded.

A few minutes before the end of the tea interval Hannah Theron found herself in conversation with Miss Reinecke. The subject was still the one Herklaas Huysmans had broached. Miss Reinecke was doing all the talking.

"Now, what I like about Mr Van Aswegen," Miss Reinecke was saying, "is that he leaves the teacher a lot of discretion in the punishment of the class. That is a very sensible policy. So good for discipline. What I mean to say is that no teacher would ever carry on like that dreadful Labuschagne."

Miss Reinecke droned on.

Hannah Theron listened with only half her brain and caught little more than isolated thoughts and phrases.

"Class has got to feel that while they have teacher's love and devotion teacher is also there to train them in right ways… I have found what works best is not to cane children just indiscriminately at any time and just after they have done wrong. I reserve last part of afternoon, every Friday, for infliction of punishment. Works ever so well. When I do punish him it is without feelings of anger. I then cane in cool sense of duty. Girls on hands. Boys bending over. Short pliable cane my brother-in-law bought for me in Pretoria.

"I talk to whole classes on Friday afternoon. How painful it is for me to have to cane. I don't mention who. No one knows for sure whose name is down in my little black book. Those who have been very naughty, whom I reserve for severe caning, I keep over for last. I am not tired by that time. In fact, I have got even more energy for caning really bad children at end of Friday afternoon than when I started caning. Because of my sense of duty, I suppose. Because I know what I am doing is not for own pleasure but in child's best interests.

"Another cane in reserve, but not so good. Swishes more, but not same weight of impact. Doesn't curve in quite same way around buttocks. Child jumps more when I discipline him with this cane. But with yellow rattan he stands and quivers. More effective. No longer impressed when child roars and bellows and jumps about floor. Good deal play-acting. When that part of body just shivers I know child has been effectively disciplined."

Miss Reinecke proceeded to discuss the whipping of animals.

"If you take a horse now," Miss Reinecke said, "spurs and things like that. And a riding crop. Now, you take a horse – "

But before Hannah Theron could take a horse, Miss Reinecke's instructive monologue was interrupted by the bell announcing the resumption of school work.

That afternoon, when she passed the windows of Miss Reinecke's classroom, Hannah Theron heard the swishing of a cane. Then she remembered that it was Friday.

3

On her way to the hotel later that afternoon, Hannah Theron passed the place, on the main street, where the new three-storey block of buildings was being erected. Bert Parsons, in consultation with Lionel Andrews, had found out where he had gone wrong. The principals had been shifted back and the other adjustments had been made, through sawing and splicing, and the stage was soon reached where the white labourers began bringing along the sheets of galvanised iron. The mistake had occasioned less delay than had at first appeared.

"It's all right that you was with me to check up," Bert Parsons said to Lionel Andrews grudgingly. "But like I said at the start, it's that bleeding architect. He says one thing and writes down another. Next time I land a contract I'll see you come with me as foreman. I'll pull you away from Neser. Who does he think he is, anyway? Just wait till I put in a tender again, that's all... Now why the blasted hell do you got to hand up that sheet of galvanised iron arse to front again?"

This latter query Bert Parsons directed at a white labourer, a middle-aged man with thick shoulders but with bent knees and with a yellowed hat pulled straight down over his ears, thereby obscuring his forehead – of which there was not much, in any case – and the upper part of his face.

"I always forgets," Van Schalkwyk, the white labourer replied, pulling the sheet of galvanised iron back on to the scaffolding planks and turning it round.

"Them white labourers," Bert Parsons announced to Lionel Andrews. "Give me a kaffir every time, that you can boot in the ribs. In that way he learns quick. Them white labourers never learns."

So the job went on.

Neither Bert Parsons nor Lionel Andrews noticed the nervousness of the labourer, Van Schalkwyk, standing on the scaffolding planks with his hat on a level with the top of the wall, ready to pass up another sheet of galvanised iron each time one of the men shouted. The sheets were stacked near at hand.

And for the life of him, in spite of the repeated and detailed instructions he had received, he didn't know what was the top and what the underneath of a sheet of galvanised iron. He knew it had something to do with the grooves. He had also studied a number of sheets, and he had seen that they were all alike. But it was in the way you handed up a sheet that it became different. It was that last groove in the sheet. If you passed the sheet up with that piece turned down, then the sheet went in under the last one, for a couple of grooves. Or was it the other way round? Honestly, he didn't know. It had something to do with keeping the rain out.

So he kept on passing up the sheets, just the way they were stacked near him on the scaffolding, and it seemed that he was doing it right. Anyway, that foreman with the red face hadn't sworn at him for quite a while now. At least ten minutes. He must be getting the hang of it now. It must be that you simply take up the sheet, carry it to the place nearest to where the man was working, turn it round once and then you –

"What's your bleeding game?" Van Schalkwyk heard Bert Parsons roar. "How the hell do you expect me, perched on this damn purline like a ruddy bird, to turn round these bloody sheets that you hand up backside to face? Next time you does that you can go down to the timekeeper and get your time! How the hell do you expect me to do this bleeding job?"

Oh well, apparently there was more to it than he had begun to imagine, Van Schalkwyk reflected. This was hard work, all right. You had to think so quick. It wasn't like putting up a shed on a farm. There you seemed to know just what was wanted. You were your own boss – on that job, anyway. You had your hammer and your punch for hitting a hole in the iron and then you knocked in the screw that you first put through a hole in the washer. And you got the job right without having to worry what sheet came on top and what came on the bottom. And then you would call your wife and she would admire it. And that roof wouldn't leak. At least, not much. Not more than any other sort of roof. And it wouldn't leak because you had put the sheets on wrong, but just because it was nearly always second-hand galvanised iron that you used, and you couldn't always fill up all the old nail-holes with hot tar. And the farmer you worked for would make jokes and be satisfied.

A sudden nostalgia for the farm in the Waterberg district where he worked as a bywoner for the best part of his life, and where he had met his wife and had had children, and that bywoner's house that he had had to quit because of the drought that had lasted for three years on end – a sudden nostalgia for that old life that he had known so well and that was deep in his blood and his being overcame Koos van Schalkwyk, standing on the scaffolding planks, with a sheet of galvanised iron in his hands that had become shapeless through the years of toil.

The result was that it was a long time before he heard Bert Parsons shout for another sheet of iron, and when he did pass up the sheet it did not at first penetrate Van Schalkwyk's brain that he had again handed up the thing the wrong way round. And it was only after he had climbed down the scaffolding and was walking over the uneven ground in the direction of the timekeeper's office that there came to him the full realisation of the fact that he had been fired off the job.

A pert youngster, eighteen years of age, whom the workmen called Boet, took Van Schalkwyk's place on the scaffolding. Boet was bright and cunning and had a lot of cheek and had on one occasion very narrowly escaped going to reformatory. He had learnt the art of ingratiating himself with people, so that he was as much at home on this building job in Kalvyn as he would have been in a Johannesburg slum. He had escaped the hardest part of the job, from the point of view of the labourers – the work connected with mixing the concrete for the foundations – and he was, as a rule, sufficiently resourceful to escape anything else of an unpleasant nature that came his way in life.

"You got a bit more brains than that old fool that's just gone off,"

Bert Parsons announced to Boet, after they had been at work for a few minutes, Boet passing up the galvanised sheets correctly and with alacrity, and with an occasional quip at the expense of both Bert Parsons and Lionel Andrews. But Boet's pleasantries were purposely unbarbed. Instead, they were subtly flattering to these men's maleness.

"There goes a nice bit of skirt for you," Boet exclaimed suddenly. "Just your style, Bert."

This was the first time Boet had addressed Bert Parsons thus familiarly, by his first name. Until then he had called him, half-jocularly, "Boss" or "Foreman."

Bert Parsons leant over to see. Crouched on a section of newly completed roof, he craned his neck down the side of the wall. Hannah Theron was passing down the sidewalk on her way back from the school. She walked up very straight, her high heels click-clicking smartly on the cement.

"I seen her before somewhere," Bert Parsons said. "Oh yes, in the Northern Hotel lounge. She's a nice piece. Except for her face. Her nose is too long."

Lionel Andrews joined his mate on the edge of the wall.

"Catch her looking at you, Bert," Lionel Andrews said. "She's got class, she has. She's not one of your sidewalk pick-ups. Better cut her out."

The implied slight in Lionel Andrews's remark annoyed Bert Parsons.

"She's just stuck-up," Bert Parsons replied, "and all about nothing. What's the betting I get her? Make it a quid?"

"Better go slow," Lionel Andrews admonished him. "She's a schoolteacher. You don't want to start no trouble with that class of dame."

"She might want to keep you in after school when you don't do your homework," Boet interjected, "like I knew a school-teacher in Wonderboom – "

"Make it a quid?" Bert Parsons repeated.

"Oh, all right," Lionel Andrews replied. "Only, remember what I said. You got to go careful."

4

Mrs Manning, the proprietress of the Northern Hotel, was in the lounge that evening when Hannah Theron came in after dinner. Mrs Manning motioned Hannah to a seat on the upholstered bench beside her.

"Come and have a spot with me, dearie," Mrs Manning said.

Ordinarily Hannah Theron disliked the type of woman who addressed her as "dearie", but, coming from Mrs Manning, that word did not have in it that particular undertone that normally roused Hannah Theron's resentment.

"You're still alone here, dearie," Mrs Manning said significantly. "Oh well, what else can you expect in a dorp like this? When I first came here I thought I'd go mad. Me being used to a life where a girl can have her fling and not too much said. But I found afterwards that this little place isn't too bad, taking it all round. There are things that go on that you don't know about until you get to know the ropes. Anyway, I've had my good times here."

Hannah Theron looked at Mrs Manning, a full bosomed blonde well on towards middle age, who nevertheless looked as though her capacity for the enjoyment of the more overtly physical things of life had suffered no diminution with the years. With her peroxided hair and her too full red lips and her cheeks smeared with a rouge the colour of a brick wall, Mrs Manning, seated in the hotel lounge, proclaimed by her appearance that she was either the proprietress or a woman whom the proprietress would not allow in the hotel lounge.

Because she owned the Northern Hotel, it was different somehow. Mrs Manning had become as much of a local institution as was the goldfish pond in front of the Town Hall. Nobody complained of the garish colours of the goldfish. And yellow and red were the colours of Mrs Manning's personality, also.

"How did you come to take over this hotel?" Hannah Theron enquired, vaguely curious about this exotic creature, whose strangeness in Kalvyn usage had staled.

"A boyfriend left it to me," Mrs Manning replied. "You could have struck me down with a coal hammer when I got the news. Georgie Green. I had forgotten all about him. Years before he had been just one of many. Ships that pass in the night sort of thing. He'd come into my life and gone out again, like they all do. And then one day a solicitor suddenly tells me that Georgie had left everything to me. Of course, I was young in those days when we went together. And he was getting on. So I must have been his last romance. His last proper romance, if you understand what I mean. And I never knew it. Although I should have been able to guess. Ah well, that's all there is in life, I suppose.

When that goes you haven't got much to live for, have you, dearie? So that must have been why he left me also. He didn't want me to know that I was his last woman – "

"Maybe it wasn't that, altogether," Hannah Theron suggested, not quite sure of what it was that Mrs Manning was seeking to imply. "Perhaps it was that he loved you, and he wasn't quite sure of it at the time, and only afterwards, when he met other girls, other women, he found that – "

"Perhaps you're right," Mrs Manning answered, not much interested. "But it isn't just enough for a woman to give herself. She's got to get the man also to – oh well, this is breaking my heart. Poor old Georgie Green. We got to have a sundowner. What's yours, dearie?"

Hannah Theron wasn't certain whether she should have a spot. She began to demur. Mrs Manning swept aside her protestations.

"Hans," Mrs Manning called, and then again, even more loudly, "Hans, you lazy-bones – two whiskies and sodas."

"Shouts at me like a kaffir, and in front of people, too," Hans Korf muttered to himself in the bar, while he poured the two drinks and opened a bottle of soda-water. "One of these days I'll quit."

But his face expressed no vestige of his inner annoyance when he set the glasses before the two women in the lounge.

"Cheer up, dearie," Mrs Manning said as she raised the whisky to her lips. "I've had good times here in this dorp, and I'm still going to have good times. And don't you worry any. Before you know where you are you will be right in the swim, also. I can see you got what it takes."

Just then the door of the lounge swung open. There were voices and footfalls. And one voice, loud and heavy and devoid of resonance, that Hannah Theron, seated with her back to the door, recognised.

"Come and sit at this table, boys," Mrs Manning called. "Let me introduce you to the nicest little girl that's been staying at my hotel for a long time."

Bert Parsons, looking very masculine in a well tailored blue suit with full drapes under the shoulders, advanced towards the table. Hannah Theron half turned to look at him. A flaming tie trailed carelessly down his shirt front. He was handsome in a heavy sort of fashion. This was Bert Parsons. Hannah Theron knew him even before Mrs Manning had made the introductions.

He sauntered up to the table, huge and ungainly and yet with an animal sureness of movement, and took Hannah Theron's slender fingers in his large paw. He pulled out a chair and sat down beside Hannah Theron, and it was only then that she noticed the other two men – Lionel Andrews, who was short and had sturdy shoulders and seemed unaccountably sheepish, and another young man whom they called Phil.

"What's yours?" Bert Parsons boomed to the company at large. Then he shouted for Hans Korf, who took the orders and returned a few minutes later with the drinks.

During this time Hannah Theron found herself glancing at Bert Parsons in those intervals when his gaze was directed elsewhere. He had a snub nose and a large mouth, and his face was very red. And there was an expression in his eyes that held her. It was a half sated sort of look that was outside of the proprieties. But there was also more to it than that, Hannah Theron felt.

A few months before Hannah Theron had found herself at the short end of a romance with a young man, Willem Retief, a clerk in the Education Department in Pretoria. Between Hannah Theron and Willem Retief there had not been that thing of flame that sears flesh. When they had met they had both been at a loose end. They had brought each other only an additional experience, which was something that neither of them needed. And when Willem Retief had decided to go, Hannah Theron had nothing with which to restrain him. And it was only after he had gone that she realised that she had wanted to keep him longer. And because somewhere along the path of their meeting and of their association she had bungled, she was left, at the end, with no means whereby to hold him. Her body had been smooth like the surface of a desert. She was foolish, and her body had no hooks.

The result was that Hannah Theron had to come to Kalvyn as a creature with a torn body. Willem Retief had made inroads into the domain of her ego. It was not in his approach to her, and in his dealings with her in her yielding, that he had outraged Hannah Theron's womanliness. And it was all an experience for which she had felt no need. Throughout the months during which Hannah Theron's entanglement with Willem Retief lasted, she was conscious, almost from moment to moment, of the fact that these were quite unnecessary passages.

And now, seated in the lounge of the Northern Hotel, and glancing at Bert Parsons every time his eyes were averted, Hannah Theron found herself, half unconsciously but with a sure deliberation, making comparisons between the man who had but recently gone out of her life and the man to whom she had just been introduced.

Well, there was that something about Bert Parsons's eyes. Burning eyes set deeply in his red face. They were the eyes of a man. Eyes in which there seemed to dwell hidden cruelties. They were eyes that spoke of the strength of a man. And a man is a strong, sleek beast; and he is also blubber. Bert Parsons's eyes seemed deeper in his head because of the prominence of his cheek-bones. Willem Retief's eyes were set shallowly. They were the eyes of a weakling. But there was this about a weakling, Hannah Theron reflected: you knew all the time how far he was pulling you in, because you were allowing him to do it. If after that you found that you had committed yourself too far, and that you had lost out, it was only because somewhere along the road you had slipped up; you had blundered; you got hurt, all right, but you had the knowledge that it was through your own fault.

But with a man like Bert Parsons it would be different. She could sense the strength that lay in his body. It was a thing from which she shrank in fear. But it was also a thing that drew her. And he was weak, of course. Hannah Theron had no illusions about that. It was a weakness infinitely more squashy than anything that could be associated with Willem Retief. Because in Bert Parsons's weakness there would be a sinister quality. Not just the weakness of hate, but a thing like the moving about of water, that would suck you under.

It was only months later, when she reflected on the circumstances of her meeting with Bert Parsons that Hannah Theron realised that her succumbing to Bert Parsons's advances had been a slow, heavy thing of the soil, in which there was none of the luminosity of the intellect or of the spirit. Indeed, in the strict sense of the word (as she discovered later), it was incorrect to say that Bert Parsons had had any need to make advances to her at all. She had been his for less than the asking.

And it was afterwards, when there was the net with steel strands about her spirit, and the nights flowed through the jacarandas that were shadowless in the night, that she struggled in the toils that held her, and she was afraid to recognise the nature of those toils for what they really were. And she tried to believe that this thing that had happened to her was an unnatural emanation from her loneliness.

It was because she had come to a small town like Kalvyn, in which there were few cultural activities, and little in the form of a higher kind of life, that she had sought shelter from the chill wind behind the ramparts of her body. That was what she tried to convince herself about.

She did not realise that it was not the loneliness in the small town of Kalvyn that had caught her up in a snare with steel strands. It was the warmth and the thickness of life in the Northern Transvaal dorp and in her own flesh that had mated her with the brown earth. She had never been lonely in Kalvyn. Her blood had sensed no loneliness there. Seedtime and harvest. The winter grass, long and blond in the wind, or short and stiff and stubbly underfoot. The soil, heavy and sodden with black life in the time of rain, red in the rust of waiting when there was drought. That was Hannah Theron's body.

O stony world, dreaming in barrenness and bringing forth trees with thorns. And summers bitter with drunkenness. How shalt thou cleave the rock under the hillside, and leave the human heart uncut?

And so it was that, whatever Hannah Theron told herself with her mind, the ultimate truth was always a deeper thing. And when her mind bade her cry to the hills in her shame, she could not obey this command, on account of the depths of her blood. It was the things she had acquired through her mind that spoke to her as a woman tarnished.

But her blood did not know anything of this shame. Her blood had beat in her temples in response to the demands of the earth, in the endless rhythm of a fructification and the growing to a heavy fullness and a drooping in tatters and the rags of a laying waste. She had come to Kalvyn, where the thickness of life was, moving in clumsy turgidities, and yet with a clean and perfect rhythm that throbbed with the blood in her temples.

Thus it was that her reason, her intellectualisation, her finer spiritual sensibilities, even, drew back in anger and red shame from the thought that the man who had come to her should have been a drunkard whom she had heard singing bawdy songs in a saloon bar. But her blood did not share in this rebellion. Listening to the importunacy of blows struck at the hard door of life, that thing of the dark blood within her had responded, not to the sullen stars, but to the summer warmth of the earth.

Chapter Three

1

Hans Korf placed more drinks before them.

"Here's to the skin off your nose," Mrs Manning said.

Phil, who – as Hannah Theron had learnt in the meantime – was a motor mechanic, spoke of the dance that was to be held in the Town Hall on Saturday.

"I suppose you are going with Dulcie?" Mrs Manning asked of Bert Parsons.

Dulcie. The name conjured up all sorts of ideas to Hannah Theron's imagination. Some doll-like creature. Sweet and feminine and with soft curves and soft eyes. But tough underneath. In her femaleness strong as whipcord. She could hold a man long after he had grown tired of her. He would be wearied of her, and he would still come back. Well, that was more than Hannah Theron had been able to do with Willem Retief. It was a secret that girls like Dulcie had, and that Hannah Theron would never acquire.

Such were the thoughts that came into Hannah Theron's mind when Mrs Manning mentioned the name of Bert Parsons's girl. Brainless ideas. Stupid and unfounded thoughts that went round and round in a wild dance. All created out of the sound of the name, Dulcie.

It was the whisky that was affecting her, Hannah Theron told herself. She felt hot under the jacket of her grey costume, which she had not yet discarded for her spring frocks. She thought of the filmy dresses that belonged to the fashion of the previous summer. They were creased and smelt of moth-balls. She must iron and air those dresses.

And she must go to the dress shop across the way tomorrow after school and arrange about opening an account. There was a tall girl in the dress shop, a girl with dark hair. Hannah had seen her on several occasions without having spoken to her. That girl looked like the manageress. Hannah would explain to her what sort of a summer frock she wanted, for a start. There was nothing in the window that attracted her. The frock must be smart but very simple. There must be pleats down the front to hide her thinness. Perhaps they wouldn't have a frock like that in the shop. She might talk to Mrs Manning about some dressmaker in the town.

There was laughter among the men after Mrs Manning had spoken about the girl Dulcie. Bert Parsons's face turned more red than ever. And there was that glint back in his eyes, a male look behind which some unslaked thing seemed to lurk. A look that frightened Hannah Theron as it drew her. The laughter seemed to go on for quite a while. Hannah Theron found herself wondering desperately as to what it was all about. She felt as though her head was beginning to swim. It must be the whisky, she thought again. Then she heard Bert Parsons speak.

"It's all off between me and Dulcie," he announced. "She says she don't want to see me no more."

And because this explanation was made in laughter, Hannah Theron thought that there was more behind it than the plain fact of Dulcie no longer wanting Bert Parsons. She imagined that something was being hidden in that laughter. She didn't know that all that was being hidden was a man's humiliation.

Before the party broke up that evening, Bert Parsons had invited Hannah Theron to accompany him to the dance in the Town Hall on Saturday night. And Hannah Theron had looked into Bert Parsons's eyes, deep-set between prominent cheek-bones, and she was drawn to that glint of danger.

And because she felt drawn, she had refused his invitation.

2

During the tea interval in the teachers' common room next day, Hannah Theron found herself in conversation with Lettie van der Walt. Lettie was talking about the police ball.

"You must get out a bit, learn the life of the place, meet people and all that sort of thing," Lettie was saying. "We are going in a party on Saturday, and we are short of a girl. I said I would ask you – "

Hannah Theron thanked Lettie van der Walt, and shook her head.

"Somebody invited me last night," Hannah Theron explained. "Somebody at the hotel. But I said I couldn't go with him because I didn't know him well enough. And if he sees me at the dance with somebody else he'll think I didn't go with him because he wasn't good enough. And I don't want him to think that."

"Well, you must please yourself, of course," Lettie van der Walt answered. "But you know how it is with men. If he thinks you won't go out with him because he's not good enough for you, it will only make him all the more keen. It's a mistake to consider a man's feelings. I've learnt that much."

Hannah Theron did not answer.

Lettie van der Walt had wide, blue eyes and a round face and a conventional prettiness. And she was young, somewhere in her early twenties. But a number of lines were beginning to harden at the side of her mouth, giving her a peculiarly set expression at times. Hannah Theron wondered whether that look had its origin in Lettie van der Walt's experience of life or it had been caused by the nervous strain of school teaching. That look, that beginning of a hardness – had Lettie van der Walt acquired it inside or outside the classroom?

"May I ask who the man is who invited you to the dance?" Lettie enquired after a pause. "Please don't think I'm being rude. I'm only asking because I am interested in you."

But she said it in such a way as to leave no doubt that she was really interested in the man. Interested to know which man in Kalvyn had singled out Hannah Theron as his partner to the police ball.

Hannah Theron flushed darkly as she answered. Lettie van der Walt observed with a half smile the wave of sudden scarlet mounting Hannah Theron's long, thin features. The colour vanished from Hannah Theron's cheeks and temples as quickly as it had come, like the falling to the ground of an hibiscus flower. So that was that, Lettie van der Walt reflected, that flush fading from Hannah Theron's face like the falling of an hibiscus flower.

"His name," Hannah answered, with the air of imparting a confidence, "is Bert Parsons. Mrs Manning introduced him to me in the lounge of the Northern Hotel last night. There were two other young men with him. I said I couldn't go to the dance with him because I didn't know him well enough, meeting him just once, like that. But that wasn't my real reason, of course. And there was something about the way they were laughing that made me feel queer."

Hannah Theron spoke rapidly, as though seeking, with a flood of words, to distract Lettie van der Walt's mind from a train of thought that she did not wish her to follow. Words. Hannah Theron was using words as a veil, as a garment to hang before a nakedness into which Lettie van der Walt's round blue eyes had looked.

"But what about that Hartnell girl?" Lettie van der Walt asked.

"Is her name Dulcie?" Hannah Theron enquired.

Before Lettie van der Walt could reply, there was a burst of laughter from Japie Kruger. The two girls looked round. Herklaas Huysmans was reclining in an easy chair, his long legs stretched clumsily in front of him, and he was talking to Miss Reinecke and Japie Kruger and Anna Coetzee. Japie Kruger rarely laughed at anything that Herklaas Huysmans said. He never knew when Herklaas Huysmans was serious or when he was pulling his leg. So something unusual must be happening.

But Herklaas Huysmans, when Lettie van der Walt and Hannah Theron turned round to listen to the conversation, appeared to be talking only of dull matters connected with the profession of school teaching. There seemed precious little to laugh about in that subject!

"I have seen it happening over the years," Herklaas Huysmans was saying. "When I first started teaching you didn't have to work much more than a five hour day. You had only to keep the register and the record of work book, and a few odds and ends like that, and you could do most of it in class, while the pupils were writing compositions, or doing sums from the board. But look what it's like today. You've got to divide your class into groups. You have got to follow out in the minutest detail what the Education Department has got the cheek to call the suggested syllabus. They don't lay it down, mind you, they only suggest it. And then let the inspector find out that you haven't followed that suggested syllabus to the nth degree. And then look at all the records and things we have to keep. And you can't bluff. It's all got to be written down. Teaching is no longer a five hour day affair. You can't get through all that work in ten hours a day. And you wait, it's going to be twelve hours a day. And still longer. And look at all the apparatus you have got to prepare. When I started teaching fourteen years ago the only apparatus the teacher knew anything at all about was a blackboard and a piece of chalk and a longer piece of stick. And all for this one reason."

"And what is that reason?" Lettie van der Walt enquired, with a faint show of interest. "I know I have to sit up almost every night until ten or eleven o'clock doing arrears of work that I can't manage in school. If I don't do that I can't go on with the class work next day."

"That's what Huysmans has been saying," Japie Kruger declared triumphantly. "He says the Education Department keeps on introducing new schemes every year as part of a deliberate policy. The idea isn't that the children should be better taught – because they are not. It is to take up every minute of the women teachers' spare time, so that they can't get into mischief."

"And we men have got to suffer for it," Herklaas Huysmans added. "When a woman teacher has a lot of spare time on her hands she doesn't just read or sit back and loaf, like a man does. She starts getting into trouble. They can advance all sorts of scientific reasons for giving the teachers all this extra work. Application of child psychology. Improvements in the theory of teaching. All that tripe. But I can see what the Education Department's game is. It's so that the women teachers should have less time for immorality. It's a stunt to keep them off the streets."

Japie Kruger winked at Anna Coetzee. "I hope you'll take that as a warning," he said.

"You're the first person who has ever said that the teaching profession is immoral," Miss Reinecke interjected.

"Not the teaching profession as a whole," Herklaas Huysmans answered, stirring lazily in his big armchair. "Only the women members."

Japie Kruger laughed again.

"I know you are only trying to be funny," Miss Reinecke continued, a note of anger rising in her voice. "But it's a queer sense of humour for a vice-principal to have. Your talk about bottles of gin hidden in the chalk cupboard, and now this rubbish about immorality. And I am surprised at Japie Kruger laughing at it. I have got a totally different opinion of him now. I always thought he was so chivalrous. And now you cast these aspersions on the women teachers of this country, and he thinks it's all a great joke."

Japie Kruger looked uneasy.

"But it is only a joke, Miss Reinecke," Japie Kruger said. "It's because it's not true, because we all know that it is not true, that what Huysmans says sounds humorous. If the women on the staff of this school, for instance, were immoral, we wouldn't talk about it. It's because they are not immoral that we can see the funny side of it – "

"A male teacher is moral," Herklaas Huysmans interrupted, "so he can't speak from personal knowledge as to whether or not a woman teacher is moral – "

Lettie van der Walt leapt to her feet, her round eyes ablaze with anger.

"We are not compelled to remain sitting here, listening to these low insinuations," she called out. "I'm going back to my classroom."

Hannah Theron looked at her watch. It was time for the pupils to fall in. It was her turn to ring the bell. She slipped out of the staff room in silence. Only Anna Coetzee noticed Hannah Theron's departure. She saw a tall, slender figure, with its dark head bent forward, gliding swiftly out of the door.

3

After school that afternoon, Hannah Theron walked through the quiet roads, where the spring was bursting, on her way back to the hotel. The kaffirboom was in terrible flower. Everywhere, in the gardens she passed, the blossoms on the fruit trees spoke of the heavy sap flowing in a slow, curled darkness.

It was spring again. But it was a spring-time that brought no rapture to her spirit. She felt that the lightness in her step was but a way of walking, something artificially acquired, like the habit you get into of holding a cup when you drink tea.

She passed by the building that was being erected in the main street. She walked on the far side of the pavement to avoid having to pass under the scaffolding, from which wet plaster was dripping in places. Something made her look up. Leaning over the edge of the roof were the heads and shoulders of two men and a youngster. The one in the middle was Bert Parsons, his face red and grinning, his broad shoulders massive against the sky.

Hannah Theron felt her heart throb. Inside her was the sense of a dark leaping, a slipping down an incline, a heavy, oily liquid washing the sides of a pool of black granite. Her being was caught into a whirlwind of conflicting emotions, so that her footsteps seemed to falter. She felt as though she were swaying in her high-heeled walk.

Hannah Theron looked down again hurriedly, but not before she had seen Bert Parsons wave at her.

"I'll see you in the lounge again this evening, kid," she heard him call in that loud, deep voice that held no resonance and no music but, instead, a tone that entered into her consciousness somewhere below the level of music. And she heard laughter. Those men were laughing.

But it was the laughter of spring. There was no mockery in that laughter that was open to the sunshine. The only mockery was in that colourless laughter inside her. Jeering at her. Hannah Theron, who could not laugh at herself, had to bear within the confines of her living, whose walls seemed all too thin, the echoes of a cracked mirth that was not any the less sunless because it was not of the grave. The laughter of those men seemed to her like bronze and steel, a war-horse prancing in the flame of pride, and it woke inside her a wretched guffaw, passionless and self afraid.

A few moments later Hannah Theron walked into Chic Modes, where that girl with the black hair was the manageress. It was a small shop. On one side was a counter backed by a high shelving. On the opposite wall hung a long row of dresses. A small girl with fair hair came forward.

"Can I help you, miss?"

Hannah Theron paused in indecision. She wanted that other girl to attend to her, the tall thin girl with the black hair, a girl taller than Hannah Theron, and not unlike her in build and colouring. Taller than Hannah, too tall, almost, for a woman, that girl dressed with a degree of taste that made her body look inviting. And her carriage was graceful. That was the girl whom Hannah Theron wanted to attend to her. But she didn't want to put the small, fair girl before her out of countenance. In the next moment her difficulty was solved.

"Engela," the tall girl called out from the little wooden cubicle at the back of the shop, "have you seen that invoice from Madeleine's?"

"Yes, Miss Hartnell," Engela answered, "it's on the file next to the – oh, I'll show you."

And so it came about that Miss Hartnell, emerging from the wood and glass cubicle, attended to Hannah Theron.

Would this be Dulcie? Hannah Theron wondered. Yes, she must be.

And when Miss Hartnell said, "You are Miss Theron, I believe. Can I help you?" Hannah Theron's feminine intuitions told her with the clamancy of brazen tongued trumpets that this girl was indeed Dulcie.

Hannah Theron's momentary confusion gave way to a peculiar kind of self-assurance. She liked this girl, Dulcie, whose very appearance was a challenge to battle.

And, of course, Dulcie knew all about her, and about the fact that Bert Parsons had invited her to the dance. And also that she had declined the invitation. In a small town like this, everybody knew everybody else's business. And Dulcie must have seen her through the peep-hole in the cubicle, and have called Engela away on purpose.

Thus these two women met – the one who had just gone out of the life of Bert Parsons, the drunken builder, the town rake, and the woman who was about to enter his life. They met in a rivalry with which there went also a queer sort of a respect for each other. They had no illusions about each other as women. They saw through each other with a cold and cruel and relentless insight, as women. But in that moment of meeting they felt for each other also a queer kind of a twisted regard, which did not in all their subsequent relationships ever depart from their spirits utterly. Even though that regard was for most of the time in their unconscious.

Dulcie Hartnell saw in front of her a girl who superficially was not unlike herself. This girl carried herself with some sort of distinction. She dressed in good taste. The grey costume she wore set off her figure to advantage. The simple cut spoke of good class, breeding and all that. Which meant no more, of course, than that this Miss Theron had been through the mill and had learnt the effectiveness of the quiet approach.

Knowing how to dress was something that life taught you. Some of the best brought up girls Dulcie Hartnell had come across didn't know the first thing about dress. It was a different kind of refinement, this thing about clothes, that people who didn't know any better ascribed other sorts of reasons to.

Dulcie Hartnell was satisfied that Hannah Theron had been through it. But she could sense these things in other ways also than from Hannah's dress. They were two women, and they could not conceal from each other what was inside them.

"I am trying to find something for spring," Hannah Theron heard herself saying, "something in pastels."

That was what her voice was saying. Her thoughts had taken a different turn.

Bert Parsons. What was his feeling for Hannah Theron? What were his feelings for this girl who had been his woman? No need for anybody to tell Hannah Theron now that Dulcie Hartnell had been both girl and woman to Bert Parsons. She knew these facts in her own blood, in her own body. It was a knowledge that curved inside her in a primitive rankness.

Hannah Theron tried to remember, once again, all she could of the way Bert Parsons had reacted towards her at their meeting in the hotel lounge. Was it an interest that would go deeper? And the way he had waved at her less than a quarter of an hour before from the top of that building. He had been aroused. Hannah Theron was sure of that. She knew it inside her. It was something nobody could argue with her about.

But then there was this difficulty. They said that when a man was tired of one girl he went to another girl who was her exact opposite. If Bert Parsons had tired of Dulcie Hartnell, he would have gone to a girl of the Mae West type. Blonde and buxom. Somebody like Mrs Manning, the proprietress of the Northern Hotel – but younger, of course. He would not have gone to somebody who was also tall and thin and dark. It must mean that Bert Parsons had not grown tired of Dulcie Hartnell, but that she had grown tired of him, likely. Or perhaps there was no other girl on the spot at the moment.

But of one thing Hannah Theron was certain. In that short while in which they had been together in the lounge of the Northern Hotel, Hannah Theron and Bert Parsons, the maleness in Bert Parsons had spoken to Hannah Theron of that which could be conveyed neither in word nor in gesture.

"I think I have something here that is just your style," Hannah Theron heard Dulcie Hartnell say. The voice seemed to come from a great distance. From a green, dim height shrouded in smoke.

So the two women went on talking about clothes. Hannah Theron bought a spring frock to which a few slight alterations would have to be made. She also arranged about opening an account at the shop.

4

Bert Parsons had had a bath and shave. The grey dust from the building had been washed off his large body and out of his thick black hair. But there was little he could do about his hands, large and calloused and with broken fingernails, under which the dark grime was embedded. His palms and the insides of his fingers were hard and rough, like dried mealie-cobs.

Seated on the narrow iron bed in his room in Mrs Ferreira's boarding-house, and dressed in a clean white shirt, his blue pin-stripe suit folded on the bed beside him, Bert Parsons contemplated his huge, shapeless hands.

The feelings uppermost in his mind at that moment were of self pity. It didn't matter where he went – in the Carlton Hotel in Johannesburg, where he had gone to stay for weekends when he was making good money out of contracting; anywhere, where there were men and women of the world – the moment they saw his hands they knew he was a workman. But he was just as good as any man he had ever come across, in a bar or a night club, in Johannesburg or anywhere else.

And when he was doing well, and didn't have to work as a foreman carpenter, like now, he could spend just as much dough as any other businessman on those girls with the made-up smooth faces and the narrow eyebrows and the slick hair and figures. And in evening dress he looked better than any of those Johannesburg businessmen.

And he had taken out those same women that held their heads up high in the places of fashionable entertainment and he had taken them to shows and to dances and had given them money, a couple of fivers, just like that, and he had bought them presents and had slept with them. But it had made no damn difference. Underneath there was a veiled sneer in their attitude towards him.

He knew he hadn't had much education. But several of the successful men of the world he had come across had told him that they hadn't had much education, either. They had made their way in the world because they had brains. And they were proud that they hadn't been educated. Bert Parsons knew that he was just like those men. They were his sort and he was their sort. Just wait until he landed a contract again.

He wouldn't be working for a boss now if it wasn't that he had gone on that drunk spell that had lasted – God, how long did it last? It looked like months. And so he missed all the contracts that were going. What sort of a chance would Neser have stood to get the contract for the new stores if Bert Parsons had been there to put in a tender? And because he had been drunk all that time he had to go round to Neser with his hat in his hand, crawling, like a bloody kaffir. But wait. He'd show them. There was the new market buildings to go up. Just wait. Was Neser a member of the Kalvyn Club? No, but Bert Parsons was. A few whiskies with the Town Clerk. That was all. Then you would see what was going to happen to that contract.

Social life. That was the secret. Neser was just an ordinary workman. He would never be anything else. How you got on in life was by mixing socially. You made a splash that put you in with the top class. Then you were all right. Then things came easy. That was something a man like Neser would never know. And if Neser knew, he wouldn't be able to get away with it. People would sense that underneath Neser was just a workman.

Bert Parsons went over to the wardrobe and took out a bottle of whisky. He poured a double tot into a tumbler and swallowed it down in a gulp. Then he felt better. He had shown them once before what he had in him. He would show them again.

Then, once more, he became conscious of his hands with the thick, shapeless fingers and the broken fingernails and the rough callouses. A workman's hands. Again Bert Parsons saw himself as a workman just like Neser. When he was drunk he didn't care. Not that much. And the women really liked being caressed by a hand that was a man's hand, and no argument. No matter what they said or pretended to think, just because they wanted to make him feel sore.

Bert Parsons had another tot of whisky, which he drank neat, and as a warm glow trickled into his veins he felt his self esteem coming back to him. He slipped on his trousers and adjusted his tie, which he had spent some time in selecting from several dozen hanging from a string on the inside door of the wardrobe.

In the mirror of the wardrobe that stood edgeways in a corner of the room, next to the wash-stand that held an enamel basin and a cracked jug, Bert Parsons surveyed himself during long moments in which the raw spirit pleasantly dulled his senses and stroked his muscles with a warming touch. Show him a better looking man anywhere. That was all. A better looking man. He held his hands in front of his chest, the open palms turned outwards. He laughed. What did he care what a woman thought of his hands, roughened with lime and brick dust and calloused from saw and hammer, when she was being his woman? Bert Parsons laughed again.

It was that little bitch, Dulcie Hartnell, that first started making him feel rotten about things like this. And she wasn't any better class than any of the waitresses, and servant girls even, that he used to knock about with in Kalvyn before he met Dulcie. All this fine lady business was just put on. And then Dulcie had the cheek to say that she had helped him to better himself. That was what she had said. As if he hadn't had it inside him all the time.

And then, because he had gone on a few sprees, Dulcie had turned sour on him. And he knew he felt rotten about it, Dulcie turning him up like that last week. He felt bloody rotten. Yes, he had to admit that. That thin cow that sold dresses and acted like a queen had the cheek to say that she had improved him. That he couldn't stand for. He had had ideas all the time. Lots bigger ideas than Dulcie would ever have. And now that she had turned him up, he felt all gone in. But he wouldn't show it. To hell with her. She was just a bitch. But why was he so blasted cut up about it? It must be that he loved her. That was it. He loved her. To hell with women. They were all muck. That was it – muck. And they gave themselves airs. Acting as though they didn't...

It was only then, after he had had another drink, that Bert Parsons thought of Hannah Theron. She seemed a bit of all right, he thought. Nothing very special. But she would be all right... And there was that bet he had with Lionel Andrews. Yes, that school-teacher seemed to be quite a decent bit of skirt.

She could never make him feel like Dulcie, of course. But she would do to string around with, to take out to dances and for weekends to the Isipi Hotel, and to have around for his girl until such time as Dulcie Hartnell came back to him – if she ever did come back to him. Or until he found some really smart dame that he could feel the same about as about Dulcie.

Well, he would see her again, this evening, in the lounge. He knew she would be there. He knew, all right. And even though she had said she wouldn't go to the police ball with him on Saturday night, he was sure she would change her mind before then. She would come to his room, too, if he wanted her. And that same night. School-teacher or no school-teacher. A girl didn't get to look that way for nothing. All that quiet smile business, and yet she didn't turn a hair at all those dirty jokes Lionel Andrews was telling, one after the other, in the lounge, before Mrs Manning had said it was time to break up. That school-teacher would be quite easy.

Bert Parsons was still admiring his reflection in the mirror when there was a soft knock at his door. It must be somebody in the boarding-house. It couldn't be Mrs Ferreira, he reflected. She knocked louder. Or perhaps it was really a loud knock, and it only sounded soft to him because he was already getting full of pots.

He went to open the door, his feet a little unsteady, his tall, thick body swaying slightly. He fumbled twice before his huge hand closed around the doorknob. He must be getting a bit tight, he thought. He would stick his head under the bathroom tap and after that a cup of black coffee would put him right again for the night. He would have a couple of quick ones with the boys in the bar and then he would go into the lounge and chat a bit to that school-teacher girl. She would be waiting for him, all right. That sort always did.

Bert Parsons got the door open. Before him stood a girl of about eighteen. He had to look twice before he recognised her. Oh yes, of course, she was old Van Schalkwyk's eldest daughter. The daughter of that white labourer he had fired off the building job the other day.

"Oh, hello," Bert Parsons said. "You want to see me? Come in. Come right in. What's your name again. I can't just – "

"Wiesie is my name," the girl answered. "Wiesie van Schalkwyk. My father he said I must bring Mr Parsons this letter."

"Come in," Bert Parsons said. "Come in and sit down."

He knew her now, of course. Wiesie. She was a bit cracked. Soft in the head. She was given to doing silly things. They all called her 'Simple Wiesie.' Nevertheless, the tone of deference which this half-wit child adopted towards him – addressing him in the third person – was flattering to Bert Parsons's vanity.

"Sit down," he said again, this time with just the suggestion of pomposity. "And give me the letter. I'll read it now."

The girl came into the room, looked around for a chair and, seeing that the only one in the room was occupied by Bert Parsons's working clothes and soiled overalls, went and sat on the edge of the bed, giggling at this immodesty.

Wiesie van Schalkwyk was plump and of an indecisive kind of fairness. She had a round face with blunt features that were not altogether unpleasing to look at. Her mouth was inclined to hang slightly open, as though the task of keeping her lower jaw in place imposed a severe muscular strain on her. She had a habit, when she spoke to people, of lowering her head and turning her eyes upwards, looking at the person she addressed through her fair eyelashes. This mannerism imparted to her features an expression of slyness that did not really form a part of her nature.

Standing in the centre of the room, his legs apart, and swaying slightly, Bert Parsons slowly deciphered the contents of the grimy note – an ill spelt and ungrammatical appeal, traced in laborious characters, to Bert Parsons to take Van Schalkwyk back on to the building job. Himself uneducated, Bert Parsons derived considerable amusement from the contemplation of another man's shortcomings in the field of scholarship. Also, it was pleasant for him to think of himself as a man of such influence as to receive a message of this nature. He had become a boss again. It was a lucky sign. It augured well for the municipal market contract.

He was on the point of informing Wiesie straight away that her father could come back. But then he checked himself. It hadn't to be as simple as all that. He was in a position of authority now. He could act like a man in authority.

"Well," Bert Parsons said, "you can tell your dad that there is lots of labourers like him looking for jobs today, and that he can't just mess around any old how and then when he gets fired think I'll take him back every time. I been a contractor for big jobs before today. Much bigger than them stores" – his imagination, inflamed by the liquor, was swelling with illusions of grandeur – "four, five storeys high blocks of flats. So if I lets him come back he has got to put his guts into – "

He was set for a long speech, and he would have continued almost indefinitely in the same strain, his blood whipped up by the alcohol, when he noticed that Wiesie was not paying any serious attention to his remarks. Instead, she remained seated on the edge of the bed, swaying her plump body backwards and forwards, slowly, and she was giggling again.

At first Bert Parsons was annoyed. Here he was going all out to play the big boss and she wasn't taking him seriously.

Then a raw understanding flooded his senses. Wiesie van Schalkwyk was a girl. Until then he had seen her only as her father's messenger.

He moved unsteadily over to the wardrobe and hauled out a bottle. He fumbled about on top of the dressing-table, trying to remember what had happened to the other tumbler. He found it, a few moments later, in a recess under the wash-stand. He rinsed the glass with water out of the jug. Then he poured out two stiff tots of whisky.

"I am sorry I haven't got any soda," Bert Parsons said to the girl. "I always drink it neat. Will you have water in yours? Just a little water?"

His manner and voice were ingratiating.

"Yus," Wiesie van Schalkwyk answered, giggling again. "A little water, please, Mr Parsons."

With a hand that shook visibly, Bert Parsons handed the girl her drink. He emptied his glass at a gulp.

Wiesie tasted the liquor and grimaced. Then she drank a little more and, seeing over the top of her glass that Bert Parsons had finished his drink, she drank what remained in her tumbler in a comical kind of confusion.

Bert Parsons seated himself on the bed beside her, his bulky form dwarfing her short, plump body into insignificance.

"How old are you, Wiesie?" he asked, his arm at the same time encircling her shoulder.

For a moment Wiesie looked startled. She felt nervous when this big man brought his red face so close to hers.

"I am nearly twenty, Mr Parsons," Wiesie van Schalkwyk answered. "The day before Christmas I am twenty."

"Twenty and never been kissed," Bert Parsons said, and before she could answer he had pressed his mouth on hers.

Slowly Wiesie van Schalkwyk found herself relaxing to the warmth of Bert Parsons's embrace; her fears left her; her body tingled in the waves of a dark urgence.

Wiesie van Schalkwyk had left off giggling.

"You can tell your father he's on," Bert Parsons said when Wiesie van Schalkwyk was ready to leave. "Tell him to report to the timekeeper tomorrow morning."

While he spoke, Bert Parsons remained seated on the bed. He had wanted to offer Wiesie van Schalkwyk another drink before she left, but he changed his mind. It would be no good if she got home looking tipsy. That wasn't what Van Schalkwyk had sent Wiesie to him for. He had sent her to him for another reason. Well, he and Van Schalkwyk understood each other now. There was nothing more to be said on either side.

Wiesie said nothing either, when she went out. She expressed no gratitude to Bert Parsons for his promise to re-employ her father. Nor did she answer when, as she went out of the door, Bert Parsons called to her, "I'll see you some more, kiddie."

She walked out of the room in silence.

Bert Parsons remained on the bed, his gaze directed straight ahead of him. There were all sorts of feelings curling about slowly inside him. The feeling that was strongest of all, and that he tried hardest to suppress, was one of disgust with himself.

But he overcame that feeling. Through thinking of Hannah Theron. He would take her to the dance, all right. She would go with him on Saturday, even though she had declined his invitation on the previous night. He thought of her as that young school-teacher who tried to look stuck up.

But she would be easy, in spite of the airs that she tried to give herself. Bert Parsons looked at his hands. And this time it was not in self mockery or self pity. Yes, that young school-teacher would be as easy as Wiesie van Schalkwyk had been.

But Bert Parsons did not feel sure as to whether he was deriving real satisfaction from these thoughts.

Chapter Four

1

THE spring was well advanced into the sullen expanses of the summer, with its slow dreams and quiet and strong stirrings at the scarlet heart of life, when Hannah Theron was again seated in Sybrand van Aswegen's office. The principal of the Kalvyn Afrikaans-medium Primary School looked at the school-teacher seated opposite him in very much the same way as he did a term and a half ago, at their first interview.

He had spoken to her at some length now, and he was waiting for her to answer. In his waiting there was a degree of restlessness that was not in keeping with the normal pattern of his emotions which he had so disciplined along the path mapped out for him by his ambitions that there was not a single person in this world who could say for sure that he knew what Sybrand van Aswegen's real nature was. The first time Sybrand van Aswegen had seen Hannah Theron she had disturbed him. She had the same effect on him now, when he was waiting for her reply to the speech he had just made: to the words which he had spoken with a directness that was unusual for him.

He had talked straight to her because he was sure of his ground. The things that had happened since their first interview – matters of which he had received at first vague tidings and afterwards first hand accounts – were all merely in confirmation of what he had felt about Hannah Theron at the beginning.

Eventually she answered him.

"Do I take it, then, Mr Van Aswegen," she asked, "that you want me to resign?"

"That is a matter that rests with your own conscience, Juffrou," Sybrand van Aswegen answered. "But I want to make clear to you that I have no facts as yet to lay either before the Secretary of the School Board or before the Department. Nor shall I go out of my way to seek such facts. I shall take no action unless I am directly approached by responsible residents of this town. As principal, my first duty is to the school. But I have responsibilities also to my teachers. And I have summoned you to my office with a view also to affording you such protection as lies within my official capacity."

"If it is a matter of my own conscience," Hannah Theron replied, "then I can only say that there is nothing which impels me either to wish to resign from the Education Department or to apply for a transfer to a school in some other town."

Hannah Theron's voice was cold, and she spoke with a tight lipped resolution which she did not feel. So far, she and Sybrand were only sparring, revealing nothing to each other of their real thoughts.

Then Sybrand van Aswegen, tired of this play-acting, and in the assurance that he held all the cards, struck bluntly into the heart of the subject.

"It is the class of men you associate with," he said. "This is a small place, and you can't blame people for talking about it. A school-teacher has to be circumspect. She has to be careful that no breath of scandal becomes attached to her name. She has a position to maintain in the community. Parents must feel that they can send their children to school with confidence – "

"The children in my class all love me," Hannah Theron interrupted him. "And there is nothing I have done, in my life outside of school hours, of which I am ashamed. Whatever people say or think about me, they can't prove anything. And when I examine my own actions frankly, I am satisfied that there is nothing I have done that I have not done in love. The only sin one can commit is to act in a loveless fashion. But if you want me to leave here, I shall, of course, apply to Pretoria for a transfer. Only, in my heart I am satisfied that I have done nothing wrong."

"But the company you keep," Sybrand van Aswegen continued. "You are expected to associate with your social equals. And now that you have gone to stay in Mrs Ferreira's boarding-house – well, you can guess what people are saying, can't you?"

Hannah Theron smiled bitterly.

"You yourself asked me to leave the Northern Hotel," she said. "The first day I came here, you said that I should stay either with a private family or in a quiet boarding-house."

"But that man Bert Parsons is also staying at Mrs Ferreira's," Sybrand van Aswegen replied. "And they tell me that your rooms are almost adjoining each other. As you have said, there is nothing that can be proved. Although if I went out to seek it, I should no doubt find that the necessary proof would be forthcoming. But that doesn't form any part of my duties. All I wish to do is to try to bring home to you your responsibilities as somebody entrusted with the care of youth."

Proof, Hannah Theron thought bitterly. Proof. If it was proof they wanted, then the thing she feared that was wrong with her would be the most convincing proof that there was. If only she could be sure, one way or the other. But there was nobody she could talk to. She couldn't go to a doctor. Not in Kalvyn, anyway. And Bert Parsons was the last person in the world to whom she would think of mentioning these fears.

And here was Sybrand van Aswegen full of all this smug talk. She wanted to laugh. He was trying to say to her that she was a harlot. But a school principal couldn't use words like that in talking to a member of his staff. She wondered what Sybrand van Aswegen would think if he knew some of the things Bert Parsons called her, when he was filled up with pots, and his passion was worked up, not for her, but for Dulcie Hartnell. Especially if they had gone to a dance that night, and Bert Parsons had met Dulcie Hartnell there, and Dulcie had lured him on with all sorts of feminine tricks, so as to be able to laugh in his face afterwards, and to be able to laugh at Hannah Theron. Yes, if only Sybrand van Aswegen knew the kind of thing that went on then, when they got back into her room, he wouldn't be so mealy-mouthed about this business.

Perhaps she would even tell Sybrand van Aswegen, just to see how he took it. Let him get her fired out of the Education Department, then, if he felt like it. It would be marvellous to shock him out of his staid respectability. If he knew that this woman member of his staff was not only a thing that a drunkard made use of to get rid of all his physical cravings, but that he treated her with nothing but the most open contempt on top of it. She had a good mind to tell Sybrand van Aswegen. There was very little to lose.

She would probably have to leave Kalvyn in any case. Perhaps it would even be better to leave now than to hang on longer, when the thing she feared would have turned into certainty, and the whole place would know the kind of trouble that she had got herself into.

Anyway, there was one thing she was determined about. And that was that Bert Parsons would never know. Not from her, anyway. She wasn't going to lower herself to the extent of forcing him to take notice of her on that account. Hannah Theron felt that Dulcie Hartnell would always remain for Bert Parsons a creature of flame and flesh and perfumed allurement, and that she herself would never be anything more than a makeshift. And her pride would not allow her to make use of this circumstance that was filling her with unspeakable dread to get at Bert Parsons's feelings – which in any case would not amount to very much.

Possibly he would even go so far as to agree to marry her. Because everybody would accept it that he was responsible for her condition. And whatever else he said and did, he didn't want his associates to regard him as a cad. No thanks, she wanted none of that. Made an honest woman out of, and all the time, in his drunken bouts, having that thrown up at her. And mouthing Dulcie Hartnell's name in maudlin half stupors.

"Whatever you think of me, Mr Van Aswegen," Hannah said eventually, "I would like to let you know that I am not ashamed of the company I keep. The people of my own class in this town – if you mean my fellow school-teachers and people like that – well, there are not many of them. And I don't think I have very much in common with them. In any case, they have never shown that they are interested in me. Look at the Cultural Society. I used to attend all the meetings, and whenever I had anything to say the other members would frown or pretend not to hear. They are all like a lot of sheep. No one has got any ideas of his own. When they read in *Literêre Tydskrif* about some new artist or writer, they all say immediately that that person is a genius. They have no originality. They have no views of their own. And if the people I associate with are, as you say, not my class, they have at least got an independence of spirit."

Sybrand van Aswegen, feeling once more that he had all the cards in his hands, suddenly decided to unbend.

"Remember, I am somebody who is friendly disposed towards you," he said. "I want you to bear that in mind, Miss Theron. In everything. I believe I understand your difficulties. And if there is anything I can do to help, please don't forget me. I suppose you think I like the sort of life I am leading. Well, let me tell you something. The sameness of it has been killing me for years. I have repeatedly asked myself what it is all about. I am a respected member of the community. I am a good school principal. I have a wife and four children. I am treated as an equal by the foremost citizens of this town. In the Kalvyn Club my views are listened to with respect – unlike the way your opinions are received in the Cultural Society. One of these days I'll be elected to the Town Council. And what do I get out of life? My life is like a desert. Petty worries. Small anxieties. Unimportant little triumphs. Pleased at a good report from the inspector. Trying to save up enough to be able to take my wife and children to Cape Town for the December holidays. Looking forward to the time when I will have paid off my house. I have had nothing out of life. Nothing."

Hannah Theron laughed bitterly.

"I know what you are thinking, Mr Van Aswegen," she replied. "And let me tell you that you are wrong. I get nothing out of life, either. Much less than you do. Going to parties and dances and getting drunk. And having weekends of debauchery. I know that is how you picture my life to be. It makes me laugh. You can ask anybody who has ever seen me at a party, or a dance, or in the lounge of an hotel, whether I have more than one or two drinks, whether I have ever been even slightly drunk. I tell you, it's misery. There is nothing more dreadful to me than the sight of people getting drunk. And that's what they call life. And that's what you call life. I tell you, it's death, Mr Van Aswegen. To be in the company of a drunk man, and to be in a state of nervous tension all the time, not knowing what he is going to do next. In terror from one moment to the next. And hoping against hope all the time that he will change, and that from being a drunkard he will become a decent human being – like he is when he is sober. And knowing, at the back of your mind all the time, that he will never become any different. My one dream in life is to have quiet, calm, serenity. A little home and children. Just the kind of life that you have got, Mr Van Aswegen. If you only knew how I envied you."

This wasn't quite correct, of course. She didn't really envy him his stodgy, dissatisfied life. Especially as that was the very life that she had herself discarded. She had flung that sort of life on the ash heap in the act of flinging herself on the ash heap as well.

But what if it was true, this thing that she suspected about her condition? What about her parents? What was going to happen to her? She would never be able to face it. She would have to find some way of doing away with herself. It would be very pleasant to be dead. The cool, green allurement of the grave. She would find some way; she would have to.

And here was this Sybrand van Aswegen jealous of what he thought was her exotic experience of life! Here was he burdening her with his frustrations and unfulfilled urges. Perhaps it would be better if she played up to him for a little while. That would give her time to think, room in which to manoeuvre.

"I am the one who is to be pitied," Sybrand van Aswegen said, getting up from behind his desk and moving slowly round to the side. "Up to the time I married I had no experience of women. You know what I mean. Of life, of sex. My wife was my first woman. You have no idea, when the years pass by, how that thought keeps preying on my mind."

Well, he had certainly made up for lost time, Hannah Theron reflected cynically. Four children and all that. Instead, she tried to be understanding. Heavens, here was Sybrand van Aswegen, the austere principal of her school, suddenly going to pieces. Going maudlin just as though he had been drinking. All men were like that. She would talk to him as she talked to Bert Parsons when he was drunk. She would try to console him.

"There is always life, Mr Van Aswegen," Hannah Theron said. "And when two people really love each other, then life can never be dull. You are filled with regrets because you think that you have missed some important experiences in life. But let me tell you that you have missed nothing. It's people like me, who don't find love, who get battered about by life, for whom existence is nothing but a sterile waste. I am in the desert, Mr Van Aswegen. I wonder how I could convince you of it."

Before she could draw back, Sybrand van Aswegen had caught her in his arms, clumsily, and was pulling her towards him. He mouthed all sorts of words, half inarticulately. He brought his face close down to hers. His lips were drooling.

Oh well, let him kiss her, Hannah Theron decided. Let him slobber over her. She would not respond to the warmth of his emotions. That would lure him on all the more, afterwards. But at the moment it would make him draw back within himself. And that was how it worked out.

Clutching her tight in his arms, Sybrand van Aswegen planted his mouth full on hers. He thrilled to the touch of her cold lips, and the next moment he released her.

Hannah Theron hurried towards the door. Her last glimpse of Sybrand van Aswegen showed him leaning with one hand on his desk, a foolish look on his flushed face. Hannah Theron opened the door and walked out quickly.

She had not wanted this thing to happen. But now that it was over she felt that there was not very much wrong with the situation. As far as the immediate future was concerned, at least, she would have Sybrand van Aswegen on her side. He would be afraid of becoming a nuisance straight away. But afterwards he might become something of a pest. Malicious, too, very probably. She would have to deal with him then in some other way.

2

Hannah Theron walked back to Mrs Ferreira's boarding-house in a state of acute despair. Men could see what she was. All men could feel that she was a loose woman. She had no feminine pride left. How quickly a man could detect a thing like that in any girl!

And then men were merciless. They could tell the moment a girl was a stricken creature. And then in filth and lust they pursued her. They no longer saw her as a woman in the way they would see their mothers, or sisters, or the girls they were engaged to marry, as women. Instead, they saw her as the unclean receptacle for their passions. Everything was fair then. There was no code left to protect a girl like that. They could cheat and deceive and seduce and rape her even, and all the things they did to her constituted only the material for low, salacious stories to be related in pubs, and hotel lounges, and in other places where men foregathered in order to talk dissolutely.

That was what they called a conquest. That was the sort of thing that to a man was a tribute to his male vanity. A plume. A star. Something that was balm to his ego. A piece of embroidery for his masculinity. It was a free for all. But Hannah Theron felt that only she and girls like her, whom these men recognised as stricken, wounded things, knew how shabby a reality was this matter of a conquest. What kind of a hunting was it, when the hunted deer saw the hunter from afar and made it easy for him, coming up to him, cowering and with its head down between its forequarters?

Since the first time Hannah had lived with a man, what were those other occasions on which she had given herself to men? She was not the spoils of a chase, but the pitiful flesh of an unbidden surrender. And these men had all got status from a thing like this. They had stuck out their chests and had thought of themselves as no end man-like, and attractive, and malely irresistible. And they had treated her with contumely. Down, bitch, down. She was a broken animal, quivering by the wayside. Because of the things that they had done to her, which they were free to do to her, they regarded themselves as virile, heroic figures, great hunters and great conquerors.

These were the thoughts that beat pitilessly into Hannah Theron's brain as she walked back, through the unmade roads and grass-grown pavements that were the back streets of Kalvyn, on her way to Mrs Ferreira's boarding-house. She no longer walked straight down the road that would take her into the main street. Although Mrs Ferreira's boarding-house was not in the main street, it was so situated that Hannah Theron could still, if she chose, walk a considerable distance down the main street in order to get to the boarding-house. In the same way that, at the beginning, she had walked down the main street in order to reach the front door of the Northern Hotel. But it was significant that she now walked along the more unfrequented ways.

And she had not heard that people had spoken critically, in the past, of her practice of walking down the main street. It was the things that had happened inside her that had made her change her route. Bert Parsons was no longer working on the Kalvyn stores. That job was practically completed, with only a couple of painters and carpenters putting on the final touches. Instead, Bert Parsons had tendered successfully for the municipal market building. He was making big money on that job. And he had also been promised the contract for the new Volkskas building. Bert Parsons was being regarded as an up and coming young man. He was doing very well for himself. But it had nothing to do with Bert Parsons's place of work, this circumstance of Hannah Theron's choosing to walk back to the boarding-house along ways where she would encounter fewest people. There were other, deeper reasons for this.

Everywhere Hannah Theron passed trees that were in magnificent foliage. Startling flowers that were in midsummer bloom. From this subtropical soil all growths curled outwards in a heavy luxuriance or shot up towards the sky in a swift slenderness. The leaves had flung away their tender shades that were sad with the questings of first youth and were now swollen with the darkness of strong greens. Huge flowers flared out in incredible scarlets, hot and voluptuous, their blood languors caught in the sun. Or they stood in the mystic silence of blues, whose breath was of a cold and almost frightening intensity.

And Hannah Theron thought of this thing that she feared was taking place inside her. And she only wished she could know for sure. The school holidays were still some time away. Otherwise she could go to Johannesburg. She could go and see a doctor who would not know her, whom she would never see again. She couldn't go to a doctor in Kalvyn. He wouldn't talk about it, of course, but she would come across him almost every day. She would not be able to face him in her shame.

If only she knew definitely, one way or the other. This uncertainty was driving her insane. And there was nobody she could talk to about it.

And here was this further complication with Sybrand van Aswegen. Just another man. Another male who had seen that she was stricken. He was obviously trying to blackmail her. But he wasn't somebody like Bert Parsons. Sybrand van Aswegen was somebody she could handle. He had better look out. Sybrand van Aswegen was not a proper man in the sense that Bert Parsons was a proper man. Sybrand van Aswegen's place in life was determined by his job, by his official standing, by the way he had worked himself up in the community. He was not a man in the naked sense of the word, like Bert Parsons was, and if he tried any funny business with her, well, it wouldn't be any good warning him. But he would find that he was embarking on something that wouldn't do him any good.

Hannah Theron was nearing the boarding-house. She was just preparing to slip across the main street at that end where there was less activity when she noticed, coming towards her, a tall, thin figure in a shirt and tennis shorts. Only when he waved his racket at her did she recognise Herklaas Huysmans. This was the first time she had seen him dressed otherwise than in the formal suits he wore to school. Hannah Theron bit her lip in momentary vexation. This was tiresome. Meeting Huysmans. After her encounter with Sybrand van Aswegen this was the last thing in the world she wanted. A further association with her job of school teaching.

Suddenly she felt that if she were not a school-teacher she would be able to face the world all over again. If a café waitress got into the sort of trouble that she feared she had got herself into, there was nothing fatal about it. Her whole life didn't go to pieces just on that account. It was very unpleasant, distressing, painful and all that sort of thing. But afterwards she could live again. It was the fact of her being a school-teacher that was responsible for at least three quarters of her present state of despair, Hannah reflected. In a city, doing some other sort of job, she would be all right. People wouldn't know about it. Or, if they did, it would be only a minor accident. It wouldn't be complete and final calamity. It wouldn't be this awful terror. This thing that was worse than death, literally.

Now here was Herklaas Huysmans, the vice-principal of the school, by his very presence, long and angular and ungainly, enforcing on her consciousness the realisation of her responsibilities as a school-teacher. In spite of his pretensions to originality of thought and boldness of outlook, he was just a good, conscientious schoolmaster. Nothing else. No devil in him. No fire. Otherwise he would have been sacked from the Education Department long ago.

And there was no way of avoiding him. If only she could wave at him, cheerily, and say "Hello" and pass on. Then she could get to Mrs Ferreira's boarding-house and in a few minutes' time, with her shoes kicked off, she would be lying stretched out on the bed. That was the one thing that she wanted above everything else at that moment. Rest, rest from her physical fatigue. Rest from the turmoil of her thoughts and emotions. Rest from her killing fears. Rest from the unpleasant experience which had ended her interview with Sybrand van Aswegen.

But by his manner she could see that Herklaas Huysmans wanted to talk to her. What a bore. With her nerves all jangled and her feeling like hell inside.

"A pleasant afternoon," Herklaas Huysmans called out, "and a pleasant meeting."

"Are you on your way to tennis?" Hannah Theron asked, purposely obvious and impersonal. "Well, I suppose you have to hurry. Ta-ta!"

"No," Herklaas Huysmans answered, "I'm not going to play tennis. It's too hot. Now, I want you to do me a favour. I am going for a long, cool beer. I want you to come with me. To the Northern Hotel lounge."

He saw Hannah Theron's hesitation. She was thinking of her bed in the boarding-house. The curtains drawn. Her body stretched at full length on the counterpane. A few blissful moments, in which she would be completely cut off from the world. But Herklaas Huysmans ascribed her hesitation to another cause.

"Bert Parsons won't mind," he said. "For that matter, you don't know, either, where he is at this moment, do you?" Herklaas Huysmans looked at her slyly.

In point of fact, Hannah Theron did not know where Bert Parsons was at that moment. The contract for the municipal market was in a certain sense a sinecure for Bert Parsons. He had got that contract through the inferior exploitation of what is known in mediocre life as 'personality.' Bert Parsons had made a set at the Town Clerk of Kalvyn. He had buttonholed him in the Kalvyn Club. He had also played golf with him. Finally, on a weekend when he told Hannah Theron that he had to go and visit a relative at Messina, Bert Parsons had taken the Town Clerk and two girls to an hotel some forty miles from Kalvyn. It was in the lounge of this hotel, over the eighth brandy, when the Town Clerk was on the verge of talking about his aged mother and of spewing, that the allocation of the municipal market building contract was finally decided, tenders or no tenders. The Town Clerk had informed Bert Parsons, on the last day, of the lowest figure so far tendered, and Bert Parsons had quoted fifty pounds lower.

The job itself was proceeding swimmingly. Lionel Andrews was doing all the calculations. He had been appointed as works foreman by Bert Parsons, and he took a pride in his job. The result was that the money Bert Parsons had to squander at that particular time was not to be reckoned in terms merely of fivers, but of sums treble that amount. The set of golf sticks he had bought Hannah Theron, almost as an afterthought, had cost sixteen guineas. Consequently it was no more than the truth, this insinuation of Herklaas Huysmans.

Of course, Hannah Theron had no idea where Bert Parsons was at that moment. But she could have guessed. And it would have been a fair bet that he was not on the job, that he was not present to see the concrete poured into the boxes on top of the wall at the second floor level of the municipal market building.

Anyway, what Herklaas Huysmans had hinted was in the nature of a challenge. Hannah Theron took it up. Even when she was most licked by life, stricken to the knee, as it were, she always knew how to rally. You could almost say that this was Hannah Theron's secret weapon. When you thought she was knocked out for keeps, battered out of the ring for good, this was the time when she came to light with quite unexpected powers of recuperation. As resilient as a tennis ball.

All right, if Herklaas Huysmans thought that this was the reason why she wouldn't go and have a spot with him – something to do with Bert Parsons getting upset – well, she would show him. As resilient as a tennis ball. And Herklaas Huysmans wasn't playing tennis, because it was too hot...

"I'll have a spot with you," Hannah Theron said coldly, and began to lead the way towards the Northern Hotel.

3

They walked in through the front door, their eyes momentarily blinded by the darkness of the drawn curtained lounge after the brilliance of the outside world. They found a table. Hannah Theron pressed the bell.

A few minutes later Hans Korf came in. He blinked. This was the first time he had seen Hannah Theron in the lounge with a man who wasn't Bert Parsons. Hannah Theron caught that expression on Hans Korf's face, a look that vanished almost in the same moment of its appearance. Hans Korf's reaction only served to spur her on.

It was a challenge. She had accepted it. Hell, she would show them.

Herklaas Huysmans looked at Hans Korf in a way that the waiter, if he had known the word, would have termed fatuous.

"I suppose the lady will have the same as I," he said, "and that will be two long beers. Off the ice."

"No," Hannah Theron interrupted him. "I'll have a double whisky and soda – not too much soda."

"You're a hard drinker, Hannah – may I call you Hannah?" Herklaas Huysmans observed after Hans Korf had retired to the bar room with the order.

"You can call me anything you like," Hannah Theron replied, "after I have had that whisky inside me."

To herself she thought – hell, what he must think of me. Of course, he thinks I am tough. He wouldn't have had the nerve to invite me here for a spot if he didn't know about my association with Bert Parsons. If he had taken me as merely a colleague, a fellow teacher, teaching at the same school, to whom he had wanted to be nice, he would have asked her into the Grand Café for tea and an eclair. But because it's me, he thinks he can invite me for a beer. And he doesn't know me. He knows nothing at all about me. That just shows what sort of reports are current about me in this place. They think I'm tough. A tough dame. A gun-moll sort of woman. Hell, if they only knew. If they only knew how soft I am inside. If they only knew about all my inferiority complexes, God, they'd be sorry for me.

"Here's how," Hannah Theron said, her glass to her lips.

"Good luck," Herklaas Huysmans answered.

He handed her a cigarette. They sat smoking and talking. A few minutes later Herklaas Huysmans pressed the button once more.

"The same again," Herklaas Huysmans said, somewhat foolishly, when Hans Korf made his reappearance. "Except that mine is also a double whisky straight – I mean neat."

"Two double whiskies?" Hans Korf asked, at the same time winking at Hannah Theron.

Herklaas Huysmans confirmed the order.

This placed Hans Korf in a dilemma. What was Hannah Theron's idea, he wondered. He had a soft spot for her. She was one of the few people whose voices had not jarred on him after he had got to hear her talk. Because he was partly deaf, most of his understanding of what people said to him was gained by way of lip-reading, but after he had got to know people for a while he made a special effort to try to catch the timbre of their voices. Mostly, the sounds that made contact with his tympanum in this way revolted him. But it was different with this Hannah Theron girl. When he had got with her to the stage where he stopped watching her lips and tried to get the sound of her voice, he was not disillusioned. Her voice to him was like music. Before he had listened intently to the sound her voice made he had, as a matter of course, watched her lips. And the movements of her lips were music to him. Afterwards, when he heard the sound of her voice, that was music to him also. And so he had a soft spot for her.

He was mildly annoyed at the things he saw Bert Parsons doing to her although, from the moment of their first meeting, Bert Parsons and Hannah Theron, when he served them with drinks, and Mrs Manning was in their company, he knew then just what would happen to Hannah Theron. He never tried to do anything about that sort of business any more. It seemed to him that that was just part of life. It belonged with the things that he accepted as belonging to the inevitable part of existence. That the butterfly should be caught in the net of the snarer. That the cuckoo should come and dash the swallow's fledglings to the earth. That he should have to stand by and watch the agony of the vlakhaas taken in the coils. That was all right. He understood and accepted all that.

But this was a different sort of a situation. Clearly Hannah Theron was enmeshed in no web of this man Herklaas Huysmans's weaving. Hans Korf knew Herklaas Huysmans only distantly, as a schoolmaster who was regarded as being something of a softie and who at irregular intervals dropped in for a beer, which he always drank in the lounge, and who never joined in the conversation that was proceeding among the habitues.

Now, what was the position? Did Hannah Theron want to get drunk in this man's company, or did she want this man Herklaas Huysmans to get drunk? Hans Korf was in a dilemma. Should he bring Hannah Theron only a single whisky, diluted with water to look like a double, in the certainty that she would get at least tipsy, or should he fulfil the order? He couldn't decide.

Then he made up his mind, and along male lines. Oh well, if she was out with this man, she must know what she was doing. She would have another double whisky. Two tots. She knew what she was up to. The moment after he had poured the stuff, Hans Korf regretted his action. But it was too late then. What was the use of his trying to save her anyway, when she did not want to be saved?

Over their second drink, Herklaas Huysmans had a great deal to say.

"My ambition was to be a lawyer," he announced to Hannah Theron, "so that when you look at me, as you do now, and in your eyes there is the contempt that one member of the teaching profession invariably has for another member of our ancient and undistinguished order, I should like you to remember that at one time I at least had dreams. If you don't believe me, come and have a look at the office desk I have in my flat. Drop in and have a look one of these days. And I'll also show you my law books. I'll dust them for you specially before you arrive. Only let me know when you are coming. Potentially, I was the greatest barrister in the country, in the world. Cicero had nothing on me. For one thing, I know Roman-Dutch law. I could make rings round Cicero at Roman-Dutch law. But it all went wrong. I'll show you my desk, though. I didn't have the guts to rent an advocate's office and put that desk in it, and put those law books in it and, above all, put myself in it."

"But it isn't too late yet," Hannah Theron said consolingly, in the same way that she habitually talked to Bert Parsons or to any of his drunk cronies, or as she had talked to Sybrand van Aswegen that same afternoon.

Oh well, men were all the same. They were just big children and just beasts. The principal of her school, Sybrand van Aswegen, had complained to her that very afternoon that she was not associating with her social equals in Kalvyn. Well, he had no cause for complaint now. She had listened to the first half of a maudlin story from her social equal – or slight social superior – Sybrand van Aswegen himself, an encounter that had terminated in her having been slobbered over; and here, on this same afternoon, and less than an hour later, she was on the point of undergoing the same experience at the hands of another school-teacher.

Whatever Herklaas Huysmans thought was going on in his mind at that moment, Hannah Theron knew only too well that if he had another whisky, on top of that first beer, he would end up by trying to kiss her – and, after a little while, he would offer to sleep with her. Here was a person of her own class: not so different from that other class with which she should not, according to Sybrand van Aswegen, associate.

And the technique with every man was the same. He had a couple of drinks in the company of a woman for whom he did not have too much respect and he would then begin to experience sentiments of self pity. He had gifts. The world had been against him. He had not been able to realise himself. That was why he was what he was. Life had been unfair to him. That was why he was only a drunken workman, when he would have been the managing director of a great industrial enterprise, given anything like a break. But life hadn't given him that break.

He would have been an artist. He would have painted great pictures. But he never had the chance to attend art school. But you should just see the drawing he had made of General Smuts, and copied only from a small photograph in a newspaper.

Or he was the greatest lawyer since Voetius or Marshall-Hall. And because they had sent him to that little school on the backveld, at an important stage of his studies, so that he didn't have access to a decent law library, just through that he had become a broken man. And so he would have to remain a school-teacher all his life, his great talents for the human race wasted in the desert.

All men were like that. Attributing their failure to unfair outside circumstances. Not seeming able to realise that difficulties are only put in your way in order that you should surmount them, if you have got any sort of guts inside you at all.

And when a man like this spoke to a girl whom he admired, whom he regarded as being on a pedestal somewhere far above him, how he would preen and strut then. Giving himself airs. Going all out to impress her with a pose of extrovert success. A man of the world. In the know, dashing, debonair. All that sort of junk. It was only when he was with a girl of whom he secretly thought nothing, because he could sense that she had been betrayed by other men, and that she was a stricken creature, a fallen thing – it was only in the company of such a girl that he adopted no sort of a pose. He let himself go completely. He became a whining poltroon, drowning in a cesspool of self pity.

He had no pretences to keep up. He thought nothing of this girl. In his heart he thought of her simply as a whore. And he could relax in the company of a whore. A whore had no moral rights. Imagine a strumpet trying to tell him to pull himself together. She had to be only too damned pleased and flattered that he took any notice of her at all, that he was willing to make her the recipient of the filth of his weakness as he would subsequently try – and successfully – to make her the vessel for catching up the ordure of his unsatisfied physical urges.

With a pang Hannah Theron realised what she had become. She had known these truths about herself and her place in life for quite a while. But at this moment, seated opposite Herklaas Huysmans and drinking whisky with him, the reality of her situation became focal. She knew exactly what was going to happen.

What Herklaas Huysmans didn't know about her was the fact that she had loyalties. She belonged to Bert Parsons. There was no question of Bert Parsons being in love with her. Bert Parsons had got her through exploiting the same technique that Herklaas Huysmans was – perhaps unconsciously and purely instinctively – making use of now. And Herklaas Huysmans didn't know how Bert Parsons was treating her. He knew Bert Parsons was being disloyal to her, that at that very moment he was probably carrying on with some other woman. But he didn't know of the things that Bert Parsons did to her in the intimacies of the bedroom. He didn't know the low brutalities with which Bert Parsons in disdainful lust assaulted her feminine pride. And Herklaas Huysmans did not know that, in spite of all these things, because of that loyalty born out of her unutterable sense of inferiority, she would never look at another man as long as Bert Parsons chose to retain her as his woman with flesh that stank.

If she were not attached to Bert Parsons in this most squalid of all fashions, it would have been quite all right. Herklaas Huysmans could have poured out the story of his failure to her. She would have listened. She would have pitied and consoled him. He would have become maudlin after a while, in his self pity. After a few days he would have reached the stage where he would have taken her to his flat to have a look at that desk which had never stood in a barrister's chambers. And he would have told her that she was the only person in the world who could give him courage, and that she would still make it possible for him to find himself, and she would have given herself to him unquestionably. He was going about it in the right way. He would want to take her and she would give herself to him. All by means of his instrument of a crawling self pity.

And Herklaas Huysmans would put out his chest in the pride of conquest. Using his frustration as the stepping stone on which to reach her body. Oh, it would have been simple and straight-forward enough. She was a broken creature, and it was her duty to give herself in that way, to respond to that kind of advance.

But the only snag, as far as Herklaas Huysmans was concerned – and it was something that he didn't know yet, sitting there ordering a third whisky – was that, for the present at least, Hannah Theron regarded herself as belonging to Bert Parsons.

Herklaas Huysmans was talking about Justinian and about the Code Napoleon. He was declaiming. He said that he was born to be not only the greatest lawyer, but also the greatest orator of his time. And he had never been given a fair chance. His hand was shaky by this time. When he lifted the glass to his lips, some of the whisky got spilt over his white tennis shirt.

Hannah Theron felt that it was time to leave. She knew that she herself was more than a little tipsy. And that in spite of the fact (of which she was unaware) that with the last round Hans Korf had relented and had diluted her whisky with a fair proportion of ginger ale and water. It was time to go.

She realised that, through force of example, she had made Herklaas Huysmans drunk. She was responsible for Herklaas Huysmans's condition. In the same way that Bert Parsons was responsible for her condition. This was a thought that came into Hannah Theron's mind spontaneously. She tittered at the closeness of the parallel. And because she found herself laughing in this fashion to herself, she knew that she was becoming affected by the drink. That wouldn't do.

They would have to leave at once. She must have been mad to have led Herklaas Huysmans on in this way. Still it was jolly. My God, a person had to live. She couldn't go on like that very much longer, day after day, like that, sunk in misery. Despair would drive her mad unless she did something irresponsible, something to lift the burden of anxiety from her shoulders – if only for a little while. But it was funny to look at old Herklaas Huysmans. What a sight. And there he was lifting the glass to his wide slit of a mouth again. He spilt some more liquor over himself.

"It doesn't matter if your hand shakes," Hannah Theron said to him, quoting an expression she had heard in the company of drinkers, "as long as your voice remains firm."

Herklaas Huysmans lay back in his chair and laughed uproariously, nearly overbalancing as he did so. The noise of his laughter drew Hans

Korf into the lounge. Herklaas Huysmans raised his head slowly and gazed bleary eyed at Hans Korf, framed in the doorway.

"Tmore," he said. "Two – more."

Hans Korf shook his head and looked significantly at Hannah Theron. A sign passed between them. In this matter they understood each other well. Hans Korf returned to the bar and did not come back to the lounge again.

The same thing had happened frequently when Hannah Theron was drinking in the company of Bert Parsons and his mates. Bert Parsons, with the cunning of the drunkard, suspected that there was some form of mute signalling between his girl and the bartender. But he had never caught Hannah out at it. Mostly he accepted it with a measure of calmness, Hans Korf's refusal to bring any more drinks into the lounge. Then he would go into the bar with his pals, and they would continue drinking there. But sometimes he got annoyed with Hans Korf. Then he would fling his glass at the bottles ranged in rows on the shelves behind the bar counter. And if there were some beer bottles handy, he would throw them also. They were used to his ways in the bar of the Northern Hotel.

He did this sort of thing only when he was earning big money. Next day he would come in and write a cheque for the damages. Mrs Manning saw to it that the bill with which he was presented was of such dimensions as to cover not only the breakages but the insult to the good name of her premises as well. But when Bert Parsons didn't have a building contract, and was employed only as a workman, he was more circumspect. It wasn't only that he had less money to throw around then to pay the damages, but his self esteem was also not equal to anything in the way of a too disorderly kind of behaviour. He couldn't carry it off with an air when he was only a workman.

Hans Korf had gone out. Herklaas Huysmans did not know that he wouldn't return. Hannah Theron sat undecided, wondering what to do next. How to get Herklaas Huysmans out of the hotel. She hoped he was not going to be difficult. It was easier to deal with an habitual drunkard, whose actions conformed to some sort of a pattern. It was an irrational pattern, of course, with all sorts of insane variabilities, but there was in it an underlying element of the predictable. But it was different with a man who didn't drink regularly and who then went on the spree. He could do anything. You had no data on which to base any sort of calculation.

4

Then, to Hannah Theron's great relief, Herklaas Huysmans announced his intention of adjourning from the Northern Hotel. So that wasn't a problem any longer. But she had passed through some moments of acute uncertainty, which had at least resulted in sobering her up completely. She found herself suddenly free of all the effects of the alcohol as she watched Herklaas Huysmans rising unsteadily to his feet. Oh well, she would have to go with him. She couldn't leave him in that condition. She would have to look after him in some sort of a fashion until he had sobered up.

Herklaas Huysmans rose to his feet. His mouth was slightly open. He looked at Hannah Theron with a fixed stare. He tried to take a step forward and lurched heavily against a chair. Hannah Theron got up quickly and took him by the arm. For a moment she felt his loose, limp body against her thin form with malicious satisfaction.

Sybrand van Aswegen had talked about the honour of the school, about the responsibilities attendant on being a member of the teaching profession. Then how did Herklaas Huysmans, vice-principal, fit into the picture? Of course, the circumstances were exceptional. Herklaas Huysmans didn't get drunk every day of his life. Even if he were seen staggering about the streets, people would think it was the heat. That he was ill, or that he was suffering from the effects of sunstroke. People would never associate him with drunkenness.

Nevertheless, assisted on his unsteady course by Hannah Theron's resolute hold on his arm, Herklaas Huysmans went out of the lounge of the Northern Hotel and shuffled along the pavement with the gait of a drunkard. He was talking incoherently by this time. Only afterwards did Hannah Theron try to piece together some of the import of his babblings.

In the meantime she had her work cut out to guide him along the sidewalk in the direction of the two-storey building in which his flat was situated. This was a bit of a change, she reflected. A school-teacher in a scandalous condition. If the inhabitants knew, it would give them quite a lot to talk about. For a change, local gossip, in reference to educational circles, would not be restricted entirely to herself as the subject. Herklaas Huysmans had been seen drunk. But he had been seen drunk in her company. Hannah Theron was conscious of an inward amusement, whose source she could not quite uncover.

They had been lucky so far. They had progressed for a block and a half and had been observed only by a couple of natives and a schoolboy in Standard Four, who had raised his hat and said, "Middag, Juffrou; middag, Meneer", as though there were nothing amiss.

But they were still more fortunate, that afternoon, for there was a taxi waiting on the rank at the side of the post office. There were three taxicabs in Kalvyn. And you rarely found one at the cab stand, which had been instituted by the municipal council for the purpose of adding to the civic prestige of the town. The usual procedure when you wanted a taxi was to go round to the office of the firm that owned Kalvyn's three cabs and, after a good deal of negotiation, in the course of which somebody was sent running out to look for one of the drivers, you succeeded in hiring a cab. Or you could telephone and wait for anything up to two hours.

Consequently Hannah Theron knew that her luck was in that afternoon, the cab stand being just about the last place where anybody would have expected to come across a taxi waiting for a fare. She knew the driver. One of his children was in her class.

"Will you please help me, Mr Vermooten?" Hannah Theron called out. "I want to take Mr Huysmans home. He became ill suddenly."

Vermooten came out from behind the wheel and looked steadily at Hannah Theron and Herklaas Huysmans. Hannah Theron was very conscious of the nature of his scrutiny. She felt very foolish suddenly. Herklaas Huysmans was milling around as though he was a member of a herd of cattle. He trod on her shoe several times. He was keeping up a running fire of incoherent comment. His white shirt was damp in places from sweat and spilt whisky.

And he looked very ridiculous somehow, at that moment, with his long, bony legs surmounted by those tennis shorts, and his socks trailing down over his canvas boots, and irregular patches of black hair on his thin thighs and unmuscular calves. If a girl went to the trouble of shaving off those hairs, why should a man be too superior to make concessions to aesthetic demands of this sort?

Suddenly Herklaas Huysmans lurched sideways. He was going to collapse. Hannah Theron flung her arms round his waist. He was a dead weight. He sagged still lower, his body bent double. His buttocks were raised in the air, partly through the support extended by Hannah Theron and partly through the circumstance of his knees not yet having given in. When Vermooten seized hold of him, Herklaas Huysmans's head was almost in contact with the reddish coloured dried clay of the sidewalk.

Vermooten sniffed suspiciously. "He been drinking?" he asked.

"Mr Huysmans did have a few drinks," Hannah Theron replied. "He was affected by the heat."

Vermooten grabbed Herklaas Huysmans under the shoulders and half led and half carried him to the car, the door of which Hannah Theron held open. The taxidriver was surly. He was sullenly reluctant to take this fare. He revealed his reluctance not only through the expression on his face but in every line of his body's movements. Hannah Theron was embarrassed. She felt uncomfortably hot.

Then she became annoyed. What a piece of smug cheek this was on the part of the taxidriver, getting sniffy because he had been asked to help get a drunk man home. Especially as this was the first time Herklaas Huysmans had been incapable in the street.

She was just beginning to feel very defensive in regard to Herklaas Huysmans; but she checked herself in time when she realised the true reason for her anger, which had nothing to do with Herklaas Huysmans. Actually, what she resented was the taxidriver's attitude towards her. An implied familiarity. It was because she was with Herklaas Huysmans that the taxidriver had the impudence to ask if he had been drinking. It was because Vermooten didn't regard her as a lady.

If Sybrand van Aswegen's wife had been in this same predicament, wanting Herklaas Huysmans assisted home because she had come across him somewhere when he was drunk, the taxidriver would not have dared to be rude. He would have pretended that Herklaas Huysmans really was ill. He would have been suave and polite – to her face at least, no matter what he said about her afterwards.

It was clear that Vermooten did not regard Hannah Theron as a school-teacher who had one of his children in her class. He thought of her only as a woman whom he had driven to Mrs Ferreira's boarding-house under peculiar circumstances, when Hannah Theron was still staying at the Northern Hotel.

There was one occasion, for instance, when there had been a dance at the other end of the town and Bert Parsons had run his car into a tree, and they had telephoned the taxicab office. Vermooten had driven Hannah Theron and Bert Parsons, who was drunk and singing, to Mrs Ferreira's boarding-house. This had been at two o'clock in the morning. And when Bert Parsons paid the fare he asked Vermooten to call back for Hannah Theron just before daybreak. Of course, Hannah Theron immediately countermanded these instructions, in shame and vexation, and Vermooten drove off without a word. There had been other similar incidents.

And now she was stuck here with Herklaas Huysmans, who was also drunk. Oh well, Herklaas Huysmans would have to look after himself.

"I'll go and ask them to keep your racket for you," she said to Herklaas Huysmans, while Vermooten stood by her side, waiting to close the door of the taxi. "I've just remembered now, that you have left your racket in the hotel."

Herklaas Huysmans grunted some reply.

Hannah Theron was on the point of turning away when she suddenly felt her wrist grasped in a firm hold. Herklaas Huysmans had slithered his body along the seat and reached out with his arms and seized her wrist in a two-handed grip. That was it. You could never tell what a man was going to do who wasn't used to drink.

"You mustn't leave me," Herklaas Huysmans mumbled. "State I'm in – mustn't leave me. Be better soon."

"Will you please make up your mind, Juffrou?" Vermooten asked. "I can't wait here all day."

Hannah Theron bit her lip in annoyance. The tone in which he addressed her. It was as though he had said, "I can't wait here all night." Her business relations with him hitherto had been affairs of the night. Nights that had drenched her body in heat and thickness.

Hannah Theron made an effort to suppress her rising anger. "I think it best that you take him to the flat alone, Mr Vermooten," she said. "There is nothing more I can do for him."

"No, I suppose there isn't," Vermooten answered in a flat voice.

Why wasn't she a man? Hannah Theron reflected. If only she were a man she could have driven that veiled insinuation right back into this dreadful person's throat. Or if she had a man. A man who loved her, who cherished her. A man whose presence would save her from these insults.

But that was just the point. Her life was such that no man would ever come to her defence in chivalry. Unless he was drunk and wanting to fight everybody, in any case. She was unprotected in the world, vulnerable to all the low taunts and bitter sneers which any oafish male chose to fling at her. This lecherous looking taxidriver would be wanting to sleep with her next. Making her feel inferior, like this.

And he might even get away with it in time. How many men had she not yielded to in the past, just out of a sense of her own inferiority? And Vermooten was no doubt quite justified in thinking that if she gave herself to other men, or at least to one other man, on those heavy nights of which he knew, then what was wrong with him?

Hannah Theron felt the tears starting to her eyes. But they were not tears of anger. She was conscious only of an intense feeling of humiliation, an awful realisation of her tarnishment. She was an abject and debased and polluted thing.

And Vermooten was making no effort to assist her in getting Herklaas Huysmans to release his drunken grip on her wrist.

This whole incident had not lasted many minutes, but it had taken place in broad daylight, and in the main street of Kalvyn. And people must have noticed what was going on. And she didn't feel too sure now, that it would be generally accepted that Herklaas Huysmans had merely been taken ill. She made up her mind suddenly.

"All right, Mr Vermooten," she said, "I'll go with Mr Huysmans to his flat."

Huysmans's hands still clutching her wrists, Hannah Theron scrambled into the back seat of the taxi next to him. It was an undignified way of entering a car. Vermooten slammed the door shut.

A few moments later they were driving to the flat, Vermooten seeming purposely to pick an unfrequented route.

Chapter Five

1

Good progress was being made with the new municipal market building, the job being ahead of schedule, in spite of the fact that during the past few weeks Bert Parsons, the contractor, had been displaying only the most casual interest in the work. His visits to the job had been brief and infrequent. He had appointed Lionel Andrews construction foreman, and Lionel Andrews – who was a good organiser within the limits of slogging his guts out in another man's interests, and who was meticulous about details – took a pride in the fact that nothing had as yet gone wrong with the erection of the building.

The carpenters had completed the construction of the wooden boxes on top of the wall. And today the labourers were mixing concrete in the machine and were carrying the buckets of stones and water and river sand and cement to the foot of the wall, from where the buckets were hoisted to the top of the scaffolding and the contents poured into the concrete boxes.

It was a sweltering afternoon – the same afternoon on which Hannah Theron took Herklaas Huysmans back to his flat by taxi. But on the building job the heat was oppressive. Only white labour was being employed, in terms of the contract, and the majority of the white labourers, on the completion of the Kalvyn Stores building, had obtained work on this new job. It is a queerly nomadic sort of life, being engaged in the building trade. When a job is finished you get paid off and, unless the man you have been working for has found another contract, you go and look for work where you see the foundations being dug on a new job.

Van Schalkwyk, father of the half-wit girl Wiesie, was one of the white labourers on this job where Bert Parsons was the boss. Van Schalkwyk's job was to assist another man, Basson, to lift the loads of stones and sand into the mixer for each new batch of concrete. The youngster, Boet, was in charge of the engine. In the mixing of concrete this was the only cushy job there was. Whatever other share you had in the task of filling the wooden boxes with concrete, you had to sweat like a nigger for your day's pay. The labourers had a cruder way of expressing the truth: they had a saying that was based on primitive physiological functionings.

After a good deal of vituperation Lionel Andrews had at last got the endless chain of operations to function with a fair degree of smoothness. Van Schalkwyk and Basson filled the heavy container first with small stones and then with sand, and then with more stones and then more sand, decanting the container each time into the wide maw of the mixer and ending up with a couple of shovelfuls of cement. Boet would then start up the engine and as it revolved he played a hosepipe into the interior until the mixture was of the right consistency. While the mixer turned, Van Schalkwyk and Basson would fill up the container with a fresh load of crushed stone.

When the batch was ready, the contents of the mixer was tipped into two wheel-barrows with which two more labourers would proceed at a brisk trot to the foot of the wall. Here they emptied the concrete out of their wheel-barrows into a number of buckets, which the labourers on the scaffolding hoisted up on ropes, thereafter pouring the wet mixture into the boxes on top of the wall. A tradesman stood on the scaffolding with the labourers to check the level of the concrete. By the time the men with the wheel-barrows returned to the mixing machine, another batch of concrete was ready to be tipped out.

The labourers grunted and sweated profusely. Lionel Andrews took up a position on top of the mound of crushed stone. From there he could watch the functioning of the chain. The hot summer sun beat down pitilessly on the uneven ground over which the men with the wheel-barrows toiled. Lionel Andrews had put two of the younger men on the job of trotting with the wheel-barrows. He judged that Basson and Van Schalkwyk would not be too sound on their pins, because of the disadvantage of their years, and that in consequence they would not be able to stand the pace to the end of the day. But they should be able to keep up with the job of filling and lifting the container.

"Vandag bars ons," young Hanekom, one of the labourers, had said when the last of the wooden boxes on the wall had been nailed into position and Lionel Andrews had given instructions for the concrete mixer to be dragged into place.

The strength of a chain is its weakest link. The job of throwing concrete had been proceeding for the best part of an hour. There could be no stopping, no interval for a breather, no couple of minutes snatched for a smoke or a rest. Concrete sets too quickly for that sort of thing. You can't do just part of it now and leave the rest for a little later. When you start on it you have got to go through until the end, until the moment when the man on the scaffolding totters up to the box with the last bucket of concrete and the tradesman, putting his spirit level on top of the mixture, announces that the last box is filled. Once the pace has been set, it has to be maintained to the end. And it is a good pace.

Basson, Van Schalkwyk's half-section on the job of feeding the mixer with sand and stone and cement, was the first to notice that his partner was tiring. In matters of this description there is nothing more pitiless than one workman's treatment of another.

When one workman detects the fact that another workman isn't pulling his weight on the job, for any reason whatsoever, a queer sort of aberration takes place in that workman's brain. It is as though he suddenly arrogates to himself the position of employer and he becomes infuriated at the thought of his work-mate having the cheek to slack. This is a peculiar kind of phenomenon. Like that of healthy chickens pecking the one that's sickly. When a workman through age or infirmity finds that he can no longer stand up to the job, he also discovers that he has all of a sudden accumulated a whole army of bosses.

Basson noticed that Van Schalkwyk was puffing. That his breathing was becoming stertorous. That when it came to lifting the heavy loads of stone to the lip of the concrete mixer there was an unsteadiness about his actions that was occasioned by more than the unevenness of the ground and the weight of the stones.

"Jy moet roer, jong," Basson called out to Van Schalkwyk when, shovels in hand, the two were refilling the container with crushed stone. Basson spoke loudly and bitterly. He wanted Lionel Andrews, the foreman in charge, to know that Van Schalkwyk wasn't doing his full share.

Van Schalkwyk grunted some reply. His mouth was too parched to talk. He felt he had no wind left. There was no more strength in his arms. His knees were trembling from the exertions he was making. Each time he assisted Basson to lift the container to the opening in the mixing machine, he felt that he wouldn't make it. Those last two inches, to get the thing resting on the side of the opening, and then heave it from underneath, sending the stones rattling into the interior of the mixer – he felt that each time was going to be the last. And those boxes on the wall were not even halfway towards being filled.

Young Hanekom and his mate had trotted off with their wheel-barrows. The mixer was at rest, its maw tilted at an angle towards the ground. The container was filled with stones. Basson and Van Schalkwyk stooped down and grasped the container by its crude handles. "Hup!" Basson grunted.

They began to lift the thing. Van Schalkwyk's arms felt like lumps of lead. His knees tottered. His back and shoulder muscles were numbed with a beast's exhaustion. He couldn't make it.

"Jy moet wikkel, man," he heard Basson call out, not so loudly this time, but in a slow, smouldering anger.

Van Schalkwyk made a last effort. He put every ounce of the strength that remained to him in that final effort. The container shook a couple of times, trembled on the edge of the mixing machine's wide mouth and, to Van Schalkwyk's complete surprise, responded to his final exertions. The stones clattered into the empty interior of the mixing machine.

His own face and body bathed in sweat, Van Schalkwyk took a quick look at Basson. No, he could see that Basson was not feeling the strain yet. Basson's face was dripping with sweat and there was a brown patch of grime across one cheek where he had hurriedly wiped his face with the back of his hand. But he could see from Basson's face that he was still comparatively fresh. There was no look of pain in his eyes. His jaw muscles didn't quiver. His breathing was heavy; but he was still far from that stage of exhaustion which Van Schalkwyk knew that he himself had reached.

Van Schalkwyk knew that with the next lift of the container he himself would go under. He would have to loosen his hold on those wooden handles, no matter how hard he tried. The container would be wrenched out of his hands. The stones would fall on to their feet in front of the mixer. Lionel Andrews would curse at him and fire him off the job, would tell him to get his jacket and go. The other labourers would jeer. He would be fired and where the hell would he get another job?

Van Schalkwyk's brain began to function again with the low cunning of a man who could not face directly up to the demands of life. There was no real viciousness in his nature, no more than there was in the nature of any other man. But in the struggle for existence he always fell just short of being able to hold his own. He had simple desires in life. He wasn't able ever to fulfil these desires completely. He had never had quite enough to eat, or quite enough to smoke, or quite enough to drink. His brain began to work in the same channel of low cunning through which he had got his job back, before, when he had got the idea of sending his daughter Wiesie to interview Bert Parsons in his room. His brain began to function again. He would have to do something. And quick.

The two men pulled the container a few feet away from in front of the machine and took up their shovels. This time it was a load of sand that had to go into the mixer. Basson was stooping forward with his shovel, sinking it into the sand. The next moment he would step back to throw. It was now or never.

Without pausing to observe whether Lionel Andrews was watching, Van Schalkwyk grasped his shovel in a two-handed grip near the top of the handle. He brought the bowl down with a shattering impact on the back of Basson's head. It was very quick, the matter of a split second. Basson was on the point then of drawing himself up to pitch the shovelful of sand into the container. That was the moment when Van Schalkwyk's shovel struck him.

Basson grunted and fell forward on to the heap of red sand. The back of his neck was red, also. The blood was running down the back of his neck into the sand.

Van Schalkwyk didn't know whether Lionel Andrews had seen what had happened, but he didn't care. He already knew what he was going to say.

Lionel Andrews came running to the spot where Basson was lying. He had not witnessed the incident. As a matter of fact, nobody had seen Van Schalkwyk strike Basson with the shovel. It had all been the matter of a single moment. And in that moment the attention of each of the workmen was engaged elsewhere.

Van Schalkwyk couldn't have timed it better if he had worked it out in the most meticulous sort of detail – which he hadn't. And if Lionel Andrews had observed the cowardly assault, he would have tried to hush it up. He would have said he had seen nothing. He wanted to get the building job done. He didn't want hours and days wasted with court cases and giving evidence and making statements and all that sort of thing.

"He got in under my shovel just when I was bringing it down quick," Van Schalkwyk explained before the foreman could ask any questions. "You was there to see, wasn't you, Mr Andrews?"

"Yes, you bloody, clumsy fool," Lionel Andrews said, "I saw the accident. Now you two men drag Basson to the other side of the sand and turn the hosepipe on him. Come along there, now. We got no time to waste. Get along. Look smart!"

Between them Van Schalkwyk and Boet dragged the still unconscious Basson to the other side of the mound of red sand. Boet turned the hose on him. The water cascaded over his head and soaked into his shirt and into the sand. When his shirt dried later on, it would be caked in stiff blood and dried mud.

Basson groaned and moved his head slowly from side to side. He had only been knocked unconscious. Another man, with a more fragile sort of bone structure, getting a crack like that on his head, would very likely have died; at the least, he would have sustained multiple fractures to his skull.

Basson merely shook his head some more, grunting and trying to sit up in the pool of red mud which his blood was steadily making more crimson. By this time several of the labourers were standing around him, laughing.

"Basson is babelas again," one of the labourers said, meaning that he was suffering from a hangover.

"There's nothing wrong with him," Lionel Andrews announced authoritatively. "Help him to get up and to get his jacket on. You take him to the timekeeper's shed and put a dressing on his head."

This last order was addressed to Boet.

"And must he come back to work again for the afternoon?" Boet enquired anxiously. "There don't seem much wrong with him, foreman."

Boet wanted Basson back again on the job, of course. He didn't want to have to let go of his cushy job of running the machine and handling the hosepipe.

"No, he better not come back till the morning," Lionel Andrews answered. "He ain't sick, but labourers these days coddle themselves in a way you got no idea. I don't want him hanging around here all afternoon, putting up a bleat that he can't work. Too lazy, that's what."

Basson staggered off to the timekeeper's shed, supported by Boet. A few minutes later, after Boet had returned, the chain was reorganised. Boet, who would have preferred Hanekom's job of pushing a wheelbarrow, was put in Basson's place in front of the mixer as Van Schalkwyk's mate in filling and lifting the container. Lionel Andrews held the hosepipe and operated the mixing machine.

When Van Schalkwyk picked up his shovel again, he noticed that a couple of black hairs were still adhering to the back of the bowl. In the next instant he scooped up a shovelful of red sand and went on helping Boet to refill the container.

Van Schalkwyk felt all right. All his fatigue was gone. He had a queer sense of exhilaration. He could go on working until nightfall. He had been too quick for Basson once. He would be too quick for him again. The fact that he had taken an unfair advantage of Basson made no difference. What he had done to Basson once, he could do again. Van Schalkwyk had lived most of his life on the veld and he had seen the same sort of thing with animals. It didn't matter how you did it, as long as you succeeded.

If Basson came back next day or the day after and tried to get even with him or to take vengeance on him, he could try all he liked. Every time he would be too slow. After you had licked a man once, you could always lick him again. And it didn't matter what means you employed. Van Schalkwyk had seen that from the animals and the birds. Even if Basson had died and Van Schalkwyk would have had to do time for it, it wouldn't have mattered. Once you licked a man you were all right.

The afternoon wore on slowly, very slowly. Van Schalkwyk was in great fettle. He was triumphant. He was a man. He swung his shovel with an air of exuberance. It was as though he had got his second wind back and a lot more. He could work faster and harder than ten men, any ten men. He could pause between lifting the container and do a few steps of a vastrap. That was how he felt.

Then Van Schalkwyk began to notice that Boet was tiring. Boet was young, but his body was soft. Always when there had been hard work to do, Boet somehow or other got round the foreman and had been let off easy. Boet was getting unsteady on his feet. And the way he puffed at the last few inches every time when it came to lifting the load of stones to the mouth of the machine. That wouldn't do.

"You must pull yourself together, Boet," Van Schalkwyk shouted loudly, so that the foreman could hear him. "You are a young man. Jy moet wikkel, jong."

The work went on. There were still several boxes to be filled. The concrete mixer was filled and its belly was whirled round and round and the concrete was spewed into the waiting wheel-barrows and conveyed to the top of the wall. And Boet felt that his arms were like lead and that his shoulder muscles were pieces of torn flesh, and his knees trembled and his back was a living mass of pain, and above all he couldn't breathe. His raw lungs no longer knew how to pump in air.

The mixing machine, which he had been working all afternoon, starting and stopping it with a lever – the concrete mixer which had been a tame thing, responding to his mastery in muted obedience – now became for him an insatiable monster, wanting more and more stones and sand for its belly cravings, on and on endlessly, like a grey devil. A beast that was devouring him inch by inch.

By this time Van Schalkwyk's exuberance had reached the point where the least diversion could make him laugh hysterically. Then he saw Boet's face. Boet was just about all in. In a much worse state than he had at first thought.

Van Schalkwyk's mood changed abruptly. A slow rage began to smoulder inside him. All that coarse jollity left him. He spoke to Boet in a deep voice, in a low, savage growl, in threatening tones charged with cold anger and heavy male lust.

"Roer jou agterent, kêrel," Van Schalkwyk called out in crude and primitive menace. "I don' want no loafing here."

2

With Vermooten's assistance Hannah Theron had got Herklaas Huysmans into his flat, which was fortunately situated on the ground floor. But when they had got him out of the taxi and were guiding him along the pavement to the front door, Dulcie Hartnell had come past.

Dulcie had greeted them. She had made some savagely friendly observation about "poor Mr Huysmans" and about its being such a hot day. Then she had walked on.

But Hannah Theron had caught the insinuations all right, both in her words and in her manner. And what Dulcie Hartnell implied was that before Hannah Theron could get her man, she had first to get him drunk.

Inside the flat Hannah Theron set about getting together the utensils for making Huysmans some black coffee. What struck her most about the rooms were their ordinariness. So singularly lacking in personality. None of those little touches even in respect of crude prints or out of the way bricabracs which even the most uninteresting bachelor got to assemble in time in the place where he stayed.

Herklaas Huysmans had floundered on to the couch. He was lying on his belly with his face twisted to one side and an arm trailing on the floor. He was only half asleep. At intervals he mumbled something about his gratitude to the sweet girl who was looking after him.

Hannah smiled. Ah well, for a man to be grateful under such circumstances was at least more than she was used to, as a general rule. But she knew from past experience that when a man got to that stage he was also, as a rule, not far removed from the stage of getting sick. So she found a small flat basin, which she placed in front of the bed in case of emergency. She did that without thinking. The sordidly realistic side of drunkenness had become deeply implanted in her knowledge of the world.

The kettle boiled. Hannah Theron poured the boiling water into an enamel coffee-pot that was badly battered in places and dented at the spout. The coffee-pot seemed typical of the way Herklaas Huysmans lived in his flat. A carelessness that was not far removed from squalor.

Next to the couch in the living room was a huge desk. That must be the desk Herklaas Huysmans had been talking about, and which he had never had the courage to place in a lawyer's office, with himself as the lawyer. The desk was littered with papers. In places where the wood showed were inkstains and splashes and old marks made by damp and soiled crockery. Hannah Theron felt a sudden wave of pity surge within her. The discoloured top of the desk seemed to speak of such utter and dismal failure.

And it was all so unnecessary. What did it matter that Herklaas Huysmans had not become an advocate? It was a silly sort of a job, being an advocate, in any case. Silly. He was just as well off as a schoolmaster, or as a workman. Those workmen who were employed by Bert Parsons and of whom Bert Parsons was one. All this foolish striving and then this shabby tragedy of defeat. It had all to do with Herklaas Huysmans's own soul, of course. That was where he had been defeated. If he could only see that being a lawyer meant nothing at all – not even being a great lawyer, not even being the greatest lawyer of his time – if he could only see that he would no longer be defeated.

Hannah Theron pushed a bundle of papers to one side and made room on the desk for the two coffee-cups. If Herklaas Huysmans was asleep she would have let him be. But he was at least half awake. She shook him by the shoulder and called his name.

Grunting and muttering what sounded like mild swear-words, Herklaas Huysmans sat up clumsily on the couch. He looked very sick. The lines in his face seemed deeply etched all of a sudden, showing up darkly against the greenish pallor of his skin. His black hair hung in a tousled mat over his eyes. He gazed unsteadily into Hannah Theron's face. Her long, thin features seemed to swim in the air. In that moment she seemed very beautiful to Herklaas Huysmans.

He was sick. He felt a nauseous stirring in his stomach. He had to keep his head very still and to exercise a strong control over some muscles that seemed situated near the back of his neck, somewhere, in order to prevent the world from going round.

And yet when he looked at Hannah Theron, as he was doing now, he was conscious only of romantic sentiments. Her face swam before him. The long black hairs hanging down over his eyes seemed like tangled grasses growing on the edge of the pool in which Hannah Theron's face swam.

He was no longer drunk. He was in that state that is always peculiarly ghastly, when the heady fumes of drink have cleared, dissipated into fabulous voids, and all that is left is the thin grey edge of the world of realities that is advancing with slow sure steps that are like hammer blows.

Shaken, tousled, dishevelled, disgusting to the sight and swinish in his estimation of himself, Herklaas Huysmans became aware of Hannah Theron's nearness. It wasn't the feeling he had had for her earlier on, when he had grabbed her wrists and had held on, clutching at her arms because her body wasn't there for him to grasp, and he had pulled her into the taxi next to him. Those were not the feelings Herklaas Huysmans had about Hannah Theron now. Instead, he felt only shame at the thought that he had dared assault her in that fashion.

He could remember the situation only dimly. He was half sitting and half sprawling in the back seat of the taxi, and Vermooten was fussing around and Hannah Theron was preparing to leave. And for that reason he had caught hold of her.

He remembered what he had thought then, too. He thought about Hannah Theron, in those moments, the same things that everybody in Kalvyn was saying about her. That she was, of course, the mistress of Bert Parsons. And that that showed you just the kind of girl she was. She didn't mind a man being a dissolute rake, a drunken sot, as long as he had a virile masculinity. In Hannah Theron's tall thin figure was the rankness of flesh lusts. The strong maleness of Bert Parsons's coarse body was what Hannah Theron needed and wanted. She cared nothing about higher things. She wanted to be wrapped only in the thick warmths of the earth. Tall and thin, with burnt-out eyes and prominent features, she was staled with the heavy sensuality of hot nights. That was what Herklaas Huysmans had thought about Hannah Theron when he pulled her into the taxi; he had thought about her those things that he had heard dozens of Kalvyn's residents say about her.

And so he had pulled her into the taxi after him, determined that if she could take Bert Parsons she could take him, Herklaas Huysmans, also. He was as good a man as Bert Parsons any time. Just because he had a better brain than Bert Parsons – that didn't mean that he didn't have as strong and as desirable a maleness as Bert Parsons. He had pulled her into the taxi as flesh that was potent in the curves of alcohol fumes; he had pulled her into the taxi under the spell of her body's rawest lure, his blood irritated to warmth by the knowledge that a sexually virile man regularly lay in her arms. And what another man could do, he could do, also.

But Herklaas Huysmans had none of these feelings about Hannah Theron now. All he hoped, sitting back against the wall, with one fist pressing into the softness of the couch to keep the world from swaying, was that he had not gone too far. He trusted that he had attempted nothing outrageous when he had been alone with Hannah Theron, and his blood had been heated by the perfume of her nearness. He trusted that the stupor of drink that had enveloped his infatuated senses in a purple amnesia had deflated his physicality as well. He saw Hannah Theron now as a distant being, cool and aloof and yet womanly, a fragrant stranger and a thing of delicate loveliness.

"I have made some coffee for us," Herklaas Huysmans heard Hannah Theron say, as she passed him his cup, which he reached out with shaky hands to receive.

He spilt some of the coffee into the saucer. And when he lifted the cup to his lips a thin trail of black coffee trickled across the crumpled white of his tennis shirt, the new soilings mingling with the dried stains of spilt whisky. It was an old, stale thing, a shirt-front splashed first with whisky that had dried and then stained with fresh coffee. The only thing about it that was new was that Herklaas Huysmans was an initiate.

And the way Hannah Theron had said, "I have made some coffee for us" – there was an intimacy about the way she said that last word. She had made the coffee for both of them. Not just for Herklaas, because he had been drunk.

"Thank you very much, Hannah," Herklaas Huysmans answered. "That was just what I needed."

There was so much more that he wanted to say. He felt a sudden furious surge of hatred for Bert Parsons. He knew that Hannah Theron belonged altogether and exclusively to Bert Parsons. No man would ever get her away from Bert Parsons, no matter how that man loved her, or how kind he was to her.

Herklaas Huysmans felt that Hannah Theron did not want kindness or understanding or devotion. Those were things that she would despise in a man. What were love and human sympathy and adoration even, coming from a man, compared with the way that Bert Parsons walked? Compared with the way that Bert Parsons breezed into a place, thrusting his body forward with a strong, clumsy grace, the light of a supreme confidence dancing in his eyes, making a mockery of all other men? What Hannah Theron fell for, because she was in reality demure and retiring, was this blatant flaunting of a man's sex. Herklaas Huysmans believed that he understood all that now.

And he was conscious of a hot, blinding jealousy at the thought of Bert Parsons. He remembered the taxi incident. It was only because he had been drunk, of course, that he had the audacity to believe that he could ever be as good a man as Bert Parsons. You could only be a man if you had the body of a man. If out of your body came raw maleness. If there flowed out of you the magnetism of an animal vitality.

On the other hand, if you were so stupid as to have devoted your best years of your early manhood to intellectual pursuits – to stupid studies in airless law libraries, bending over dusty tomes and allowing all your rich, red life to dry up in the brainlessness of scholarly research – then it was only to be expected that a girl like Hannah Theron, whose temperament was also naturally that of a recluse, would not have very much time for you.

She could understand you. She could pity you. She could have all sorts of warm, tender feelings for you. An infinite compassion. But she would not be able to thrill to your striding in to her. The blood would not rush hotly to her temples, burning in white fires her veins, drowning in a purple drunkenness her flesh and nerves. Only a man like Bert Parsons could do that to her. Only a man with untamed lusts, with the wild freedoms and the magic and the reckless urgencies of a healthy animal, could draw out of Hannah Theron's body the inner springs of her hidden life.

"So this is the desk you have been telling me about," Herklaas Huysmans heard Hannah Theron say. "Well, I have seen it quicker than we expected, haven't I?"

Yes, Herklaas Huysmans reflected gloomily. Towards him she could no doubt be capable of an infinity of compassion. He did not deign to reply. He read only a pitying condescension into her enquiry about his desk.

They went on talking like that for some time, aimlessly. Herklaas Huysmans found that he was recovering from his drunken spell without having had to go through the stage of getting sick. He noticed, for the first time, the small flat basin that Hannah Theron had placed before the couch. He had not needed that basin, after all. He had pulled himself together somehow in time.

He felt proud to think that he had not got sick in Hannah Theron's presence. She had expected him to spew up the contents of his belly into that basin, and she would no doubt have ministered to him in the slime of his being sick. And he had spared her that. It filled him with a sense of pride, the thought that he had overcome his physical nausea.

At the moment a sense of bitterness again crept into his soul. Obviously, Bert Parsons had often been sick like that, with Hannah Theron tending him. And obviously Bert Parsons hadn't cared a damn. He would obviously be as disgusting as he chose in Hannah Theron's presence, confident that nothing he did could change her feelings towards him. That was the manly way to carry on. Bert Parsons knew the right way to deal with a woman. The man had to be master. The man had to strut with his chest and body out. He could also slobber at full length on the earth. That was only another part of his masculinity.

And what a woman respected, above everything else, was to have a man who was her lord and master. Especially a girl like Hannah Theron would feel that way. She would want to be mastered. And mastery was a physical thing. And so it had all sorts of ramifications, which included the aggressions of violating chastity with the strength of the flesh and of ravishing the outer decencies through allowing a brutally frank expression to the functions of elimination. This latter was a form of sadistic display. It was part of the physical crudities of male mastery. It was self assertive, a kind of orgiastic exhibitionism.

"I must be going now," Herklaas Huysmans heard Hannah Theron say. "I am sorry you got ill. It was my fault, I am afraid. I'll see you in the morning at school, I suppose."

This time he did not try to stop her from going. He felt no impulse to restrain her. He knew, also, that if he had wanted to, he could not have stopped her now. She would have an appointment with Bert Parsons, of course. It was getting on towards evening. And the nights belonged to Bert Parsons.

"Goodbye, Hannah," Herklaas Huysmans said. "And thank you."

He did not turn his head to see her go. He heard the door open and shut behind her.

A few moments later Herklaas Huysmans had crawled to the edge of the couch. His head hung down over the side, a good way down. His long body gave a couple of preliminary heaves. His hand shot out for the flat basin. He drew the receptacle nearer the edge of the bed. He was just in time.

3

Hannah Theron had left. Sybrand van Aswegen was alone in his office. Leaning against his desk, the principal of Kalvyn Primary School stood looking at the closed door. He had caught Hannah Theron in his arms and had kissed her. She had broken from his embrace and hurried out of the office.

Deep in thought, Sybrand van Aswegen took up his black hat with the wide brim that conferred on him the dignity, not merely of a pedagogue, but almost of a predikant, and walked slowly towards the door. He waited a few minutes. Then, when he judged that Hannah Theron would be off the school grounds and out of the front gate, he locked the door of his office behind him and sauntered to the back of the school where his car was parked.

He sat back in the seat and took out the ignition key. It would be all right now. He could drive home, out through the back gate, without any fear of encountering Hannah Theron. Sybrand van Aswegen's face was clouded. There were things about himself that at that moment he felt he could not understand.

It was as though all his securities had suddenly been swept away. All the years of his toil and striving, of his pinching to make ends meet, years of fawning on his superiors, on school principals and inspectors and Education Department officials in Pretoria, years of intrigue amongst his colleagues – it seemed as though all the achievements which had come his way through the lonely bitterness of his heart were being snatched away from him. He was on the edge of a precipice. It could almost be said that he was balancing this way and that. It was almost as though he had already gone too far, and that there would be no coming back for him.

He had let go of himself. It had all been just the matter of a moment. But if he could do it once, what would not happen afterwards? It wasn't anything very much that he had done, perhaps. He had only kissed a girl in his office. But think of the circumstances. He had ostensibly called Hannah Theron into his office to reprimand her, to lecture to her from the height of his moral probity. To be blunt about it, he had regarded her as a whore. The town was talking about the way she was carrying on with that drunken rake, Bert Parsons. In the interests of the school, of the teaching profession, of his own status as principal of the school, it had been his duty to talk to her seriously about her mode of life.

And he had failed in his duty. Through his one action, of seizing her in his arms in that fashion – when he was trembling with lust and saw her thin body through a crimson haze of passion – he had undermined the discipline of the school for ever.

She would be able to do what she liked after that. How did he not know that she would talk about what had happened? He could imagine Hannah Theron relating to Bert Parsons and his associates the details of what had taken place in the office; he could imagine their laughing about it; they, young men and a young woman, ridiculing the follies of middle age. No. He couldn't imagine that happening. Hannah Theron wasn't that kind of a girl. You could say what you liked about her. But she wasn't cheap in the sense of trying to get some sort of a meretricious standing out of the fact that her principal had fallen for her, and had in that way made a fool out of himself.

But then, how did he know that she wasn't like that? He knew so little about her. He knew next to nothing about himself for that matter. He had no guarantee that, through her association with people like Bert Parsons, Hannah Theron had not become debased to the extent of blabbing out the whole story just to make it appear that she was somebody very attractive. Or perhaps she felt it was her duty towards Bert Parsons, her man, to tell him everything that happened.

Seated before the steering wheel, getting ready to start the car, Sybrand van Aswegen squirmed. What if Bert Parsons was of a jealous disposition and wanted to make something out of it? What if he got drunk and came round to the school, thirsting for the principal's blood? That would be a scandal, all right. That would be something he would never survive.

No wonder he felt his whole life going to pieces. The work of years crumbling. Getting beaten up by the town rough because he had taken liberties with his girl – and under the most inexcusable of all circumstances. He had taken advantage of a young school-teacher on his staff, after having summoned her into his office to give her a morality talk.

He could be chucked out of the Education Department and be discredited in the community, as easily as he had flung his arms around Hannah Theron. It all rested with her. She had it in her power to ruin him. She merely had to say a few words to Bert Parsons, goading him with a stray hint or so, and the fat would be in the fire.

And even if she said nothing about it to Bert Parsons, or to anybody else, if she kept it all to herself, the position would still be the same. Sybrand felt that he would never be able to face Hannah Theron again. He had revealed himself to her as a cheap hypocrite. She could no longer have any respect for him as her principal and her superior. She could feel for him nothing but scorn. That feeling she would communicate to the other members of the staff. Consciously or unconsciously, through this knowledge that she had of him, she would communicate to the world the fact that Sybrand van Aswegen was a fraud.

There was something about that in the Bible. In Proverbs, Sybrand van Aswegen seemed to remember. About a sinful woman. That was what Hannah Theron was. And that if you had anything to do with a sinful woman, she dragged you down to destruction. He could see now what it meant. If you had anything to do with a harlot, she automatically got you into her power. You were lost, after that. You had no more self-respect after that than what she had.

And it was so dreadfully unfair. Here had Hannah Theron been living as a loose woman for years and years. She had come into his orbit. He had not wanted her. He had not asked the Education Department to send a harlot down to Kalvyn. And it was inevitable that, with her cunning, she would get him down. He was naive. He knew nothing of the world from the point of view of its viciousness.

And Hannah Theron had come along and had struck him down – not deliberately, not as part of a plan and of set purpose, but merely because that was part of the curse of being a harlot. A woman of sin was like a plague. Where she went she destroyed men. That was what the Bible said. The right place for a woman like that was the lazaretto.

Sybrand van Aswegen began to wonder whether he shouldn't talk to the predikant about his trouble. Actually, if the predikant really was what he professed to be, a man of understanding and a man of Christ, one would be able to go to him. But the predikant did little more than preach on Sundays. You could not go to him for human understanding when your mind was in a state of acute misery.

Sybrand van Aswegen knew he had to talk to somebody. There was one person he could talk to. And the stronger that knowledge came to him, the more he sought to reject it. The knowledge that there was a person to whom he could tell the whole story, and who would be able to comfort him and who would be able to give him advice that would remove all his fears.

But he felt he dared not tell his wife what had happened in the office. Not that he was estranged from his wife. They understood each other very well, he and his wife. They had struggled together. They had built up a home and a family together. And if they had not suffered adversity together, in the cruder sense of the word, they had known a more grinding sort of a squalor together: the baseness that went with having to keep up certain appearances on an inadequate salary; the vileness of having to present a facade to the world on the comparative penury of a school-teacher's earnings. Oh, they had been through the rough and the smooth all right, and together.

But they had in some way got separated. In those things that belonged with the deeper intimacies of a man's relations with his woman. At one time he would have been able to talk to his wife about Hannah Theron. He would have been able to tell his wife exactly what had taken place. She would have been pained, of course. Jealous. No matter how understanding she was, she would have known the bitter hurt of jealousy. But he would have chanced that, knowing that after a while she would get over it.

And she would certainly have been able to set his mind at rest. A woman, she would have been able to understand what it was that another woman was up to. In a few words his wife could have brought him comfort. She would have said that he was overworked. That he had been living under very great tension over a period of years, and that the holiday at the Cape over December would put him right again. And that in the meantime he had nothing to worry about. What had happened in the office was an everyday occurrence. Where didn't that sort of thing happen? And it was only because his nerves were in a rotten state that he had allowed himself to become so upset by it.

Of course, it was a wrong thing he had done. But what was that compared with all the years of an honoured and responsible citizenship? And Hannah Theron would not dare to make mention of it: if she did, there was nobody who would believe her. It would look as though she was trying to blackmail him, because he was threatening to expose her sin to the school board.

All these things, Sybrand van Aswegen realised, his wife would say to him if he broached the matter. She would laugh away his fears. She would be hurt inside, of course. But she wouldn't show that hurt. She would be afraid of giving him pain; she wouldn't want him to realise that through his actions he had, indeed, been unfaithful to her.

Thinking along these lines, Sybrand van Aswegen found a certain measure of rest for his overwrought emotions. God, he was just being silly! He was panicking, and all over nothing. The world had never yet got him down, not even when he was a child. He could always see clearly into any kind of a situation. He always knew, in every sphere of activity, what were the essential things to go for, and what were his strong points, and what his weak. He was certainly not going to allow this thin-faced prostitute, who had no right to be in his school anyway, to bring him to his knees, merely because he found himself involved in a situation in which the currency was unfamiliar to him.

She knew the ropes and he didn't. That suited him. He didn't want to know the ropes, in this smeary world of sex. Hannah Theron could have her world. He wasn't trying to chisel in on it. He had made one blundering attempt to get there, and not because he wanted any of that dissoluteness, either. He had been overmastered by his feelings on that one occasion. It had all happened just in that one moment. And he had been made a fool out of. Good. That suited him, too. He felt rather proud to think that he didn't fit into that sort of life. He had been made into a figure of ridicule. And all just because of his innocence. Well, let them laugh all they wanted to – if they wanted to.

They had laughed at him in the orphanage also, those other orphans. Because of that sordid little tragedy that had made orphans out of his sister and himself. They had laughed because his father had died under circumstances of half comedy and half melodrama. That python story. Well, let those other orphans, his fellows, his mates, his contemporaries, whatever they chose to call themselves, let them try and laugh at him now – if they could. There was not one of them today who was not some sort of a poor white, a bywoner, an unskilled labourer. Not one of them but would have to doff their hats to him and call him Meneer. Let them all laugh.

But he still had to find a situation that could lick him. Hannah Theron or no Hannah Theron, Sybrand van Aswegen was going to be elected to the Town Council of Kalvyn before he was very much older. Before much more water flowed under the bridge that separated the old part of the town from the new, Sybrand van Aswegen was going to be Mayor of Kalvyn.

All his anxieties replaced by a newfound confidence, Sybrand van Aswegen started up his car and drove slowly out of the school grounds. When he got on to the sandy road that passed under thorn-trees and led to the fashionably residential part of the town, he accelerated.

When he had locked his car in the garage, Sybrand van Aswegen, as was his wont, walked into his house through the kitchen door. His wife, Sara, was bent over the coal stove.

"You are late, Sybrand," she said. "I have given the children their dinner. Ours is very dry in the oven by this time, I'm afraid."

"That's all right, vrou," Sybrand van Aswegen replied. "There were one or two little things I had to do in the office."

Sybrand van Aswegen looked at his wife. She was a well preserved woman, several years his junior. She was shortish and inclined towards stoutness. Her hips were wide from child-bearing. Her hair, thin and of an undistinguished shade of yellow, hung in wisps over her forehead on which beads of sweat shone.

He could almost tell Sara what it was that had kept him at the office, Sybrand van Aswegen reflected. He could tell her the whole story, just about. After all, it wasn't anything so very shocking, if you saw it in its right perspective. The sort of thing that could happen to any man. He must have been mad to have allowed it to upset him, like that. Still, on second thoughts, he wouldn't mention the incident to Sara. There is no sense in upsetting a woman over nothing.

With the help of the native girl, Sara van Aswegen laid two places for her husband and herself on the kitchen table. It was more convenient eating in the kitchen when there were only two of them. In spite of the heat from the stove.

She wondered what was wrong with her husband, though. Her woman's intuitions told her that something had happened to him. And something unusual. It was almost as though he was trying to hide something from her. Perhaps she could find out by asking him about it indirectly.

Halfway through the meal she plucked up the courage to do so. She tried to make her voice sound as matter of fact as possible.

"Your staying behind at the office, Sybrand," she said. "Did you have a lot of work to do this afternoon?"

"Yes," he answered abruptly, "I had work to do. Don't I often stay behind late?"

There was just the suggestion of testiness in his voice. He had given himself away. Sara van Aswegen was satisfied that her intuitions had been correct. There was something her husband was trying to hide from her. Otherwise he wouldn't have got annoyed at her apparently innocent enquiry.

"You poor man," Sara said, "I can see you are very overworked. No wonder your nerves have been all on edge these last months. Never mind, the holiday at the Cape will do us both a lot of good. Just think of it, six weeks in which to do nothing but enjoy ourselves."

"What makes you think my nerves were upset this afternoon?" Sybrand van Aswegen asked suspiciously.

"Nothing," Sara replied, her tone all conciliatory. "Oh, nothing at all."

To hell, Sybrand van Aswegen thought to himself. What a dog's life he was leading, anyway. You couldn't call your soul your own, married to a woman who watched you like that. Hell, he might as well tell his wife the whole story. Why not? There was nothing in it really.

But on second thoughts, why should he? Damned if he would. A man had to live. You couldn't be just an automaton all your life. You couldn't be just a piece of wood. He jumped up from the table suddenly.

"I'll tell you what we'll do, vrou," he exclaimed. "It'll do us both good. I'll get that bottle of brandy out of the sideboard. You get the glasses. We'll have a drink. That'll put us right. We're getting too dull in our domesticity, you and I. Let's have a bit of a break."

Sybrand van Aswegen went into the dining room and fetched the bottle of brandy. That bottle was taken out of the sideboard very rarely. And then it was only on very special occasions, and when there were visitors.

Sara van Aswegen shook her head in disapproval. To drink brandy like that wasn't right. Something must be worrying her husband. But he shouldn't try to get over it through drink. So many people whom she knew had acquired the sundowner habit, which she despised. And it no doubt always started just in this way. Nevertheless, she brought out two brandy glasses and a cut glass jug, which she half filled with water out of the tap. Sybrand van Aswegen came back into the kitchen with the bottle.

"Very little for me, please," Sara van Aswegen said. "I want a lot of room in the glass for water."

They went on with their meal in silence.

Back in the dining room, Sybrand van Aswegen poured himself another brandy. It was no use asking his wife to join him. He knew she would say that she couldn't drink. He also knew she would regard the idea of his having another drink with extreme disfavour. Oh well, he couldn't help that. You only lived once, anyway.

Unconsciously, somewhere in the dim recesses of his mind, he was comparing the trim litheness of Hannah Theron's figure with his wife's plump body. Sara should exercise more. She should make time to go out more regularly for tennis. She should also go to the swimming baths some mornings, now that it was going on for midsummer. Sara was quite young. There was no need for her to start putting on weight like that. Especially as that extra flesh she was carrying didn't make her look soft and attractive; it didn't give her soft curves. It only made her body appear set and heavy.

Yes, he was thinking of Hannah Theron again. He tried to remember in detail what had happened in the office. Hannah Theron's eyes had closed when he kissed her. Of course, the incident had not been distasteful to her. Did she kiss him also? He couldn't remember. But she must have. Her lips were very cold. And the contact with her lips had thrilled him all the more on that account.

She was a sly one. Deep as they make them. Perhaps she had in some subtle way, through the suggestiveness of how she sat in the chair, of the way she carried her body, lured him to that embrace. Why not? The girls had always found him attractive. They had said that he was a bit slow for a young man. That had been in his youth. But they had never complained that there was anything physically undesirable about him.

And now he came to think of it, Hannah Theron had not actually broken out of his arms. She had not struggled to free herself from his embrace. She must have liked it. It was only after he had let her go that she hurried out of the office like that. He had let her go in the very instant of his realisation of his daring in suddenly flinging his arms about her.

Sybrand van Aswegen was day-dreaming. He embroidered the incident in the office. In his mind's eye he saw Hannah Theron as somebody secretly drawn to him, in spite of the disparities between them. He had held her in his arms. He had felt her thin, lithe body against his own, all the way. She had not resented his kissing her. She must have invited it. He fancied for a moment that he could again breathe in the animal fragrance from her hair. His thoughts took a sensual turn. . .

He remained seated in the armchair in the dining room for a long time, the empty brandy glass in his hand.

Hannah Theron. . . He regretted nothing.

4

After leaving Herklaas Huysmans's flat, Hannah Theron walked through a number of back streets to Mrs Ferreira's boarding-house.

It was just about supper time. When she neared the boarding-house she heard the supper bell ring. But she wasn't hungry. All she wanted was to get into her room and lie down to rest. The fatigue that had gripped her in the early part of the afternoon had come back again.

She was glad that there was nobody about when she entered the front door of the boarding-house, which was built in three wings, each consisting of two rows of rooms on either side of a long passage, with a stone-flagged courtyard in the centre.

Hannah Theron tiptoed down the passage to her room, passing Bert Parsons's door. He occupied the room adjoining hers. The fact that they had gone to live next door to each other had already occasioned a good deal of scandal in Kalvyn. At that moment Hannah Theron felt that she did not want to see Bert Parsons.

She did not know whether he was in his room. She had a momentary fear of his door opening and his inviting her into his room. There was the vague feeling at the back of her mind that if she never saw Bert Parsons again, she would not regret it. Rather, it would be almost a relief to her. But now. Now, in these next few minutes, all she wanted was complete rest.

Thank heaven it was getting cooler. Like always in that part of the Transvaal, the hottest summer's day ended with a sudden cooling off of the atmosphere. Dully Hannah Theron wondered if that was what was taking place also in her feelings in regard to Bert Parsons. But it wouldn't be like that. There were loyalties that would remain inside her. Things she couldn't betray.

Also, she knew Bert Parsons had merely to come to her, any way he liked, drunk or sober, and in that heady thing that emanated from his body she would be caught again. All over. There was no escape. If not her spirit, then at least her senses were enthralled. The bonds of the flesh did not part as facilely as the flesh parted.

Once in her room, Hannah Theron kicked off her shoes and pulled off her light summer frock and flung herself face downwards on the bed. This was wonderful. It was peace. It was not the mercifulness of oblivion, but it was a rapturous numbing of the capacity for feeling pain. The soft wind that stirs from sleep at the beginning of dusk blew in at the window of her room, ruffling the white curtaining edged with lace and sweeping over her pink slip and making cool contact with her prostrate body. Hannah Theron lay with her mind at rest and her flesh becalmed. She couldn't worry now, not about anything.

The events of the afternoon crept back into her memory. Her encounter with the principal, Sybrand van Aswegen, in his office. Her meeting with Herklaas Huysmans. Their visit to the Northern Hotel lounge. Vermooten and his taxi. And Dulcie Hartnell coming along just as she was accompanying Herklaas Huysmans into his flat. Even the thought of Dulcie Hartnell could no longer afford her any sort of emotion. For the first time she could think of Dulcie Hartnell without any feelings of distress – without any feelings at all.

All the events of the immediate past, of that same afternoon, came back into Hannah Theron's mind. And she felt nothing about it all. The outside world was just a blur of sound and colour and silences and a greyness, and in all this there was nothing that could reach her heart. There was only the numbness of an unutterable peace.

Then she remembered her fears about her condition. There they were. Those fears. Ever since she had first had anything to do with a man, she had had those same fears. She now realised that for longer than she cared to remember there had always been in the background of her thoughts these same fears that went on from month to month. They never came to an end, really, those fears. Each time that she was reassured, there would only be the beginning, soon afterwards, of that same anxiety all over again. And now that it seemed that her worst terrors were being realised, she suddenly found that she no longer cared.

That consciousness of the world's being unfair to a woman in this way, burdening her with troubles from which the man was free, that age-old resentment that had brought her a mute bitterness in the moments of ecstasy – all those things were gone. Gone out of her life utterly. It didn't matter what the morrow would bring. What the next year would bring, or the next hour.

All Hannah Theron knew was that now, with her face sunk into the pillow, she was far beyond all joying and all grief, and that the light breeze of the evening was laving her hot skin, lifting her petticoat at its lace edge, ever so slightly, like a diffident lover – lifting her petticoat's lace as it lifted the lower part of the curtain in front of her window. Lifting her body's curtaining playfully, with oh, so light a touch.

The residents of Mrs Ferreira's boarding-house were at their evening meal: plates clattering, knives and forks slashing into roast meat, jaws going up and down in the movements of chewing, sweating native waiters rushing about with trays, loud and empty conversation. And Hannah Theron was at rest.

Far off sounds came to her. From the street and from the dining room. The sounds seemed to grow louder at first, and after that they receded further and further into the distance. A low, almost pleasant hum. A murmuring as of bees. Bees before the hive, their wings stationary in the blue air. Everything motionless, like a sculptured world. The only movement being the slow fragrance of midsummer heat lying on the fields and curling outward and outward, past the long furrows and the brown sods and the unmoving grass and through the stationary bees with their wings carved in the blue air, and then outward and onward. And for ever.

Hannah Theron was asleep.

Chapter Six

1

Several hours later Hannah Theron was awakened.

And then it was not the wind that pulled at her petticoat. The frills at the bottom of her slip were grasped in a rough hand. It wasn't the gentle tugging of the wind, that had lulled her to sleep. She was awakened by her lover's hand on her petticoat, a rough hand that sought to rend the garment from her prostrate body.

Only in the most intricately technical sense of the term – in its most floridly physical application – could Bert Parsons at that moment have been described as her lover. His red face was contorted with rage and body lust. He was half kneeling before her, but not in the attitude of a lover making supplication. One knee was pressed into the bed. He held on to the edge of the bed with his left hand, to support himself. With his right hand he was wrenching at the lace edge of Hannah Theron's petticoat.

By the time she woke he had pulled the garment as far up as her buttocks. He couldn't get it up any further without tearing the pale cream silk fabric. In the next moment the garment tore. The tearing of Hannah Theron's silk petticoat was to Bert Parsons like the pouring forth of blood from a wound is to an enraged savage.

"Get this bloody thing off you, you bitch," he roared.

Hannah Theron sat up very quickly. One look at Bert Parsons's face told her everything. He was full of pots. But that wasn't all. His features were convulsed in a mad rage that she had seen glimpses of once or twice before. But those had been only presages of the real thing, which she knew that she was looking upon now. She saw Bert Parsons in the throes of passion and animal fury. What had happened? What had come over him like that so suddenly? There was no time to think.

"Please don't tear my petticoat any further, Bert," Hannah Theron heard herself saying. "I'll take it off myself, if you want me to."

Before she could divest herself of the slip Bert Parsons had seized hold of her with his left arm. With his right hand he stripped her, brutally and methodically, of all her underwear. Up to that moment Hannah Theron had been afraid. The unexpected savagery of the attack that had awakened her from sleep had served also, until then, to keep her in a condition of cowed uncertainty. The menace in Bert Parsons's onslaught had brought nameless fears into her brain.

But with her clothes torn from her body she found herself divested also, suddenly, of her terrors. She leapt up from the bed. She seemed very tall in that moment, almost as tall as Bert Parsons, who had got on to his feet as well and stood in his shaggy, panting bulk, poised as though to strike her down.

"I've had just enough of you, Bert," Hannah Theron flared out. "You get out of my room at once, or I'll call Mr Ferreira."

"I know what you want Ferreira for," Bert Parsons shouted. "And it ain't to throw me out. A dozen Ferreiras couldn't throw me out. But that's not what you want Ferreira for, see? You would like a dozen Ferreiras now, wouldn't you? But you got only me. How you like that? No Ferreiras, see? Only me. No Ferreiras for you, my girl. You got all your clothes off and then you want to start yelling for Ferreira. Not on your life you don't."

Naked and fearless – fearless because it was in utter nakedness – Hannah Theron stood up to Bert Parsons. She was totally unafraid as she faced him. All she felt for him was an unutterable contempt.

"You either get out of here right away," she called out, "or I'll throw you out myself. I'll break something over your head, you drunken mad sot." She was suddenly beside herself with anger.

"Who are you to call anybody else names?" Bert Parsons demanded. He laughed satirically. His laughter, always unmusical, now had in it an animal undertone that made Hannah Theron feel uneasy all at once, and in spite of herself.

"What right have you got to call me anything?" Bert Parsons repeated, the truculence coming back into his voice. "After all I know about you? You was a stinking whore before I met you. You been no better since I known you. You fell for me easier than any girl I ever had. Not even trying to pretend that sleeping with a man wasn't up your alley – "

"That's only because I'm honest," Hannah Theron retorted. "But you wouldn't understand that, of course. Now will you get out?"

"Not on your life I won't," Bert Parsons answered. "And what you want me out of here for, anyway? Waiting for your schoolmaster husband to visit you, I suppose. Let me tell you that if I catch that blasted Huysmans anywhere near you again, I'll break his neck, and yours. You tell your Huysmans that from me. That long slab of misery. I'll break him in two with my little finger, the bastard."

So that was it. Suddenly Hannah Theron saw the whole situation. Bert Parsons had run into Dulcie Hartnell somewhere; had called on her, no doubt, in the hope that she would relent towards him, and accept him again on the same basis as before. He had gone to Dulcie Hartnell, taking her his body that she had rejected and that still ached for her. And Dulcie had told him that she had seen Hannah Theron and Herklaas Huysmans going into that flat together.

So that was the whole story. Bert Parsons had got jealous. It was funny. It was very funny. The funniest thing about it all was that Bert Parsons wouldn't have got jealous if Dulcie Hartnell had taken him. If she had accepted the offering that Bert Parsons had brought her, once more proffering her the gift of a passion that only Dulcie Hartnell's body could slake. If Dulcie Hartnell had taken him, Bert Parsons wouldn't be here in the room now, carrying on like a fenced-in bull. He would be lying in Dulcie Hartnell's arms now, soothed and at peace, sleeping the night with her, stirring only at those times when his body's urgencies roused him. Sleeping with Dulcie Hartnell as he had slept with her before she had turned him up, and as he slept with Hannah Theron now.

That was the whole thing. Bert Parsons had been frustrated. Dulcie Hartnell had sent him from her with his desires unsatisfied, with the slow lusts burning in his heavy body. And when he had gone away baffled, Dulcie Hartnell had, as a parting shot, informed him that she had seen Hannah Theron going into his flat with Herklaas Huysmans.

That was the whole story. And so all Bert Parsons's mad carryings-on were only a piece of play-acting. He was jealous, of course. But not of Herklaas Huysmans. All his jealousies were centred about the woman who had refused to have any further traffic with him, who had only further exacerbated his physical urges, making a mockery of his needs. That was what his rage was about. He was frustrated. A man. A bull. Yes, it was all very funny. Hannah Theron relapsed on to the edge of the bed and gave way to wild gusts of laughter.

When Bert Parsons had come into her room and started wrenching at her underwear, he had been mad enough. And rightly so. But for a reason altogether different from what he had pretended. He wasn't outraged at the thought that this girl had gone with another man into his flat. He was put down a number of pegs in his male vanity because the girl he really was in love with had scorned his burning flesh.

"What are you laughing about?" Bert Parsons enquired, staring at

Hannah Theron with his mouth wide open. His manner was no longer threatening, but he still spoke loudly. Hannah Theron was not deceived. She knew his bluster by that time. She knew that through her laughter he was caught out. And whenever Hannah Theron in the past had caught him out in a lie or a subterfuge he had, invariably, resorted to bluster that was quite harmless and never took her in.

"I am laughing," Hannah Theron answered, the tears of a mirth that was dangerously poised rolling down her cheeks, "at you. At nobody else. At you!"

She got up from the bed and went to the wardrobe. She took out a pink slip and started pulling it over her head. The garment was no more than halfway over her shoulders before Bert Parsons came up to her and began pulling at it again, clumsily trying to get it off her, over her head.

"Be careful, Bert," Hannah Theron called out through the folds of the petticoat. "This is the only clean slip I've got left. If you tear this one as well, I'll have nothing to wear to school in the morning."

"But you don't need it on, kiddie," Bert Parsons said in a thick voice. "I want you. I'm helping you to take this darned thing off again."

Hannah Theron did not try to struggle. Bert Parsons flung his arms about her in a tight embrace.

She relaxed into his nearness, soothed, a feeling of dark comfort stealing over her limbs, a feeling of being alive in a small world in which she was wanted. She raised her arms and Bert Parsons withdrew the petticoat over her head. She was still standing on the green carpet in front of the bed when Bert Parsons, feeling clumsily along the wall with his huge hand, found the switch and put out the light.

Through the long night hours Hannah Theron lay awake.

Bert Parsons was snoring. She had tried to wake him a few times, but it was no use. She didn't mind being kept awake by his snoring, since she knew that she wouldn't be able to get much sleep in any case. But she was thinking of the boarding-house. Anybody passing her door at that time, in the middle of the night, would know that the snoring was coming from her room.

Oh well, she had already compromised herself up to the hilt with Bert Parsons, as far as the small town of Kalvyn was concerned. This that was taking place now would only give people something more to talk about. And it wasn't anything very much, compared with some of the other things that they knew about, and that they had already discussed to their hearts' content.

Still, Hannah Theron would never be able to get used to it. No matter what she pretended, any new scrape she got into with Bert Parsons, any new situation that was potentially invested with scandal, brought her almost that same measure of hurt as the things that had happened when she had first lost her maiden purity.

Hannah Theron had long ago grown to accept the world's interpretation of her mode of life. She had struggled for a while against making this inner concession. She had tried to argue with herself that in everything she did she was acting in accordance with her own individual principles. When she had given herself to a man, to the first man, it had been in love. She had not acted selfishly. She had believed that the demands of love were paramount, and that whatever one had to offer one had to lay on the altar of love.

And she had always been loyal to the man to whom she had given herself. When she was with a man, no matter how she grew to feel about him later on, as long as he wanted her, she was his. And she would have nothing to do with any other man. It was only when this man no longer wanted her, when he had already discarded her in favour of some other mistress, that she would permit herself to feel that she was no longer bound to him in the most utter loyalty.

But somewhere along the path she had slipped up. She thought, also, that she knew where she had gone wrong. In the first place, when you gave yourself to a man it had to be in love. If it was anything less than love it was immorality; it was prostitution. It was what the Bible meant by being a whore, by fornication. And Hannah Theron had grown to accept the fact that in her relation with the men who had come into her life she had acted, in reality, as a loose woman. Love wasn't just a soft, easy thing of the senses. It was hard, deep, austere. Love was not merely a warm infatuation of the body, a hot yearning in the night, dreams wrapped about in flesh, a rapturous wave that first leapt sunwards and then cooled glisteringly. Love wasn't just that thing.

So she could not say that she had really ever given herself to a man in love. She might have thought so at the time, at each time, but circumstances had proved that it had always been a matter of self delusion. At the best she had on each occasion deceived herself. At the worst she had known she was a whore, and she had not had the honesty to face up to this reality. She had not had the guts to see the truth about herself nakedly for what it was. She had not minded stripping her body naked for a man. She had been too cowardly to strip her soul naked for her own contemplation.

And she still didn't know where she was. She could not feel, at the time, that she had been sinful in yielding her body to Bert Parsons. She had loved him; he had wanted her; she had given herself to him. She had loved him and therefore he had but to ask. But she had known that he was not in love with her.

Oh, she had known all right. You couldn't bluff a woman about a thing like that. She knew that that night in her room, when Bert Parsons had come to her in his passion, he was still in love with Dulcie Hartnell. And she had hoped that his feelings might undergo a change, and that in having her as the woman to whom he could turn for the satisfying of his sex hunger, he would forget his body's hunger and thirsting for Dulcie Hartnell. But it hadn't worked out that way. She should have known it wouldn't work out that way. It wasn't that she hadn't known life. It wasn't as though she was an inexperienced schoolgirl.

And after the first few weeks, when in his physical cohabiting with her Bert Parsons no longer experienced the thrill of newness and of the unexpected, he had made no secret of the fact that he wanted only her flesh. He had told her bluntly, explaining with the limited degree of introspection of which he was capable, that as far as his feelings were concerned she was no more than a substitute for Dulcie Hartnell. In his emotional life Hannah Theron was fulfilling a vicarious function. Bert Parsons was really Dulcie Hartnell's man.

And every time Hannah Theron took him she was acting like a thief. She was stealing from a man those urgencies that belonged to another woman. She was a thief and a polluted thing. She was tarnished in that, in her relations with this man, she was playing a prostitute's role. Permitting a man to pour into her night after night the passions that another woman had awakened in him. She was a smeared thing. A receptacle into which you cast ordure.

With Bert Parsons lying snoring next to her – sprawled across the greater part of the bed and relaxed in the deep slumber following on the stilled transports of a wild wantoning – Hannah Theron lay with her eyes open, gazing at the dark ceiling that was slashed with two wounds of yellow light coming from the passage through the fanlight.

She couldn't sleep. There was the pain of unfulfilled desire at her breast. She would go on lying awake for a very long time.

Bert Parsons had not bothered about her. He had grown singularly careless of her in that regard of late. His passions sated in the fury of an embrace that had only partly awakened her, he had dropped off to sleep within a few minutes, snoring into the dark and expelling deep volumes of alcohol-laden breath into the room. And with the passing of time that light spark that had been dropped athwart her limbs in the course of Bert Parsons's ruthlessly hard mating with her had warmed into a flame that was licking at her thighs, and that was unquenchable because it had come unbidden. The slow warming of her blood during the long night hours in which Bert Parsons snored had swelled into pain. She would not be able to sleep while those fierce white teeth were gnawing at her limbs, biting into her thighs.

Instinctively she reached under the sheets for Bert Parsons's hand. Her fingers passed over the firm material of his shirt that he still wore in sleep and that was damp under the arms from perspiration. She felt the hair on his chest where his shirt lay open in front. In his slumber of satiety, Bert Parsons nevertheless made unconscious response to her caress. His lips mumbled some incoherent remark and he turned his great body half over towards her.

Then his mouth dropped open and he went on snoring. His breath, stale with brandy, was partly deflected into the pillow-case; part of it burnt into Hannah Theron's eyes and forehead. She felt disgusted. But the throbbing of the blood in her limbs would not be stilled. The pain of the flesh that had grown dark in the long hours would not subside.

Eventually, reaching slowly down his huge, barrel-shaped chest that rose and fell portentously with his breathing, Hannah Theron passed her hand under the sheet to below his shirt that had become pulled up through the movements of his heavy frame in the stupor of sleep. Below his crumpled shirt her hand made contact with the side of his body that was hard with muscles. She slipped her hand down his leg, his flesh warmly coarse to her touch. Then she found his hand that was lying bent across his thigh.

It was a large hand, the fingers rough and calloused, the inside of his palm crudely unsmooth like a mealie-cob that had been long dried in the sun. Her long, slender fingers curled inside his rough hand and in his sleep Bert Parsons let his big hand close over the soft fingers of the girl lying beside him.

Hannah Theron seized his hand in both hers and brought it out from under the sheet to her lips. She kissed the knuckles, bit into them almost, and then slowly restored Bert Parsons's gnarled paw to its place under the sheet.

From the change in his breathing, Hannah Theron knew that Bert Parsons was now awake. She did not speak. Neither did he. She knew that there was no need for words.

Bert Parsons eased himself over to one side, slowly disengaging the arm on which he had been lying. And in the next moment Hannah Theron, after she had felt his breath come suddenly very near, found Bert Parsons burying his face in her hair.

He drew her to him, under the sheet and in the dark. She felt the weight on her of a heavy knee. His breath came very hot on the side of her face. She hardly noticed now that his breathing reeked of stale brandy. She snuggled in closer to him. The animal smell of his body in strong lust swept into her nostrils.

It was a long time before Bert Parsons spoke. And then he had already released her, and he was lying on his back, with his legs stretched out to their full length and his hands were clasped under his head, and his breathing had become steady again.

And he said, "I wish it was Dulcie and not you." In his voice was a wavering note, almost like a sob.

To Hannah Theron it didn't matter very much, this thing that Bert Parsons said. In any case he was only reiterating something that he had said often before, and that she knew long ago, and before he had ever made mention of it. She lay becalmed now.

Within a few minutes she was asleep. She fell asleep even before Bert Parsons did.

But she woke up before the boy came round with the coffee. It was a matter of long habit, her remembering to wake before the coffee was brought round when she had a man in the room with her in the early morning. She slipped on her dressing-gown, and when the boy came to the door with the coffee she was there before he knocked.

"Will you give me Baas Parsons's coffee also?" Hannah Theron said to the native waiter. "He will be coming to drink it in here a little later."

The boy handed over a second cup without question. He had long since bothered to work out problems of that description. He only knew that it was something that happened quite often, a missus asking him to leave a cup of coffee in her room for some other baas who was to come round later. And it had happened in other boarding-houses where he had worked, and not simply in Mrs Ferreira's establishment.

Bert Parsons was hard to wake. Hannah Theron shook his shoulders repeatedly. Then she put her hand over his nose and mouth playfully, to stop his breathing. But she thought of something, and took her hand away again.

Eventually Bert Parsons woke up and she gave him his coffee.

"You must go now, Bert," Hannah Theron said to him. "You can go on sleeping in your room. The other residents will be coming out into the passage any moment from now on. I don't want you to be seen coming out of my room."

" — the other residents," Bert Parsons replied, sullen with sleep.

"Yes, you can," Hannah Theron answered. "But not now. Some other time. I am sure they heard us quarrelling last night. They might even have heard some of the things we said. I don't want it to be made any worse."

Bert Parsons was morose. Among other things, he had a hangover. He drank his coffee and he sulked.

But eventually Hannah Theron got him to leave. He made a pass at her before he went. But he put no real heart into it. It was almost as though he did it because he felt that that was what Hannah Theron would have demanded of him. She was not insulted. She felt that she was past that somehow. She merely ushered him out of the door. Her attitude towards him had in it little more than politeness.

After Bert Parsons had left, Hannah Theron slipped on the dress she had worn on the previous day and smoothed her hair quickly. She didn't bother to powder her face. She was in a hurry. She wanted to get through with her breakfast before there were many guests in the dining room. She could not help feeling that some of the things she and Bert Parsons had said to each other had been overheard. She did not want to walk into the dining room to receive those curious stares that she knew so well.

She went out of her room and tripped lightly across the courtyard that was flagged with square grey stones and took a seat at her accustomed table. She was pleased to see that only old Mr Grimbeek, who worked in the post office, and whose room was in one of the other corridors, had so far entered the dining room. She wouldn't mind facing the rest of the residents later in the day. But she hadn't the courage to encounter them now.

She greeted Mr Grimbeek as she sat down. He smiled back at her, then he went on with his breakfast. He didn't try to make any sort of conversation, as he generally did, about the weather or about what he had read in the morning newspaper – which was Johannesburg's newspaper of the night before. It was a relief, anyway, that he wasn't talkative.

"I'll have an egg and some toast and tea," Hannah Theron said to the native waiter. That wouldn't take long to serve or to eat. When the rest of the guests arrived she would have gone out of the dining room, and she would have a reasonable chance of finding one of the bathrooms disengaged.

There was a bathroom at the end of each of the three wings of Mrs Ferreira's boarding-house. There was no system about the way you occupied the bathroom. The result was that it not infrequently happened that Hannah Theron was not able to get into a bathroom before leaving for school in the mornings, with the result that she had to perform a perfunctory ablution in her bedroom in the basin on the washstand. But this morning she felt that she must have a bath.

As soon as she had drunk her tea she rushed to her bedroom for her toothbrush and towel. Her luck was in. She got to the bathroom at the top of her passage at the same moment that a sergeant in the Air Force came out. That was fine. She would have her bath, after all. And she didn't mind facing a dozen Air Force sergeants after last night. It was the prim women that she was afraid of meeting.

"Is the water hot?" Hannah Theron asked the sergeant.

"It will be in a few minutes," he answered. "There's a lot of wood in the geyser."

Hannah Theron entered the bathroom and locked the door behind her. She opened the metal door of the geyser. The wood fire was roaring away. She put her hand on the copper cylinder. It was hot. She added a few more sticks to the fire from the chopped wood in a box beside the geyser and began to disrobe.

A few minutes later she was lying at full length in the bath, laved in the luxury of steaming water that flowed over her thin body, stimulating her flesh with its curved warmth. This was delightful. She remained in the bath until the water began to cool, heedless of the fact that at least three people had knocked at the door while she was occupying the bathroom.

With a few flicks of the towel she was dried. She slipped on her frock quickly, and over that her dressing-gown. Carrying her shoes in her hand and with the towel over her shoulder, she ran barefooted down the corridor to her room.

She pulled off her frock and the dressing-gown hurriedly. Then she went to the wardrobe and took out a clean set of underwear that was spotlessly white and freshly laundered. On top of that went a filmy organdie frock that was cool and frilly where it touched her skin. Then her suspender belt and stockings and shoes. Hannah Theron had not done these things altogether consciously, cleansing her body and decking herself in fresh apparel as a symbolical purification of her flesh from the heavy stains of the night.

But none of these things worked somehow. Half an hour later, clad in the radiance of newly laundered springtime clothes, and with school books under her arm, Hannah Theron set off down the road on her way to school. The summer morning was clean and virginal. In the air was the fragrance of bursting flowers and ripening fruit.

But as she walked down the leafy road with the school books under her arm, Hannah Theron felt about her body that it was unbeautiful and sullied with knowledge; she felt about her limbs that they were stale like Bert Parsons's breath after he had been drinking brandy.

Later that day, just before school ended, Hannah Theron made another discovery about her body. She found that what she had suspected about her condition was altogether groundless. There had been no foundation to her fears. It had been merely one more of many false alarms – except that this last fear had persisted longer than any of the others, and that for that reason it had occasioned her a greater degree of misery.

But the relief that this knowledge brought her was only short lived. She knew that quite soon again her state of being frightened would begin all over.

2

A few days before the end of the school term Herklaas Huysmans received an official letter from the Education Department containing the intimation that he had been appointed to a B-post at the Kalvyn High School.

This was by way of promotion. Or, at least, that was how Herklaas Huysmans chose to regard this change, although his colleagues at the Kalvyn Afrikaans-medium Primary School were in two minds about it.

Some of them said that, of course, a B-post in a high school was not something to be sneezed at, and they wondered what means Herklaas Huysmans had employed to get it. He was a dark horse, all right.

Others said, again, that the advantages associated with being a vice-principal of a primary school were very obvious, and that Herklaas Huysmans's appointment to the High School had come about not so much through his own efforts as through a lot of underground work that the principal, Sybrand van Aswegen, must have been putting in over a considerable period in order to get rid of a rival who was too near the throne. After all, it was easy to understand that Sybrand van Aswegen was not the type of man who would be glad to tolerate the idea of having, as his immediate subordinate, a man with superior educational qualifications to his own, and with almost as many years of teaching service.

In support of this contention it was noticed later on that nobody else was appointed, either from the staff or from outside, as vice-principal in Herklaas Huysmans's place. The argument was that the Kalvyn Afrikaans-medium Primary School was not large or important enough to justify the appointment of a vice-principal. The whole matter was very involved, as most things are connected with the Transvaal Education Department.

Nevertheless, the general consensus of opinion was that, in receiving this appointment to a high school B-post, Herklaas Huysmans had succeeded in bettering himself. Consequently he was congratulated almost on all sides by his colleagues in the primary school. About the only person who felt that the occasion was not one calling for felicitations was the elderly Miss Reinecke, who merely informed Herklaas Huysmans that she was sorry he was leaving, since he was in that way breaking an old and honoured association with a school and a school staff where he was held in high regard.

Herklaas Huysmans himself professed jubilation at the change that had come about in his fortunes. He said that this appointment was both the turning point in his career and its greatest achievement. But because he had on numerous occasions expressed his scorn for the whole of the teaching profession, himself included, his colleagues were doubtful as to how far his assertion was to be taken seriously. They did not know to what extent he was sarcastic also, when he said that this appointment was something for which he had worked all his life.

"It took me a long time to get this job," he announced in the staff room during the luncheon interval. "But I feel I have deserved it."

Because this was a special occasion, Sybrand van Aswegen had considered that it was meet that he should depart from his usual custom of having his tea and sandwiches alone in his office, and for that reason he graced the assembly with his presence.

"We shall, of course, make a presentation to Mr Huysmans," Sybrand van Aswegen announced, "as a small token of the high esteem in which we all hold him. I shall be glad to receive contributions towards this parting gift which we shall all find it a great pleasure to present to him on the last day of the term. He has been with us for many years, and the warmth of our feelings for him is by no means in proportion to the very inadequate nature of the presentation which we shall make."

"Why has the gift to be so very inadequate, anyway?" Herklaas Huysmans demanded suddenly. "I would rather that you held me in less esteem and made the present more worthwhile. You can each of you afford to subscribe at least a couple of pounds. I'll help with the collection of it. And after I have bought myself something that I really like out of the money, I'll stand you all to drinks at the Northern Hotel out of what is left of the proceeds."

The other teachers did not quite know what to make of Herklaas Huysmans's suggestions. They felt that if he was trying to be funny then his humour was in extremely bad taste. On the other hand, if he meant it seriously, what he had said was in even worse taste. His remarks were received in a dead silence. Japie Kruger tried, but with only partial success, to retrieve the situation.

"I am willing to subscribe two pounds," Japie Kruger said, "but that is too much for a girl or for a married man. The rest of you can subscribe what you like. But I shall see to it that Mr Huysmans fulfils his share of the bargain. Whatever he spends on his present he has also got to turn up at the Northern Hotel with enough money to buy us all the liquor we want. Even if he has got to pay for it out of his own pocket."

Herklaas Huysmans went up to Japie Kruger and grasped his hand. "That's a deal," he announced. "That suits me. I want to explain that it was not the money or the present I was after. I was only terrified of the formality of an official leave-taking. An orthodox send-off, with farewell speeches and all that sort of thing. I was frightened of that. But now it's all settled. I'll arrange for a ta-ta function to be held in the lounge of the Northern Hotel on the last day of term, and I invite you all as my honoured guests, and nobody will be allowed to make speeches before his seventh drink, and if there is any money left over after Japie Kruger has drunk himself under the table – which there won't be – I shall buy myself something or other that I shall have suitably inscribed with all your names."

The members of the school staff expressed themselves as satisfied. All except Miss Reinecke. She said she didn't know what the world was coming to. It was all right decrying orthodoxy and making fun of the conventions, but as school-teachers, people who had a responsible calling, they owed certain duties both to their own and to the coming generation, and there were certain occasions that had to be treated with solemnity, no matter how one felt about things like that ordinarily. Occasions to which dignity had to be accorded included funerals and farewells. Above all, she could not reconcile herself to the idea of the farewell being held in what she termed a tap-room.

But it was on this issue that Japie Kruger came to Herklaas Huysmans's aid in a manly fashion. "I am not a drunkard," he announced, "and I seldom go into the lounge of the Northern Hotel – no, that doesn't mean to say that I go into the bar. But even Dominee Zietsman has attended wedding receptions in the lounge of the Northern Hotel. It's all right if it's for a social occasion. In fact" – here his voice faltered slightly – "if the day should come when I get married, and the woman of my heart is like I am, somebody living in a boarding-house in Kalvyn and with no relatives nearer than the Cape, then I know that I shall hold my wedding reception in the lounge of the Northern Hotel as well. That is, if, perhaps, some day, she will have me."

There was a muffled sound, almost like faint applause, when Japie Kruger concluded his speech. They knew he was referring to Lettie van der Walt, whom he took out to dances occasionally and to the local bioscope, and whom he visited quite frequently in her room in one of Kalvyn's boarding-houses. It was said that he had some time in the past proposed to Lettie van der Walt and that she had rejected him. But it was also known that he still had hopes. As far as was known in Kalvyn, Lettie van der Walt was still heart-free. She seemed to have no particularly strong attachments to any of the young men in the place, several of whom were in the habit of taking her out. One or two of them even seemed more than ordinarily keen on her.

Hannah Theron stole a swift glance at Lettie van der Walt to see what effect Japie Kruger's words would have on her. But whatever feelings

Lettie van der Walt had, she succeeded rather well in covering them up. Lettie van der Walt had large blue eyes and a round face and small and regular features, so that if you looked at her just superficially you got the impression of a doll-like prettiness, behind which there lay nothing very much.

It was only after a second glance, when you studied the contours of her mouth, and you saw those straight lines at the edges, that you realised that there was more about Lettie van der Walt's mouth than the rosebud sweetness of her lips, and that there was more about Lettie herself, also, than a mask of unstained prettiness and the empty simplicity of a doll.

Now, after Japie Kruger had spoken, hinting publicly of his hopes, Hannah Theron looked quickly at Lettie van der Walt, in a feminine curiosity as to her reactions. All she saw was that, after having been caught momentarily off her guard, so that a slight flush crept into her cheeks, Lettie van der Walt successfully maintained an outward composure. Her mouth first tightened, but then she smiled. It would have been an open and natural sort of smile also, were it not for the fact that when that tightness left her lips it crept as a hard light into her eyes that were wide and blue. These other things Hannah Theron saw after the first moment of tension following Japie Kruger's speech had worn off, and she could look at Lettie van der Walt without any feelings that she was studying her.

"Have you any objections to attending Herklaas Huysmans's send-off in the hotel lounge?" Hannah Theron asked Lettie van der Walt, talking to her of an unimportant matter in order to put her at ease after the tension created by the underlying implications of Japie Kruger's remarks.

"Of course not," Lettie van der Walt replied, looking in Miss Reinecke's direction and pouting slightly. "I think it's a very good idea. She can have tea, if she wants to, that suppressed old thing. It's all hypocrisy with her, I'm sure. I wouldn't like to see her alone with a man, that's all. I wouldn't like to think, either, of the sort of thing she would get up to, if she got half a chance."

Japie Kruger had not heard Lettie van der Walt's remarks. But when he spoke again he repeated part of the argument she had used.

"We can also order tea and cake in the Northern Hotel lounge," he explained. "So it will be all right also, for those of us who won't want a spot."

Quite a lot of excitement was introduced into the discussion after that, and all the members of the staff in turn again went up to Herklaas Huysmans and told him how they felt about his promotion, and that it must no doubt give him a queer sort of feeling to be leaving a school where he had been teaching so long, and that they were sure he would get into the routine of high school work very easily; and that it wasn't as though they wouldn't go on seeing quite a lot of him still, in the future, because he was after all not leaving Kalvyn, but that perhaps he would feel too high and mighty to want to associate with ordinary primary school folk, and that if he felt lonely, he would perhaps consider getting married, too, one of these days. And so on.

The principal, Sybrand van Aswegen, made another short speech again, along slightly less formal lines. The upshot of it was that a very pleasant atmosphere prevailed in the staff room, and Herklaas Huysmans really began to feel, for a few moments, that his colleagues were genuinely interested in him, and it actually happened, for the opening of the second school session that day, that the bell was rung ten minutes late.

Those were the circumstances, then, under which Herklaas Huysmans left the primary school to take up his appointment at the high school.

On the last day of the term practically the same things were said over again in the lounge of the Northern Hotel. Miss Reinecke had so far overcome her scruples that she not only entered the lounge and took a seat at the long table that had been specially brought in for the occasion and had been covered with a white cloth, but she unbent so far as to drink a small port wine to Herklaas Huysmans's future. It was a cosy little send-off. The speeches were few and far between and, as though by general consent, were lacking in formality.

After a while the guests started to leave. The principal, Sybrand van Aswegen, was the first to go. He was followed soon after by Miss Reinecke. A little later Japie Kruger and Lettie van der Walt left together.

After she had given them a reasonable start, Hannah Theron took up her bag and began to get up also. Herklaas Huysmans put up his hand to restrain her. Hannah Theron looked at him swiftly. No, he wasn't drunk. She had a sudden terror of Herklaas Huysmans's going through the same performance as on the last occasion, when they had met outside of school hours. The memory of that afternoon was still fresh in her mind.

Herklaas Huysmans caught the drift of what she was thinking. "No," he said, "we don't need to drink any more. In any case, with the guests departed, this table with the white cloth and the empty glasses looks depressing. Let us go and sit on that couch near the door, and we'll have a last drink together. One for the road. For the road that leads over the hill to the High School."

Hannah Theron allowed herself to be persuaded. "But I can't have more than one," she said. "And you know I haven't got much time to spare. I am going to Pretoria for the holidays, and from there I have arranged to go with my mother to Cape Town. And I still have a few things to pack."

"But the train leaves only at eleven o'clock tonight," Herklaas Huysmans insisted, after they had seated themselves on a brown leather couch near the door, in front of a small round-topped table. "I could even see you off. Although I wouldn't be able to, of course. I mean I wouldn't be able to stand on the platform and wave, seeing I am going down on the same train."

He rang the bell for Hans Korf.

Hannah Theron said she would have a brandy and ginger ale. Herklaas Huysmans ordered a brandy and water for himself.

"Water," Herklaas Huysmans explained, "I refuse to drink anything else but water with my brandy. I don't believe in disguising the taste of the alcohol with some flavoured soft drink. I believe in having the raw taste of life and the raw taste of brandy. I want to live raw and naked. I want to feel things raw."

Hans Korf came in with the brandies. He looked suspiciously at Herklaas Huysmans, and then at Hannah Theron. He wondered what was on the go. This looked like funny business to him. Only a few days ago Herklaas Huysmans had got drunk here with Hannah Theron. And God knows what had taken place after they had left. And here they were together again, after the other members of the party had gone, and Huysmans looking well set now for another booze-up. What must Bert Parsons think about it, anyway?

Hannah Theron began to have misgivings also, but in a different direction. She didn't like the way Herklaas Huysmans kept on repeating himself. It seemed as though he was up to something. She didn't think he was tight. It must be something else. The other thing. This was going to be awful. It was all right with Sybrand van Aswegen. She wasn't going to worry about him any more. She was satisfied that she knew how to handle him. He wasn't turning out the problem she had at first feared he might become.

But here was Herklaas Huysmans seeming to start up all over again. Anyway, it was a good thing that Herklaas Huysmans had left the school, that she wouldn't have to see him again at the beginning of the next term. It was very embarrassing, her being pestered in this way by men who were approaching middle age and who ordinarily would have taken no notice of her, would not have seen her even, if it were not for various external circumstances: the fact that they had not, in the world about them, found true fulfilment for their desires, and that they had now, as a consequence, begun to feel restless, believing that they were missing the things life had to offer them. They saw in her a woman who was not, as they thought, outside of the current life, and that was what had drawn them to her.

Hannah Theron told herself that in all this there was no question of these men ever being able to have any genuine regard for her, any feeling for her, other than a burning of the flesh. Their approach to her was insulting. It was openly contemptuous. They might bluff themselves that they were concealing from her the underlying disdain for her body that motivated their advances to her. But she was not being bluffed.

They would never think of loading some other girl with insults of this nature, a girl like Lettie van der Walt, for instance. For it didn't matter what experiences Lettie van der Walt had had in the past; she had not been broken by those experiences. These men could see in Hannah Theron a broken creature. They saw in Lettie van der Walt a girl who was icily sure of herself, aloof, proud, self-possessed. It was only when things had happened to you in the night that had so humbled you, so far deprived you of all self-respect and hope and faith in your flesh, that men could come to you in the manner in which Sybrand van Aswegen and Herklaas Huysmans had come to her.

Hans Korf brought the drinks. Herklaas Huysmans started talking. For Hannah Theron it was hell. She knew what he was going to say. Each sentence he uttered, each phrase even, was part of the battered currency that men employed habitually in seeking to win her favours, with the result that she could feel in his remarks only an insincerity. In what he said, the only part that was not false was the brandy.

"I want to tell you," Herklaas Huysmans began. "I know you won't believe me – "

"Oh, I believe you all right," Hannah Theron answered, making the cynicism in her voice as broad as possible, secure in the knowledge that he was not in a condition to detect any sort of nuances. She was satisfied that Herklaas Huysmans was more than a little tight by this time. She could introduce any kind of note into her speaking and he wouldn't detect it. He was barely in a condition to understand words.

That was the worst of being an habitual school-teacher – something much more debauched than being an habitual drunkard – you couldn't drink more than a couple of brandies and still retain a clear intellect, if you taught school.

"Well," Herklaas Huysmans continued, "what I am telling you is the honest God's truth. I don't suppose you know why I am leaving Kalvyn Primary School, do you?"

"You have got promotion, haven't you?" Hannah Theron answered, smilingly, "at least that's what they all say. You are not going to tell me now, I hope, that you have been thrown out? At least, I hope that isn't what I am going to hear now."

"Thrown out!" Herklaas Huysmans repeated, making an effort to push out his chest. "Thrown out. I like that. I'd like to see anybody throw me out. Out of anywhere. Out of the Kalvyn Primary Afrikaans-medium School or out of a pub. Let me tell you that a Huysmans never gets thrown out. When he wants to leave, he leaves on his own recognisances – I mean, at his own volition, and he leaves with dignity. When my ancestors, who were Cape aristocrats, and kept slaves, left any place at all they were escorted out with decorum; they were bowed out, as far as the door, by the host's servants, and from there onward, from the pavement into the waiting coach, or palanquin, or curtained chair, they were bowed by their own lackeys. No, ma'am. They never got thrown out anywhere."

By this time, more through gestures than actual speech – through the manipulation of his glass and through other more esoteric signs – Herklaas Huysmans had succeeded in getting Hans Korf to bring two more brandies.

"You'll have to drink them both," Hannah Theron said. "I'm not going to help you. I dare not have another drink or I'll get tight. And this time you'll have to find your way home alone. And I've got the feeling that, if you have another drink, ancestors or no ancestors, you are going to be thrown out of the lounge of the Northern Hotel. And there won't be anybody to bow you out. All you will be able to look forward to is having Hans Korf holding on to you by your coat collar and your sleeve."

"Have you heard of Ryk Tulbagh's sumptuary laws?" Herklaas Huysmans continued as though Hannah Theron had not spoken. "And that was within the first generation of the foundation of the Cape. Well, those laws were introduced to stop my ancestors from carrying on like Eastern potentates. When they went down 's Heeren Gracht they weren't allowed to have more than about seven slaves preceding them with umbrellas. I mean, I have studied our country's laws – "

"But they were my ancestors as well," Hannah Theron interrupted him. "You ought to see the silver plate that my grandfather has still got on his wine farm just outside Paarl. Remember, I am as good an Afrikaner as you are. And you ought to see some of the napery and the candlesticks and the cutlery. I am going to pay a visit there during the holidays. But I still want to remind you that you are in the Transvaal now, and ancestors or no ancestors, Tulbagh or no Tulbagh, if you drink any more brandy they are going to throw you out of here. And that will be a very bad start for a new high school teacher. Or is this your idea of an initiation? Do you want to wet your B-post in the right way?"

"B-post!" Herklaas Huysmans sneered. "They can keep that B-post. I'll tell the Director of Education where he can put that B-post, too. That's how much I care about it. But now that you have mentioned it, I'll tell you the inside story of my leaving the primary school. The reason I am leaving is you."

Herklaas Huysmans paused dramatically. Before Hannah Theron had been able to stop him, he had poured some water into the glass of brandy with an unsteady hand and had swallowed the contents at a gulp. He had then made a grab at the second brandy.

"Don't be silly, Herklaas," Hannah Theron said, trying to be patient with him and trying to introduce into her voice a note of gentle authority, which she found had worked, on rare occasions in the past, on men who were trying to get drunk for no other reason than that they wanted to show off in front of her.

Her quiet admonition achieved partial success. Herklaas Huysmans paused with the glass of brandy somewhere halfway in the air.

But, actually, it was no real satisfaction to her, this matter of his not having swallowed down the last brandy as well. She was so little interested in him, really. The last school term of the year had ended. The holidays had started. She was going away to the Cape. She would be travelling down with her mother. It was going to be quiet. And to have a man on her hands now, at this stage, was not like a holiday at all. It was as though she was still working. Herklaas Huysmans merely left her cold. She had absolutely no feeling for him, one way or the other. And this time, if he got drunk, he couldn't blame it on her. It was his party. It was not her fault that he had drunk excessively at a party where he was the host. She looked at him with a thin amusement in her eyes.

"The reason I am leaving the primary school," Herklaas Huysmans repeated, putting down the brandy and looking fixedly into Hannah Theron's face, "is on your account. I want to tell you. That last time, when I got drunk and you saw me home, and you made coffee for me – that time. After you had gone, I knew that I was in love with you."

"What a shame," Hannah Theron answered. It was the old story. Why couldn't these suppressed males go and find some other sort of outlet for their neuroses? Why couldn't they take up something like golf, or fretwork? After all, handicrafts were taught in school these days. And a teacher should be able to benefit, no less than a pupil, from the study and practice of his subject. But then Herklaas Huysmans did play tennis. All right, if it was that he wanted a woman, there was no reason in the world why he should have to pick her. Furthermore, it was almost incredible that he should have the impudence to think that she would look at him.

"It is a shame, right enough," Herklaas Huysmans pursued, in a voice that was growing thicker. "I'll play fair with you. I'll tell you just what happened. When I met you that afternoon, and I invited you to the hotel lounge – to here where we are sitting, in fact: we are sitting here again all over – well, I had the idea that you were a bit of fluff that was going to be easy. Do you get me? There were all sorts of reasons why I wanted you as a bit of fluff. I thought that if other men could have a bit – "

"Of fluff," Hannah Theron added, nodding her head in mock understanding.

"And so I thought to myself that I was just as good as the next man," Herklaas Huysmans explained.

"Oh, better," Hannah Theron said firmly. "When it comes to dealing with a bit of fluff, you are much better. I can tell you from my experience that that is so. Just grabbing a girl by her wrist and lugging her into a waiting taxi and then out again on to the pavement and hauling her into your den – oh, I forgot, you couldn't walk by that time. No, that's right, it was I that hauled you into your flat. Anyway, at the first meeting – well, you weren't bad. You can take that from me. Next time you feel you would like a bit of fluff, you just go about it in the same way, and you'll click. You can even go a bit further, and when you are in the taxi you can bite the girl on her leg. That's also very effective. So you know what to do now. Only, next time you pick up a girl, I want you to look at her twice, to make sure that it isn't me. Otherwise you'll get into more trouble than you've bargained for. Now I must be off."

Hannah Theron glanced at her watch. Then she leant forward to pick up her bag which was lying on another chair.

And of course Herklaas took that opportunity of again seizing hold of Hannah Theron by the wrist.

Hannah Theron thought quickly. She could easily reach the bell with her free hand to summon Hans Korf from the bar, and Herklaas Huysmans would go out on his neck.

She felt that that was what he deserved. He was somebody almost unbelievably callow. And then he had the cheek to chuck his weight around when he thought he was dealing with an unprotected girl. He confessed that he had picked her up, the other day, when she had met him on the pavement, for no other purpose than to seduce her with the minimum of delay. There was a piece of downright impudence for you. He wouldn't have treated a prostitute like that. He would at least have asked a professional harlot first what she charged. And the chances were that if he had been told her price, he wouldn't have been willing to pay it, either.

Hannah Theron was furious at the thought that this gangling person, with his long weak face and his long unattractive body, should have had the cheek to approach her in a way that even Bert Parsons would not have stooped to. Bert Parsons at least treated her with a measure of consideration, during those days before she had yielded herself to him. And even today he was generous to her, after his own fashion. In spite of what he said to her, in spite of the things he did to her, there was still, in the background of his relations with her, a pretence of chivalry, which she valued nevertheless – even if that chivalry went no further than Bert Parsons giving her an occasional present and taking her out to dances and out of town for weekends. There was no need, actually, for Bert Parsons to engage a room for them at an hotel forty miles out of town, on occasional weekends. For he had all the access he wanted to her in her own room in Mrs Ferreira's boarding-house, or in his room. Even though Bert Parsons's primary motives were selfish, in his dealings with her he was still capable of all sorts of little gestures – the sort of thing that went to a woman's heart: the foolish heart of a woman that could forgive a man so much if he was nice to her in small ways.

And here was this long oaf of a man, with no knowledge of the world, explaining that all he had wanted to offer her was the nakedness of seduction. His flesh had been irritated by desire and in order to satisfy this desire he had picked on Hannah Theron, in a realism that wore no disguise of play-acting even, and all he had offered her was the body's gratification.

Hannah Theron's first impulse was to have Herklaas Huysmans thrown out of the lounge. She was white with anger. She would teach him a lesson. He would never again molest any girl, picking on her in the impudence of crude lust, because he thought she was outside of the pale of respectability.

Her hand on the bell that would summon Hans Korf, Hannah Theron paused. There was something in Herklaas Huysmans's attitude that made her hesitate with her hand on the bell, in the same way that in Hannah Theron's tone there had been a quality, some minutes before, that had made Herklaas Huysmans put down the glass again, when the brandy was halfway to his lips.

Hannah Theron felt suddenly that it was wrong to judge Herklaas Huysmans by the standards in terms of which men are judged. And if she was concerned only with the fact that her pride had been outraged by his frank confession of what his intention had been, then it would obviously be a most inhuman thing to do – getting Herklaas Huysmans trampled upon, his pride in the dust, in order to save her own feminine vanity.

She knew that salvation for herself did not lie in that direction. Because somebody had insulted her, it wouldn't do much good making him realise that he couldn't go round insulting girls like Hannah Theron. After all, the fact that she was open to this sort of approach from men was a thing of her own shame. It originated from her own sin. It was a shame that she had to bear alone.

And here was Herklaas Huysmans, who was not a man at all, merely seeking to take advantage, for himself, of the fact that men had made a broken creature out of her: somebody who dared not arrogate to herself the right – as Herklaas Huysmans thought – of scorning any man's advances, as long as what he brought her was his body in lust.

Hannah Theron looked at her watch again. Another few minutes wouldn't make any difference. She would talk to him and explain that she was not a loose woman in the sense that he thought she was.

Herklaas Huysmans was, after all, just a fool. He didn't know about men and women and the world. Because he had no sex appeal, he was in his way perhaps as much of a lost creature as any woman that the world regarded as a harlot. He was so long and ungainly. His movements were so lacking in grace. He looked so scholarly, with that beginning of a stoop. He might pass muster in a city. In a small town like Kalvyn he was lost. In a dorp it was almost like still being on a farm: a man had to have the physical attributes, or he was made to feel his inferiority. That must be a galling thing inside you. She hadn't thought of that before, quite from that angle, or with that degree of intensity.

"All right, Herklaas," Hannah Theron said, speaking gently to him, as to a child, "you don't need to hold on to my arm like that. I can stay a little longer."

"Of course you must stay," Herklaas Huysmans answered. "You don't understand what it is that I am trying to say to you, Hannah. All this will have been for nothing unless I can explain to you. My going to the High School. My giving this party. All this. It's all about you. I must explain – "

"But I must first tell you something," Hannah Theron interrupted him. "I know that you thought, and that you still think, that I am a loose woman. And for that reason you wanted to take liberties with me. And I don't care if you still want to take liberties with me, any more than I care what you think of me. If you want to think of me as somebody immoral, in the way that you do think, I want to let you know that that makes no difference to me. I really don't care a scrap what you think of me. But for your own sake, because I don't want you to make a fool of yourself, I want to tell you something. And that is that when I am with one man I have got a sense of loyalty to him that I mightn't even have for him, to that same extent, if I was legally married to him. Do you understand that? And it doesn't matter how badly he treats me either, I'll never show any outside person what passes between us – not if I can help it, that is. And this is what my being a loose woman consists of. If I love a man, I feel that I have got no right to withhold anything from him. I have got to yield whatever he demands. And if he gets tired of me, and starts subjecting me to all kinds of abuse, I feel that I am still bound to him, and that I am free to look at or think of another man only when the man to whom I have belonged until then has cast me aside. So of course you are right when you think of me as immoral. But I only want you to remember that I am loyal in what you choose to regard as my looseness. And so, if you start getting hold of the idea that I am what you call a bit of fluff, somebody that you can pick up on the pavement, or in the staff room of a school, I want to let you know where you are going to make a fool of yourself. I belong to a man now, at this moment. That's all I want you to know. That's all you need to know. For me you are somebody that just doesn't exist as a man. As somebody to talk to, now and again, when we meet accidentally or like now, you are all right. But, for your own sake, I don't want you to get wrong ideas about me."

Hannah Theron stopped talking. She couldn't altogether decide, in her own mind, as to whether Herklaas Huysmans was sufficiently sober to take in the full purport of her remarks.

Still, he had let her go and he had listened. He hadn't tried to interrupt her. And she felt that he could at least have no more illusions left as to where he stood with her.

Herklaas Huysmans pushed the glass of brandy, which was still untouched, to the far rim of the table. It was as though in this gesture he sought to convey to Hannah Theron the fact that he was still sober, and that he was determined to convince her that, in the thing he was now going to say, there would be no question of his feelings being coloured by the purple fumes of alcohol.

"I know all that," Herklaas Huysmans answered. "And I wish it wasn't so. You can't tell me anything about yourself that I don't know, that I didn't discover for myself in my flat, both when you were there and after you had left, and since then. You don't know what I have suffered here – " he put his hand to his heart with an awkward gesture.

That was old stuff, Hannah Theron reflected, all of it. She had heard it so often before from men. Only other men hadn't gone through these same actions quite so clumsily.

"What I want to say," Herklaas Huysmans continued, "is that, for whatever reason I got you to come with me to my flat – and it was for the lowest reason – by the time you left I knew I had fallen in love with you. I have known since then, naturally, the sort of contempt in which you hold me. And I couldn't stand it. I couldn't stand seeing you, day after day, in the staff room at the school, where you acted as though I meant nothing to you – just a fellow school-teacher. And all the time I was eating out my heart. I even tried, once or twice, to stay out of the staff room, pretending that I had work to do in my classroom, just so that I shouldn't have to endure the pain of sitting near you, and you as unconscious of my presence as though I was this table. But I felt I would sooner have this pain of your overlooking me completely, rather than that I shouldn't see you at all. And that was the reason why I applied to the Department for that post in the High School. I want to remain in the same town where you are. I couldn't stand the strain of your proximity, day by day, in the staff room when I felt about you the way I do, and to you I was nothing. What is he to Hecuba? Nothing at all. That's why there will be no wedding Sunday week down in old Bengal. Do you know that song? No, I don't suppose you have ever heard it. It was long before your time. And I used to think it was a silly nigger song until I fell in love with you. And since then that old song has been with me all the time. And I know just how the singer felt. And I feel it means more things than the person who wrote it ever understood about that song. Hecuba. It isn't a name you hear very often. And why out of all the women in the world has it got to be Hecuba? And, of course, he can mean nothing to her. Nothing at all."

This time, in spite of his resolutions to the contrary, Herklaas Huysmans reached out heavily for the brandy glass on the edge of the table. Without a word, and without spilling much of it, he poured the liquor down his throat.

"I must go now," Hannah Theron said softly. She again caught up her handbag, and slipped out from behind the table before Herklaas Huysmans could detain her. "Goodbye."

"All right," he answered, and his voice had become thick again. "I'll see you on the station. I'm taking the same train tonight. What's he to Hecuba?"

As Hannah had foreseen, Herklaas Huysmans was eventually thrown out of the lounge of the Northern Hotel.

He was very drunk by that time. And after Hans Korf had refused to serve him with any more drinks – a circumstance that had taken some little while to penetrate his consciousness – he had become obstreperous, first shouting loudly and then smashing the empty glass in front of him. He was endeavouring, with no great degree of success, to detach the round top of the table for some obscure purpose of his own, when Hans Korf came in and with professional skill raised him from the couch and walked him out of the door and on to the pavement.

Herklaas Huysmans blinked when he got outside. Then he started to stagger.

Hans Korf relented. There were, after all, certain proprieties to be observed. You couldn't really treat this Huysmans fellow like just an ordinary small-town drunk. He was, when you came to think of it, a school-teacher with a standard of dignity to uphold, and even if he seemed to be taking to drink lately, you had to give him a bit of a chance. Consequently, Hans Korf went out into the street after Herklaas Huysmans, whom he seized once more by his jacket collar and one sleeve, and started propelling him back into the lounge.

To any passer-by who had witnessed that incident the whole thing must have seemed peculiar. After all, it is distinctly unusual for a bartender to throw a drunk, not out of but into, a pub.

Hans Korf went right through the lounge with Herklaas Huysmans. Then he called a room boy.

"Unlock that spare room," Hans Korf said to the native servant. "Let the baas lie on the bed for a while, until he gets well."

3

Bert Parsons drove Hannah Theron to the station in time for the eleven o'clock train to Pretoria and Johannesburg.

Several of the school-teachers were already on the platform. They were, of course, happier even than their schoolchildren were at the thought of a holiday at the coast. Sybrand van Aswegen was taking his family to the Cape by car. The others were going by train. The platform was crowded. The teachers from the various schools in Kalvyn were leaving by the eleven o'clock train. And mothers with their children, the fathers having to stay behind and work.

"Look Bert," Hannah Theron said, "there's Japie Kruger. And he's without Lettie van der Walt. I thought they were going as far as Johannesburg together. Japie said that if the train was very crowded they were going to sit up all night in the dining car, rather than swelter in a crowded compartment."

"Lettie van der Walt has been and changed her mind," Bert Parsons said, "at the last minute. She's going to the Northern Transvaal instead, Messina. She asked me to tell Kruger."

"Messina," Hannah Theron repeated, her heart sinking. "You have had nothing to do with it, have you, I mean her changing her mind like this, and saying nothing to Japie Kruger about it?"

Hannah Theron looked keenly at Bert Parsons. He wore an expensive suit. His red face was newly shaven. A brightly coloured tie flared in front of his pale-blue shirt. He had a swollen look about him, somehow. He seemed flushed with a sort of animal confidence that he hadn't got merely from whisky. There was something about his swagger this evening that made her wonder, wonder.

"On my dying oath," Bert Parsons replied, a queer light coming into his eyes – or so Hannah Theron thought: although she told herself it might be the way his face was half turned to the light coming from the open door of the waiting room. "Don't be silly, kiddie. Just as I was getting into the car, you know, I went to pick up Lionel Andrews and we had a quick one in the bar before I came back for you, and just before I got into the car Lettie van der Walt came up and said would I tell her boyfriend, Japie Kruger, as she had decided to go to Messina instead. Hell, you don't think there is anything between us, do you, kiddie? On my dying oath – "

He passed his arm around her waist swiftly, furtively, withdrawing it in almost the same moment so that the passengers on the platform should not observe the action.

But Hannah Theron was comforted by the warmth of his caress, by its tenderness. She looked up into Bert Parsons's face and smiled. The light she had seen in his eyes that had made her suspicious was gone.

"Forgive me, Bert," she said, "I am so silly. It's only because I love you. And my nerves feel all gone in. This term has been a terrible strain. The last term always is. And I felt I couldn't stand any more shocks."

She reached up suddenly on her toes and planted a swift kiss on Bert Parsons's mouth. He smiled down into her eyes. The incident was over. The momentary qualm it had occasioned in her emotions was gone.

Together Hannah Theron and Bert Parsons went to inform Japie Kruger of Lettie van der Walt's last-minute change of plans. Japie Kruger's face fell. Young, in his twenties, the expression that came into his eyes had a queerly ageing effect.

But the next moment that look was gone. Hannah Theron could sense the iron grip that Japie Kruger was keeping on his feelings, so that after he had given way, for a few seconds, under the direct impact of that blow, he did not again reveal the extent to which this piece of news had hacked into his feelings.

"You know what it is with women," Bert Parsons said, in an attempt at being profound, "nobody knows when they wants to change their minds. Look at me now. I never knows where exactly I am with Hannah here, neither. Do I, kiddie?"

Hannah Theron did not answer.

Shortly afterwards the train for Johannesburg and Pretoria roared into the station. Bert Parsons helped Hannah Theron to find the compartment into which she had been booked. Besides herself, there were two other women and three children, one of which was in her class. Oh God, it was as though the holidays had not yet started. It was as though she was back at school.

Bert Parsons stood by the window of her compartment to see her off. The husbands of the other two women were there also, to say goodbye to their wives. Hannah Theron felt a bitterness sweeping into her heart. Those two women with their husbands. And she with a man who was in the baldest reality her husband, and about whom she had to pretend innocence to the world.

Then, just before the whistle blew, Bert Parsons produced suddenly, as though from nowhere, a pound box of Black Magic chocolates – Hannah's favourite. The train moved off slowly, then faster. On the platform, Bert Parsons stood and waved.

The chocolates clasped tightly in both hands, Hannah Theron looked out of the window until the last lights of Kalvyn station had faded into the night. There were tears in her eyes.

4

They had forgotten Herklaas Huysmans in the room in the Northern Hotel. He lay there, hour after hour, sleeping off his drunkenness. Because he wasn't much used to strong drink, it took him a long time to get right.

By the time he woke up and remembered that he had to get to the station, the train had already gone.

Chapter Seven

1

THE next term came and went, and the term after that, at the Afrikaans-medium Primary School in Kalvyn. The months passed. The summer departed and over the Northern Transvaal the winter lay.

Hannah Theron did not see much of Bert Parsons in the months that followed her holiday visit to the Cape. He had not written. He had even overlooked sending her a Christmas card. And when she got back to Kalvyn after the holidays, he was not waiting for her at the station to drive her to Mrs Ferreira's boarding-house.

His business was flourishing. He was regarded as being potentially one of Kalvyn's most prosperous citizens. Before the market building was completed, he had indeed landed the contract for the new Volkskas building. Several minor contracts had also come his way. Everybody said that there was a building boom in the Northern Transvaal, that if it hadn't actually come it was just around the corner, and Bert Parsons was well to the fore.

Shortly after her return from her holiday Hannah Theron had once more moved back to the Northern Hotel.

This time no one asked why she had moved. Sybrand van Aswegen seemed to think it was no longer any of his business, a school-teacher on his staff residing in an hotel. But if she had been asked, Hannah Theron would probably have told the enquirer why she had changed her abode. But even Mrs Ferreira did not ask her. She even allowed Hannah Theron to leave her boarding-house without giving formal notice. About the nearest anybody came to hinting openly at the circumstance of Hannah Theron's again taking a room at the Northern Hotel was the proprietress, Mrs Manning. That was on the second day of Hannah Theron's return to the hotel.

Mrs Manning came in, ostensibly to find out if Hannah Theron liked her room, but when she was followed into the room, a few minutes later, by a native waiter with a tray and some glasses of brandy, Hannah Theron knew that Mrs Manning had come in for a chat.

Hannah Theron was agreeably surprised to find that Mrs Manning had not come to elicit any confidences. She asked no questions and by her manner she made it clear that she expected no explanations from Hannah Theron. Instead, the plump proprietress of the Northern Hotel, after taking a seat at Hannah Theron's invitation, shook her ash-blonde curls a couple of times, as though to get herself comfortable. She took up her glass, before plunging into a rather pointless monologue about the sort of things that life did to you, illustrating her remarks with little anecdotes of a personal nature.

"Cheer up," Mrs Manning said, when she went out again. "Cheer up, dearie. We must all learn to grin and bear it. The rough with the smooth, you know. There's as good fish left in the sea as any of the bastards that fall into your lap and then leave you flat."

"Oh yes, of course, Mrs Manning," Hannah Theron answered. "I am not worrying. Really I am not."

"You poor thing," Mrs Manning called out from the door. "Your time will come. But if it doesn't come, don't let that make no difference, either."

Vaguely pondering the import of this piece of philosophy, Hannah Theron flung herself on the bed. Then she remembered that there was still some of the brandy left in her glass. She got up and took up the glass standing on the tray that the native had placed on the dressing table. Hannah Theron drank the rest of the brandy and went back to the bed.

Only after Mrs Manning had left did Hannah Theron realise what it was about Mrs Manning's personality that filled her with a queer sort of nostalgia, a sweetness that seared. It was because Mrs Manning's way of speech was similar to Bert Parsons's. Not only in the language she employed, in her expressions culled from rough life and in her raciness of phrase, but even in her intonation, there was a lot of Mrs Manning's manner of talking that reminded Hannah Theron of Bert Parsons.

Hannah Theron's wounds were very raw.

2

It was no more than a nine days' wonder in the life of Kalvyn, Bert Parsons's suddenly dropping Hannah Theron in favour of Lettie van der Walt, at the time when Hannah Theron was away from Kalvyn during the school holidays. The thing was no more than something in the nature of a mild scandal, which occupied the attention of the town gossips for no longer than the second half of the Northern Transvaal summer. By the time the autumn had come, the story of Hannah Theron and

Bert Parsons was reduced to lower than tenth place as a topic of local interest. People could just not be bothered to talk about it any more.

What scandalous interest was left was now attached to Lettie van der Walt in respect of the assumptions that were being made about her relations with Bert Parsons. They could prove nothing, as yet.

In any case, in matters of this description it was very hard to get first hand evidence, a great deal of weight having to be placed on an intelligent interpretation of each set of circumstances. In view of how much of it goes on, it is to a high degree surprising how rarely a couple get caught *in flagrante delicto*, in an act of copulation. This is, of course, a sore point with the scandal-mongers. Why can't people be caught at it red-handed? That is what the scandal-mongers want, in this way revealing the fact that their heated interest in the illicit sex lives of others is actually derived from their own neuroses, caused in most instances by suppressions.

Anyway, the fact of the matter was that, in their relations with each other, Lettie van der Walt and Bert Parsons maintained a certain degree of circumspection, enabling the gossips to think what they liked, but leaving them at the same time in the position of having to found their suspicions only on circumstantial evidence, and that not always of the most direct sort.

When Bert Parsons was still with Hannah Theron it was rather different: the actions of the two parties in that affair were not characterised by the same amount of discretion. They say it is the woman that sets the tone in matters of this nature. The obvious inference was – since no woman likes the clandestine things of her conduct to be bruited about – that Lettie van der Walt was able to exercise a restraining influence over Bert Parsons that Hannah Theron had not the power to do. When they were together, Hannah Theron had not been able to stop Bert Parsons from flaunting his triumphant masculinity, parading the inner secrets of their two lives before the public gaze.

It appeared that Lettie van der Walt was able to restrain Bert Parsons, if not completely, then at least to a very great extent. There weren't so many loose ends lying about. There were less bedroom boys to tell queer stories in the kitchens of hotels and boarding-houses. There was less gossip among taxidrivers about rendezvous terminating at daybreak. There was less hard news obtainable from the chemist's assistants. There was plenty of material for surmise: there was little in the way of solid, concrete fact.

So, because she could exercise a restraint over Bert Parsons, imposing on his conduct an outward discretion which Hannah Theron had been unable to put there, people came to the conclusion that Lettie van der Walt was more the sort of woman for Bert Parsons. She could keep him in order better than Hannah Theron had succeeded in doing. And with every man, it didn't matter who he was, what he really needed was a woman who could keep a hold on him. A woman who could curb him in her own interests. And then it would turn out, as a rule, that it was in his own interests also.

That was what people thought, in a constructive sense, about what was going on between Bert Parsons and Lettie van der Walt. In a purely salacious sense, of course, they said and thought many other things.

But in the essentials of their thinking they were wrong. They omitted the one important factor. And that was Dulcie Hartnell. In the long run, although neither Hannah Theron nor he himself was fully aware of what was going on, Bert Parsons had used Dulcie Hartnell as the pestle with which he had smashed Hannah Theron's heart to pulp, as kaffir women use a block of wood for grinding dried mealies into very fine pieces in the mortar.

And the point of it all was that – in spite of the fact that Lettie van der Walt, with her round face and plump body and baby-blue eyes, was for him a much needed change from Hannah Theron's dark grace in which there was not much outside prettiness – yet Bert Parsons's feelings for Dulcie Hartnell had undergone no substantial alteration. He still felt about Dulcie Hartnell as he had always done.

Actually, Dulcie Hartnell had caught him. By discarding him just before he would have discarded her. He would have grown tired of her inevitably. And the joke of it was that Dulcie Hartnell had wearied of him first. What Bert Parsons felt for Dulcie Hartnell was not real love. It was not even the semblance of love. What he had for her was an infatuation based upon the simple fact that she had chopped him down in his male vanity.

All that Lettie van der Walt meant in Bert Parsons's life was that her body was for him a change from Hannah Theron's body, of which he had wearied. Lettie van der Walt was merely affording for his emotions an outlet that was still thrilling because it was new. She had made no attack on his ego. She knew none of Dulcie Hartnell's tricks, employed consciously or otherwise.

Lettie van der Walt, with her soft skin and her child-like countenance, and her doll-like prettiness that was all on the surface. But with that queer tightness at the sides of her full mouth. With her blonde, wavy hair and the dimple in her chin and her round white shoulders. But with that hard light that came into her eyes when her lips smiled.

Lettie van der Walt. Perhaps she had already felt the first impact of the pestle. The block of wood pounding at her heart. The hard, heavy stamper crushing the mealies in the piece of hollowed out tree-trunk, breaking them into rough pieces and then grinding them into a coarse powder.

Watching them from the outside, the people in Kalvyn who gossiped about Bert Parsons and Lettie van der Walt saw only that Lettie van der Walt appeared to have a grip on Bert Parsons, which Hannah Theron never seemed to have had.

3

In the months of that winter which lay leafless on the Northern Transvaal, Hannah Theron remained for a while alone in the hotel, trying with a barren futility to immerse herself in her job of teaching, otherwise withdrawing herself almost entirely from the living world around her.

Sometimes a stranger to Kalvyn, meeting her at dinner in the hotel, or running across her in one of the corridors or in the lounge – which she avoided studiously for a while – would invite her to go out with him. Mostly it was to the local bioscope. Some times, if the man who took her out was a commercial traveller, the evening would not end after the show with a couple of spots in the lounge or in her room. And these occasions would be greatly distressing to Hannah Theron. She had not recovered emotionally to the extent of being able to accept life in a ready, if rough, fashion. She had not reached the stage where she would be able to say, meaning it, that it was not any use crying over spilt milk, and that a slice from a cut loaf was never missed.

The probabilities were that she would never reach such a stage. This was an outlook that was in actuality foreign to her. And because she found that, if she accepted an invitation to a show from some commercial traveller, a bird of passage who was alone in that small town, there were almost invariably strings attached to that invitation, she declined all chance invitations of this description in the end.

Hannah Theron was not promiscuous by nature. But through her having been dropped in that fashion by Bert Parsons, without warning and without explanation, she felt the whole structure of her life, in terms of her own principles and her individual conceptions of morality, undermined to such an extent that she was left with nothing to cleave to. If a man took her out for the evening, and when they got back to the hotel he became importunate in lust, she felt that she had no sure moral grounds for refusing to yield to him. She was a worthless creature, a lost and soiled thing, and to hang on to her torn shreds of virtue in the face of a man's impassioned demands seemed to her a piece of hypocrisy, of shabby play-acting, a pretence to the possession of some jewel which she knew she had cast in the slime long ago.

And yet, at the same time, she was not able to reconcile herself to the realism of her position. She could not accept her situation in the starkness of its logic. She could accept it that from the world's point of view she was a whore. What she was unwilling to accept, in its entirety, was the fact that being a whore implied on her part a willingness to give herself to all who summoned. Whatever she had left inside her by way of spirit rebelled at the thought of her having to yield herself in terms of a promiscuous fornication.

Her mind did not boggle at accepting these facts about herself, that that was all she was, and all she had become, but in the translation of this theory of her position into the practicalities she found that her deepest instincts rose in protest. The result was that, after a while, she no longer accepted invitations from the men she met in the hotel – whether they were invitations to the bioscope or requests to join them in the lounge for a couple of sundowners.

On a few occasions Hannah Theron accompanied Japie Kruger to some local dance. She went only because of his insistence. And there was no enjoyment for her in these dances. She found less pleasure in going with Japie Kruger to a dance than she had obtained from accompanying a commercial traveller to a bioscope show. In the first place, Japie Kruger was several years her junior. She always felt very self-conscious in the company of a man younger than herself. Then, again, apart from the fact that she was almost certain to encounter Bert Parsons and Lettie van der Walt at the dance, which was like a sharp knife being turned in her wounds, it was only too obvious to her what people must be thinking about her and her escort. She could sense what was being said about the fact that she and Japie Kruger were going out together. Two people who had been rejected in love – Japie Kruger having been almost as unmistakably thrown over by Lettie van der Walt as Hannah Theron had been discarded by Bert Parsons – were comforting each other in their loneliness. She didn't like that.

At first she was resentful at the thought that people could be so stony in their attitude. But afterwards she grew to dislike the idea, for her own sake, of going out with Japie Kruger. When they went out together she felt as though they were a couple of orphans who were allowed to attend a treat through the charity of others. She and Japie Kruger were two poor whites of love. And she knew that Japie Kruger was as sensitive about this thing as she was.

The fact that they had both been flung on the scrap heap in this fashion did not serve as a bond between them. They were not knit together by the links of a common sorrow. The fact that they knew the same things – that they had endured and were continuing to endure the same pain – did not draw them close to each other, either in the spirit or the flesh. Instead, Hannah Theron knew, deep within her soul, that she in reality despised Japie Kruger because Lettie van der Walt had cast him aside. And she could not but believe that Japie Kruger must have a similar contempt for her, because Bert Parsons no longer wanted her as a mistress.

On the other hand, Lettie van der Walt had a new kind of glamour for Hannah Theron. Hannah Theron avoided Lettie van der Walt whenever she could. But circumstances threw them together so much, during the course of each day. Hannah Theron could not help meeting Lettie van der Walt in the staff room during the lunch interval. And then she spoke to her only when she had to, saying only the conventional, non-committal things, and always in terms of a cold politeness.

But they had to collaborate in certain subjects. There was the singing class. Hannah Theron had to play the piano for Lettie van der Walt's pupils. And they had to assist each other with the annual kunswedstryd, where the competition was very keen. Sybrand van Aswegen had always asked them to work together in the presentation of a number of items for the school concert. At first Hannah Theron had felt that Sybrand van Aswegen, in making this arrangement, had been actuated by motives of some secret malice. But afterwards she wasn't so sure.

But the strange thing was that, after a while, after she had grown to accept as irrevocable the fact that Lettie van der Walt had supplanted her as Bert Parsons's mistress, Hannah Theron found that there was left only a dull kind of pain in her dealings with Lettie van der Walt.

Lettie van der Walt represented for her a person with superior feminine allure. She saw in Lettie van der Walt the rival who had taken her place. All right. Lettie van der Walt had all the qualities of female attractiveness, of the intricate captivation of the flesh, which she herself lacked. But because Hannah Theron had no belief left in herself, no faith at all in her capacity for creating desire in a man, she had no difficulty in looking on Lettie van der Walt simply as a girl who knew how to win men.

And as she herself, in her own estimation of herself, was somebody who stood outside of this category of women with feminine seduction, it was not hard for her, after a while, to meet Lettie van der Walt in the staff room with the other teachers, or alone in the school hall, and with very little feeling other than that of a natural inferiority.

Lettie van der Walt was not able to understand Hannah Theron's attitude. They never discussed the question, of course. Lettie van der Walt had, at the start, been unable to resist the temptation of preening herself on her triumph, and she had made one or two remarks, subtly galling in their implication, in order to assert to Hannah Theron to her face the fact that she stood no chance of ever winning Bert Parsons back to her.

"I must tell you about something that happened last night," she said to Hannah Theron on one occasion. "It was so funny. I know that if you hear it you'll laugh. Lionel Andrews was talking about a girl – you know Lionel, don't you, Hannah? – about a girl who thought that a man was in love with her. We all laughed. It was really funny."

She told the story. And she felt sorry for it almost immediately afterwards. Only then did she realise, through the completely dispirited nature of Hannah Theron's reactions, that she would never essay a comeback. Only when she had said that thing to Hannah Theron did Lettie van der Walt realise how completely Hannah Theron was licked. She had not simply been jilted. She had been beaten into fragments. Her heart had not merely been made into mealie-meal in the mortar; Hannah Theron herself had been made into porridge.

And it was when she realised, finally and conclusively, that she had nothing more to fear from Hannah Theron, that she would never stage a return, that Lettie van der Walt's attitude towards her underwent a change. Perhaps it was even that by that time things had happened that had made Lettie van der Walt herself feel doubtful about the future. It might have been that what Lettie van der Walt saw in Hannah Theron had made her shudder. At all events, when she understood that she had nothing more to fear from Hannah Theron as a potential rival, Lettie van der Walt relented.

Of course, Hannah Theron herself had not accepted the new situation straight away. At the start there was something in her spirit that had fought. But it was a very feeble sort of a revolt. It lasted for hardly any time at all. But during this very brief period, in which she entertained some sort of hope of getting Bert Parsons back again, Hannah Theron had had all the conventional feelings about Lettie van der Walt that a jilted woman has about the woman who has taken her place. Only, it didn't last very long.

She thought of Lettie van der Walt, during this brief period, as a common, scheming trollop who had caught Bert Parsons in a net of her low, sex-hungry designing. She had seen Lettie van der Walt as simply a heated female who had wanted Bert Parsons to sleep with her. In this respect she saw Lettie van der Walt's blonde hair and doll-like features as weak bits of obvious feminity. She saw Lettie van der Walt as a woman who had used unworthy means for ensnaring Bert Parsons, who would one day come to his senses and return to Hannah Theron, chastened and remorseful. One day Bert Parsons's eyes would be opened, and he would see Lettie van der Walt as Hannah Theron herself saw her, as a cheap cow using a cheap kind of perfume that the local chemist retailed at eight and six for a large bottle – the kind of perfume that the railwaymen's wives also used – and that Lettie van der Walt was using this perfume to disguise from Bert Parsons her body's stink.

All sorts of things like this Hannah Theron thought of Lettie van der Walt, for a very brief period, right at the start, when she had returned from her holiday visit to the Cape and had found out why, instead of going to the coast, Lettie van der Walt had gone to the Northern Transvaal town of Messina. In order that she should be within easy reach of Bert Parsons.

But Hannah Theron's attitude towards Lettie van der Walt changed soon afterwards. It might almost be that, through the very violence of the shock she had sustained, her capacity for self-analysis had suddenly gone into a track where it was, for once, accurate. At all events, her obviously feminine reactions had lasted only for a short period.

After that she gave Lettie van der Walt to Bert Parsons, in her own mind. And she recognised a thing that is almost incredibly impossible for a woman to do – that Lettie van der Walt must have qualities of attractiveness that she herself lacked in order to chain Bert Parsons's interest. It might even have been that the very shock to her feminine pride, which the manner of Bert Parsons's jilting her had occasioned, had also made her realise, somewhere in the unconscious depths of her spirit, that what Lettie had gained was not something that would bring her happiness. There was the spectre of Dulcie Hartnell. It was a ghost that had haunted Hannah Theron during all the time she had been living with Bert Parsons. And she could not but feel that this wraith must be lying in the same bed also, night after night, with Lettie van der Walt when she slept with Bert Parsons.

And so the situation between the two women resolved itself ultimately into Lettie van der Walt having a feeling of something like security in respect of an attack from the rear launched by Hannah Theron, in the realisation of the fact that the serious menace was the tall thin figure of Dulcie Hartnell – Dulcie who was taller than Hannah Theron, and thinner even, and with darker hair and eyes, and with a hold over her lover's affections that Lettie van der Walt could not altogether fathom. She came near making a right guess several times, but the true inwardness of the situation eluded her really, right to the end.

And Hannah Theron's feelings about Lettie van der Walt had soon become almost neutral, insofar as any active rivalry was concerned, and as a woman Hannah Theron began to feel in a queer way inferior to Lettie van der Walt. But, in any case, Hannah Theron had for many years suffered from a pronounced inferiority complex, so that she had come, in time, to make use of this inferiority complex as a refuge, as a dark, cosy region into which she could escape when the realities of life had become too burdensome.

But in regard to Japie Kruger Hannah Theron's emotions were not complicated. She did not dislike him. She had for him only a deep-rooted contempt that sometimes expressed itself as pity for him. But she could not bear the idea, after a while, of being seen out in his company. She did not like the idea of being associated with him in people's minds. Two derelicts holding hands, comforting each other, because both had been rejected. Two stricken creatures cast on the scrap heap of love.

And Hannah Theron knew that if the feelings she had for Japie Kruger were not entirely reciprocated by him, because in a situation like this a man's reactions are slower than a woman's, she was also satisfied that he did not look on her as a glamorous heroine with a fabled past.

But there were also times when Hannah Theron could not bear Lettie van der Walt's nearness. And in those times it was also possible that Hannah Theron was the nearest to being her true self, a creature who had broken out of the clay mould that her introspective self-analysis had made of her – for the intricacies of human nature defy the psychological searcher so utterly. And then Hannah Theron would feel for Lettie van der Walt everything that there was in the world of a dumb bitterness.

These occasions occurred only at rare intervals, and then it would happen in a place like the staff room. And Hannah Theron would know about Lettie van der Walt those things that she was half proud of in the presence of her colleagues, and that she was also anxious to conceal from them.

It would happen at a time when Lettie van der Walt came into the staff room bearing with her an air of silence, walking as though she was draped in a far-off quiet. And Hannah Theron would read those signs correctly. In spite of the fact that Lettie van der Walt had taken a bath, and had put on freshly laundered clothes, and had dripped perfume from a bottle on to her frock and her flesh, it was as though in Hannah Theron's nostrils there would lie, on such occasions, the heavy aromas of the night in which Bert Parsons and Lettie van der Walt had lain in bed together.

There was no gall like the sense of bitterness that would then eat into Hannah Theron's heart.

4

It was a few months after she had been going out with Bert Parsons – towards the end of the second term of that year – that Lettie van der Walt was summoned into the office of Sybrand van Aswegen, one afternoon after school.

Whatever uncertainties there were in Lettie van der Walt's mind before the principal spoke to her, in Sybrand van Aswegen's thoughts there were, if anything, even darker doubts. He had been one of the first of the citizens of the small town of Kalvyn to learn, in the early days of January, of what it was that had taken place in the relations that had existed between Hannah Theron and Bert Parsons. And the queer thing was that he had welcomed this news. He was glad that Hannah Theron had been jilted. That thought gave him a strange sense of satisfaction.

Without bothering to work it out, he felt that somewhere, in all this tangle, there was the hand of God. Hannah Theron was no more associating with Bert Parsons.

When he first heard this story, which was related to him by the postmaster in the Kalvyn Club, a couple of days before the school reopened – for Sybrand van Aswegen always came back from his holidays several days before the commencement of the new term, so that he could prepare new schedules of work – then he felt pleased about it, and in an intimate way, almost as though he were next in line for Hannah Theron's favours. This wasn't the case, of course. And he knew it. All he was aware of was that he had certain feelings for Hannah Theron. How these feelings could be gratified was a matter that he had devoted a good deal of thought to during the holidays. But always the question of making a physical reality out of these day-dreams was hedged about with so many difficulties that he had almost reached the stage of contenting himself with lusting after Hannah Theron in his imagination. But not quite.

And when the postmaster had told him that, during Hannah Theron's absence, Bert Parsons had been going out regularly with Lettie van der Walt, fetching her into Kalvyn by car from Messina at least twice a week, and that those in the know were satisfied that when Hannah Theron came back from her vacation she would not have a snowball's hope in hell of re-establishing herself in Bert Parsons's favours, then it seemed to Sybrand van Aswegen that a new world, pregnant with unheard of possibilities, was opening up for him. The fact that it was Lettie van der Walt, another school-teacher on his staff, who had cut Hannah Theron out with Bert Parsons, was a matter of very secondary interest to Sybrand van Aswegen. Who the girl was had only the slightest sort of significance for him. The fact that she was also a school-teacher at his school meant nothing more to him except that perhaps, in some obscure way, as one sees now only as in a glass, darkly, it just had something more to do with the mysterious hand of destiny.

And then this astonishing thing happened. Sybrand van Aswegen looked at Hannah Theron narrowly the morning the school opened, when she came into the principal's office to report for duty and to receive whatever special instructions Sybrand van Aswegen had for her. And he saw then, right away, that she knew. Her whole demeanour gave it away. She had been jilted by Bert Parsons and she knew it.

And suddenly all the artificial glamour that she had had for Sybrand van Aswegen was dissipated. Just like that. It was incredible. He motioned her to sit down and he talked to her about the work for the coming term. By the time she had got up to walk out of his office, he saw Hannah Theron as just an ordinary girl – like hundreds of other girls, like any one of all the women school-teachers who had at various times been on his staff, and for whom he had had no feeling whatsoever other than that they were persons who did such and such work and got such and such reports from the school inspectors. He just couldn't believe it. Her mysteries for him as a woman were gone.

Take it or leave it, but the fact was that, as a woman, Hannah Theron meant just nothing to him any more. He couldn't understand that. Perhaps it was that the period of six weeks during which she had been absent from him in the flesh, and had haunted only his thoughts, had worked some sort of a queer change in his emotions. He could not believe, altogether, that the mere fact that Hannah Theron had been jilted by Bert Parsons could have brought about this transformation in his own feelings towards her. She was just nothing to him now. All he felt for her was a weak kind of pity.

When he gave her a fresh set of instructions in regard to the school work for the new term, he spoke to her gently, with a kindliness that had a hint in it almost of condescension. This was the woman he had feared as much as he had felt drawn to her. The woman he had been afraid of, thinking that, in the power of the flesh that she had over him, she would succeed eventually, and whether she wanted to or not, in undermining his whole life. He had seen the discipline of his school crumbling under the spell that her body's allurement had cast over his senses. He saw himself going to pieces inside, with no confidence left with which to face his fellow men; he saw his home life perilously poised on the brink of an abyss; he saw himself dragged by the feet through the gutters of the small town of Kalvyn, because he had allowed his heart to yearn after the dark mysteries in the body of a young unmarried woman.

Hannah Theron, without doing anything about it, without being conscious emotionally of his presence even – he had to admit that to himself now – had attracted him as she had repelled him. And that was the kind of attraction that was the most difficult ever to get freed from. Hannah Theron had brought him to the edge of a precipice. She had dragged him into the very jaws of a danger such as he had never had to face before. Through the feelings that he had conceived for her, he had been brought into mortal peril.

And all that was gone. It was as though his eyes had been suddenly opened. That must be what they meant by scales falling from before your eyes. But it couldn't be, this vast and incredible change that had now come over his feelings, merely because Bert Parsons had grown tired of her and had dropped her like a rotten pumpkin.

Sybrand van Aswegen liked that image. A rotten pumpkin was the last thing in the world he felt that he would ever be able to compare Hannah Theron with. She wasn't like that at all. Even now, he couldn't think of her in exaggeratedly undignified terms. But nevertheless, that was what happened to her. It was the way she was dropped that was like a rotten pumpkin.

It was strange that a thought like that should give him some kind of faint pleasure. Not that he felt anything more about Hannah Theron. She did not exist for him any more as a woman. But there seemed to be some queer sort of a rightness about the way she had been let fall. It seemed that there was some sort of justice about life that didn't always strike you straight away, but that with time became part of a true pattern. He must think along those lines some more later on, perhaps, when he had more leisure.

And so Hannah Theron had gone out of his office on the first day of the new school term, after he had spoken to her about her work, and when she had left there was nothing of the fragrance of her presence left lingering in the office, and all he had had for her was a modified kind of pity. He felt about her only as somebody rather bedraggled and, yes, if he had to be truthful about it, as a girl who was slightly dirty.

Now, about six months later, Lettie van der Walt was seated in the chair opposite him in his office, waiting as Hannah Theron had done a long time ago, shortly after she had first started work at his school – waiting for the principal to make reference to the matter of her association with certain men in the town who were not of her class and standing.

"I never presume to interfere in the private lives of members of my school staff," Sybrand van Aswegen announced sententiously, speaking in studiedly measured tones.

"No, of course not," Lettie van der Walt answered. "Naturally, it would be incorrect."

"But there are times when I feel it my duty to offer a little timely advice," Sybrand van Aswegen continued imperturbably. "As in your case, for instance, Miss Van der Walt. You are very young and, if I may presume to say so, not unattractive. And I should like you to accept it from me that what I am now going to say to you is uttered in true sincerity and with a view to extending to you such help as is in my power. I should like you to forget for a few moments that I am your principal. I should like you to feel only that I am talking to you as a friend. As somebody somewhat older than you are in years, if perhaps not in actual experience. I trust you do not take this remark amiss – "

"If you are telling me that you know I am friendly with Bert Parsons, and that you object to it," Lettie van der Walt replied, "then I can only say that there is nothing I can do about the matter. Bert Parsons is no better and no worse than any other man I have ever been friendly with, and if there has been tittle-tattle about our friendship – "

And so it went on. Lettie van der Walt's attitude towards Sybrand van Aswegen was openly contemptuous. The word at the back of her mind, when she thought of the principal's interference in her private affairs, was 'impudence.' She would tell him that, too. She would say that she had as much right to criticise his behaviour, if she wanted to. She would make sneering remarks about his wife as well, if it came to the push. You wait. A light of battle started to shine in Lettie van der Walt's eyes. She had guts.

Sybrand van Aswegen saw that. He tried to forestall the things that he knew Lettie van der Walt was going to say now. But he knew that he was already too late. All he could hope for was to save some shards of himself, if he fought, from then onwards, as skilfully as possible on the retreat.

"Because I am on the staff of this school under you, Mr Van Aswegen," Lettie van der Walt said, "and even if this is a small town, don't think I am alone in the world and unprotected. What you have just been insinuating are low attacks on my moral character. If you will put your accusations in writing and sign them, I'll see my solicitors about the matter straight away. If I find you saying anything of a scandalous nature about me anywhere, I'll have you taken to court for it. And if I find you trying to intimidate me because of this, with my school work, I'll also know how to act to expose you. So far I have been trying to understand what this little interview has been all about. I thought that perhaps you really felt that you had to talk to me like a father in my own interests. I realise now that you are just an interfering old busybody. I have never come across impudence like this before in my life. I am warning you. You have forfeited the respect I owe you as my principal.

If you have anything to say that you can face in court, I demand now that you put it in writing. I don't know whether you have been in the habit up to now of bullying girls on your staff in this impudent fashion, but what I do know is that this is the last time!"

Lettie van der Walt paused, breathless.

Sybrand van Aswegen felt that all he could do was try to run away. He knew he was licked. Lettie van der Walt would never have been able to flare up at him in this way if she wasn't sure of her moral ground, if she couldn't detect in him that weakness, somewhere in his character, which Hannah Theron had unconsciously penetrated, thereby undermining his spiritual integrity. There it was again, the whore pulling the mighty down from their places. Because he had got up from behind his desk on that other occasion, and had embraced Hannah Theron, acknowledging his moral defeat because his flesh had betrayed him, he was unable to put up a strong stand against Lettie van der Walt. His guts had given in. He wasn't able to face people any more with an inner feeling of security.

"You mustn't take it amiss, Miss Van der Walt," Sybrand van Aswegen replied. "I feel that you are young and I am, as you have said, old, and perhaps too old-fashioned to be able to accept the more modern views of life very easily. But you must please understand that I have had no intention of trying to bully you. I have not spoken to you as somebody in authority over you. I have spoken only as a married man with children of my own, and I wanted to utter a few words of warning – "

"More of that rubbish," Lettie van der Walt shot back viciously. "More cheek. Oh well, let me warn you instead. I want no interference in my personal affairs from anybody. Least of all from a complete stranger, such as you will always be to me. I suppose you thought I had a guilty conscience, or something stupid like that, and that you imagined you could trade on it. Mr Van Aswegen, before you make any mistake like that again, my advice to you is first to search your own heart. It must be very filthy, if you can do things like this."

Lettie van der Walt got up to leave. She had triumphed. With weaklings like that, she said to herself, you had to take a strong line. You had to put your foot down, or they would sit on you. There was a hard glitter in her blue eyes. The lines at the side of her mouth seemed suddenly bitten in deeply. To look at her in that moment you would think almost that you were looking at a man's face, and not a doll's face. It would look to you almost as though the brain working behind that smooth white forehead was the brain of a man.

She knew she had said enough to Sybrand van Aswegen in his office. Shortly afterwards she was gone.

Sybrand van Aswegen walked slowly to his car parked on the grounds at the back of the school. He walked in a state of acute misery. He sat in his car behind the wheel and began to feel for the ignition key. Life was hell. If you had a chink in your armour somewhere, all the forces of life would concentrate on breaking through it. The Greeks were right. That story of Achilles. Life attacked you only in a spot where you were vulnerable.

That was why Hannah Theron had come to his school. She was immoral in the sense that she knew she was immoral. And in that she had undermined him. He felt satisfied that Lettie van der Walt was no worse than Hannah Theron. But Lettie van der Walt had not allowed life to lick her. Lettie van der Walt was strong. Hannah Theron was weak. That was the difference. You could be immoral in a strong way or in a weak way. If you were immoral in a weak way, then you were a whore, and you were a menace to any man you came across. That was what the Bible knew. That was Hannah Theron's sin. She was weak. Weak. She did all sorts of things she should not have done, going into life with her eyes open, and then getting smashed down, and feeling sorry for herself. That was the way a whore acted.

And it was the weakness in his own nature that had responded to the weakness in Hannah Theron. That was why Lettie van der Walt could make rubbish out of him in the way she had done. Because Hannah Theron, the whore, had first undermined him. Lettie van der Walt would never be a whore, no matter if she slept with every man in Johannesburg. She would still preserve her moral integrity. When that went you became a whore, and then you undermined and contaminated the soul of every man who responded to you with his flesh in weakness. Who lusted after you in his heart, as Christ said.

Sybrand van Aswegen buried his head in his hands.

"I am ruined," he said to himself. "What did life want to go and do that for? If I hadn't acted in such a sloppy way with Hannah Theron, this Van der Walt girl would never have been able to outface me. I would have said to myself that that fury in her eyes was just put on in order to give the impression of outraged virtue. I would have known that Lettie van der Walt's high-handed attitude was just bluff. And how many people's bluff haven't I pulled in my time?"

Sybrand van Aswegen got home late that afternoon. And before he went into the kitchen for his supper, he got himself a stiff brandy out of the cocktail cabinet. Ah well, perhaps he was just getting old. Taking life too seriously. He shouldn't get so upset at trifles. Lettie van der Walt flaring up like that was just a woman's tantrums. She would no doubt be ashamed of herself by tomorrow morning. Good Lord, didn't he know from the way his own wife carried on sometimes that women were unpredictable and temperamental and all that?

Gradually the brandy began to suffuse his arid spirit with its stealthy warmth. He poured himself another drink, somewhat smaller than the last. He understood about Lettie van der Walt now. She had merely staged a strong bluff that had worked. She hadn't seen into his inside, into that white thing cowering behind his blood. It was all right. Life could go on again, just like before. You'd see. It was all nothing. Just a woman's nerves giving in suddenly. We were all of us more or less nervous wrecks, anyway.

The only bitterness that Sybrand van Aswegen still retained in his soul was against Hannah Theron.

Chapter Eight

1

Hannah Theron did not remain at the Northern Hotel very long. She moved into a furnished room several blocks removed from the main street, ostensibly because it was nearer to the school and quieter than the room in the hotel. Actually, she felt it was too painful staying in the place where she had met Bert Parsons and where she was constantly liable to come across him, either in the lounge – which she had latterly done her best to avoid – or as he was coming in or leaving the public bar.

It was also difficult for her, when she came across people with whom she had been friendly while she was still associating with Bert Parsons, to know how to act. There was Lionel Andrews, for instance. She had on several occasions run into Lionel Andrews, once on the pavement in front of the hotel. And when Lionel had invited her in for a drink, she had not known quite how to refuse. She had the fear at any moment that Bert Parsons would come and join them.

And she knew also that, with that fear, there was a warm expectancy which she was afraid to acknowledge to herself in shame, but which nevertheless coloured the moments of her conversation with Lionel Andrews. She hated to have to admit that there still burnt inside her a flame at the thought of Bert Parsons. And then Lionel Andrews, each time they met, had so studiously avoided making any mention of Bert Parsons. To spare her feelings no doubt. Some sort of idea like that. How foolish men were.

Anyway, Hannah Theron felt that, if she were to recover at all from the wound inflicted on her by Bert Parsons's desertion of her, she would have to give herself some kind of a fair chance. For that reason she had decided to leave the Northern Hotel.

The room where she now stayed faced out on to a garden that was yellowed with the parched desolation of winter. The dried and leafless stalks of flowers that had bloomed in the summer stood black against the world that did not want them any more, and of whose existence they had forgotten long ago, after the last flowers had faded. Hannah Theron felt at home with these tattered stalks. Her life hung in the same sort of tatters. Only she still tried to cover herself with the rags.

That was where she felt that the winter tarnished stalks standing in a hard bitterness in a garden that did not want them any more were stronger than she was. They were defiant and they did not care; they had shed all their pretences. They would be pulled up before the spring rains and the first sowings. They did not look forward to any future summer. In the cold wind shaking their brittleness they had no dreams of a slow life sap stirring, flowing, beating. If only she could lose this useless emotion, this wan thing that was not a hope and that had in it no element of caressingness, then she could at least stand on level terms with those things that did not regret the passing of their coloured times.

Hannah Theron threw herself into her school work with an energy that seemed to her at first to have about it an unnatural quality. It was almost as though she abandoned herself to this thing of work, to this determination that every detail should be exactly right. And there was this conflict about it also, that it was hard for her so to abandon herself in that way. She flung her whole soul into the littleness of the daily round. She cast herself into the details of routine, as a means of escape from life, in the way that a suicide throws himself into a lake, and then finds that it is harder than he thought it was to drown.

In her new life, in that room facing out on a ruined garden, there was a sense of orderliness that clutched at Hannah Theron's heart, at times frightening her with the thought of spinsterhood, a flowering fern and a canary and a cat. And she would want to break away from this feeling of order created out of chaos. She would go to a café a few blocks away in the main street for lunch, and she would go to that café again in the evening, for supper. In her room she had a hot plate on which she boiled water for tea or coffee. And she began to notice, after a while, that she was putting the kettle on to boil at set times. It was not long, however, before she surrendered to this old-maidish orderliness also, without any qualms. As her life had become, so she was willing to accept it.

Furthermore, in the deepest part of the winter, when the hard frost lay on the ground, and the stars looked frozen in those early hours of the morning into which she had lain unsleeping, then it was a matter of strange pleasure for her to feel that, within the four walls of her room, she was sheltered from the world, and that the switch for the electric heater was near at hand, and that in the starkness of a winter's night it was possible for her flesh to feel snug. It didn't seem to matter so much, then, that her spirit strayed so far away from her body, on wounding trails under the chill light of the stars.

After she had stopped going out with an occasional stranger whom she would meet at the hotel, and after Japie Kruger had also stopped taking her out to dances and other functions – something that had begun and had ceased almost by mutual consent – Hannah Theron had few visitors. And she seldom went to visit other people.

At the beginning, when there was a knock at her door, in the evening or late afternoon, she had entertained the hope, in spite of herself, that it might be that one person whose name she was almost afraid to allow into her conscious thoughts. But afterwards she began to tell herself that the wound had healed. That was when it had turned out, with the passing of the months, that the person knocking at her door was never the one she had feared and hoped that it might be. It was never that visitor whose coming would awaken wild remembrances, tearing asunder those tissues that had begun to knit.

And by the time that the winter was almost over, when the spring was just around the corner, and the bare earth bore no tokens any more of the life that had grown too heavy in the autumn and had turned to withering thereafter, it was then that Hannah Theron began to feel, and for the first time strongly, that the sorrow into which she had been plunged through Bert Parsons's leaving her, had lost the bitterness of its edges.

If Bert Parsons were to come round now she would be able to face him.

2

During those months that were bleak with winter Hannah Theron learnt to the full the vicious strength that life has when you view it from the one angle from which only those who are lost in this world see life. She caught a glimpse of that side of life and she shuddered. That was the real reason why, during those winter months of her soul's hunger and the thirstings of her flesh, she had not made application for a teaching post elsewhere. After all, she had the whole area of the Transvaal to pick from.

Now, here is an interesting point. There is no doubt about it but that many more people, men and women, would spend those three years after matric in qualifying for a teacher's certificate if they knew what it involved, other than those materialistic features bound up with shillings and pence and also, incidentally, with pounds. If you don't mind a job that destroys your soul and that carries with it a salary that any qualified tradesman would sneer at, then you have right at your feet an occupation that offers almost as much variety – if you want to make use of it – as an able-bodied seaman's profession. It's like this. Once every quarter the *Transvaal Provincial Council Gazette* carries an education supplement. This consists of a list, extending into many columns, of the vacancies occurring in schools throughout the length and breadth of the Transvaal, and which anybody may apply for if he holds a T2 or a T3 certificate.

Think what that means. Think of this concentrated list of names, each one of which is impregnated with the spirit of the purest kind of romance. And there is no law to stop you from applying for any one of these vacancies. You apply for the whole lot if you like, on the T. E. D. 1 form specially supplied for that purpose.

And the list of the schools, the place names. It reads like a dream. Like the sort of thing Milton, for instance, used to go mad about, when he filled line after line of his poetry with place names. And the geography of Milton's time held nothing as colourful and imperially splendid as what the Transvaal Education Department has to offer in its quarterly list of vacancies: Heimweeberg 255 School, Groot Marico; Jewish Government School, Doornfontein, Johannesburg; Pietersburg English-medium Primary School, Pietersburg, Northern Transvaal; Afrikaans-medium School, Zwartruggens; farm school near Leydsdorp: a Government bus passes twice a week within fourteen miles of the school; Jeppe High School – a graduate who has taken Latin as a major subject preferred – can live in at Tsessebe House. (Were you an Oribi or an Eland when you were at Jeppe High? You don't mean to say you were a lousy Impala? No, you were a Duiker? Shades of Manduell and Vines and Cheeseman, of Candy and Vincent and Ince and of Childe and – don't say we have forgotten his name now – no no, of course not, De Graaff – and of A. H. C. Cooper and Catterall and – but look, what I want to say is that, sooner than being a Duiker I would almost as soon, yes, I know, malo, mavis, mavult, be a Koodoo. Were you there when the Elands were top house and the Victor Ludorum was an Eland? No? Then what are you talking about?) And Rooikleilaagte, Postbag Welverdiend, in the area of the Potchefstroom School Board.

Those are the sort of vacancies you can apply for, if you have the spirit of adventure, and you hold a T2 or a T3 certificate, a degree being essential today for a high school post.

Several times Hannah Theron had got as far as the office of the Secretary of the School Board of Kalvyn, a shortish, bald-headed young man known to all the school-teachers by the peculiar nickname of Klokke. Nobody knew why he was given that nickname, of course. Any more than that no more than a small proportion of the teachers knew what his right surname was. And Klokke had given her the latest number of the *Provincial Gazette* with the list of Transvaal Education Department vacancies, and he had supplied her with a number of forms that she had to fill in.

And he had said that they would miss her in Kalvyn. Everybody would miss her, Klokke had said. She was so bright and so conscientious and so – if she didn't mind his saying it, but then he was, as everybody knew, married and even happily married – so attractive to men. He had also said that she shouldn't allow a single disappointment in love to affect her like that. She should rather go on and try and forget her unhappiness, and in that way she would find out, in the long run, who were her real friends and who weren't. Klokke even tried to pull Hannah Theron on to his lap once or twice, when they were in the inner office together, and the door separating them from Klokke's typist was closed.

But these manoeuvres on Klokke's part did not interest Hannah Theron very much. What shook her was the realisation that everybody in Kalvyn knew her story, knew what had happened between Bert Parsons and herself. Klokke had naively disclosed this fact.

Hannah Theron had never experienced any very great difficulty in getting off Klokke's lap, in disengaging herself from his somewhat crude attempts at embracing her, and getting back to her room with the latest copy of the educational supplement and a large number of T. E. D. 1 forms under her arm. That part of it was comparatively easy. What wasn't so easy was sitting down and completing those forms. Filling them in and applying for some vacancy. That part of it was hard. She didn't know how hard it was until she tried each time.

And then it was that Hannah Theron came face to face with the realisation of how vicious a thing life is if you allow yourself to view it from only one angle. She understood then that it is an easy thing – once you have been so battered by life as to have lost the essential spiritual thread whereby all living processes are joined together – to see that life is only a law, a vicious thing, smooth as glass and hard as steel, and you can't get past that law. Every poet and every artist that has ever been in the world has got past that law: it was his first duty in life to get past that law. But they could just as easily have been bound by that law, which was invented for them along with the rest of mankind. And those of them who in the end were forced to subscribe to that law were also, as it turned out in the following centuries, not true poets or artists.

But these were all aspects of the matter that Hannah Theron did not understand, of course. All she knew was that the law had laid an iron hold on her. You had to work in order to eat. You had to pull your weight or you were less than scum. The poor laws. It was all a machine, and unless you clung to your place as a cog in that machine you were nothing. Cause and effect. You couldn't beat the system. All that. And if you grew old, and you were alone in growing old, who was there in the world who would have you? And that made Hannah Theron afraid to change.

At one time, when she was still with Bert Parsons, she thought of Sybrand van Aswegen – she thought secretly of him and his complaints, his insinuations about her and her mode of life – oh well, what is the whole of the Transvaal Education Department, anyway? If I get the sack from the Education Department, and I can still have Bert Parsons, why, I can get a job behind the counter in Omar's shop. There are several shops in Kalvyn. They need lady assistants. I am presentable. I am intelligent. I can talk to people in a nice way. I can get people to like me if I put myself out a little. And if the white shops won't have me, well, what's wrong with all the Indian stores in Kalvyn? I am as good as the next girl. You can't keep a good man down.

No, but that line of reasoning broke down. It collapsed the moment Bert Parsons deserted her. And what are known as economic fears began to obsess Hannah Theron's mind. And that was the reason why she could not bring herself to apply for a new appointment, why she could not fill in one of those forms that would get her shifted to some other school, in some new part of the country.

She felt that she would not be able to pass muster. She felt that the principal and the other teachers at the new school, her colleagues, would be able to tell everything about her. They would spot right away that she was immoral. They would regard her as a flop. It was silly to think that they would not be able to sum her up from the word go as a woman who had lived with a rake, as man and wife, and who had been deserted by that rake, and who was now a creature who had no right to a job in the Education Department – or to any job at all, outside of a brothel.

The result was that during all those empty months of winter, which would shortly give way to the time of spring, which would in all probability be equally barren, Hannah Theron had not been able to bring herself to apply, through the orthodox channels, for a transfer to some other school.

3

One night, when the hour was already fairly advanced, there was a knock at Hannah Theron's door, in that room in the wing of a building that had once been a boarding-house. Hannah Theron was already in bed. She was in two minds as to whether or not she should admit the caller.

Ah well, it was very difficult. Human company. She craved human company, even though she would not be too anxious to confess to herself either the nature or the strength of this desire. And if it turned out that this visitor, arriving rather later than the usual hour of visiting, should be a man, she had to admit to herself that his call would not be altogether unwelcome. Hannah Theron made up her mind quickly. She got out of bed. She slipped on her dark blue dressing-gown. Barefooted, she made her way in the direction of the door. All the thoughts that assailed her then. Doubts and fears and hopes and uncertainties.

But on her way to the door she made up her mind about one thing. If the man at the door – and she had a feeling of certainty now, that the visitor was a man – turned out, after all, to be none other than Bert Parsons, she would not be weak; she would not be vacillating in her reception of him; those months of trial through which she had passed had been a testing time. She knew now what was meant by a testing time. She would be strong in her resolve. She would let him come inside. There was no harm in that. He would find her, as he had often found her before, in a dressing-gown with no more than a night-dress underneath. But there would be this difference about their meeting now, and that was that Hannah Theron herself was a changed person. She had been tried in the fire. Those winter months of cold neglect. Bert Parsons would find no warmth in her response this time. He would have to go to Lettie van der Walt for that thing he was looking for. And if Lettie van der Walt would not give it to him, so much the worse. Perhaps some waitress working in a café and finishing work at half past eleven would be willing to oblige him. He would learn, and within the first few minutes of this meeting, that Hannah Theron was not the girl who was once more going to provide him with that thing that was going to slake the urgency of this physical needs.

It was with those thoughts in her mind that Hannah Theron walked barefooted across the uncarpeted floor of her room to answer the door. It was a man who had come to visit her. That man was Hans Korf, bartender at the Northern Hotel.

"Oh, come inside, Mr Korf," Hannah Theron said, not quite able to conceal her surprise.

"I was thinking lots of times of coming along to see you," Hans Korf announced, standing at the door in uncertainty. "But I didn't know, for sure, how it was that you would receive me. I only want to say that even if I am only what they calls a barman, I got a heart of gold. I don't mean that my heart is better than any other man's heart, or any woman's heart neither, but I know that when a person has been badly done by, if that person is a man or a woman, or a child even, then you can always depend that Hans Korf is going to take that person's part. Now, as I was saying – "

"Please come inside, Mr Korf," Hannah Theron repeated. It was embarrassing having the bartender of the Northern Hotel standing in the doorway saying all these things that could be heard a considerable distance down the corridor. Hannah Theron thought that possibly, on account of his deafness, Hans Korf had not heard her invitation the first time.

Hans Korf took off his battered brown hat, which he twisted round nervously in his fingers, and shambled into the room. He took a seat on the only chair in the room and, sitting bolt upright, his hat on his knee, tried to give the impression of refinement and breeding as combined with human understanding.

Hannah Theron felt that it was all going to be rather difficult, somehow. There was no need for Hans Korf's having to tell her that his intentions were strictly honourable. She could see that sticking out a mile. But it would be very hard for her to get him to understand that she had no doubt of his intentions; that she knew perfectly well that he was not calling on her in the capacity of some Don Juan. But it would be very difficult to get him to realise all that. It wasn't Hannah Theron's fears that had to be set at rest; it was Hans Korf's. And what would make it all the more difficult was Hans Korf's deafness.

She couldn't, Hannah Theron reflected, very well shout out at the top of her voice, "Yes, it's all right, Mr Korf, I quite understand. I know you haven't come here to rape me." A little speech like that would possibly make Hans Korf feel at home; he would conceivably understand then that there was no question of his visit being construed by Hannah Theron as an unholy attempt on his part at setting up as the Snake of Kalvyn. She would have to find some other way of putting him at his ease.

It was funny though, Hannah Theron thought, how different a man was when once you took him out of the environment that he was used to. Here was Hans Korf carrying on in her room like some unsophisticated yokel. Like the kind of person that she had heard men in the Northern Hotel lounge describe as a 'skapie.' And yet, put him back behind the bar; put a towel over his arm and stick a tray into his hand, and he was a totally different person right away. As a bar steward he had poise, suavity even. Nobody could ruffle him. Certainly not Bert Parsons. Hardly even his employer, Mrs Manning. In the carrying out of his duties as a bar attendant he had an air of self assurance that you couldn't ignore. The way he walked. The way he asked you for your order. Everything about him spoke of something or other that fitted in with a public place, and that wasn't quite human. A kind of cheap aloofness that you couldn't penetrate. A sort of pose that sneered at you – all the more even, when you thought that you saw through the hollowness of it.

And here was this same Hans Korf, no longer the automaton, no longer the slick bar steward with a towel over his arm, balancing a tray of brandies and ginger ale, but an ordinary man, thin and a bit deaf and awkward, sitting on a chair in her room and dressed in a worn suit and nervously twiddling his hat in his fingers.

Hannah Theron decided that the only way in which she would be able to make him feel at home was to take his visit as a matter of course, to such an extent that she would not bother even to affirm that his visit was quite in order and did not in any way outrage the proprieties. So she sat back on her bed, with a pillow behind her shoulders, and her legs curled up under her, and she allowed him to talk on uninterruptedly. The only kind of response she made was by way of nodding her head up and down a number of times, in sage agreement with his remarks, every time that he paused for words or breath.

This way of handling the situation worked well. After a while Hans Korf was noticeably at ease in Hannah Theron's room. First he stretched out his legs, then he lit a cigarette. Then he flung his hat on to the bed. In the end he sat back in his chair, his body relaxed and his head at a comfortable angle.

"It's not for me to have to tell you what they says about you in the bar, or in the lounge of the hotel even, Miss Theron," Hans Korf was saying. "I only says as the man or the woman that talks evil of somebody else must have a good reason for it, and that reason isn't that the person that gets talked of is bad, but that the person that says such things has got a lot more on his conscience than what he would like the dear Lord to know about, if you understand what I mean."

The dear Lord. The incongruity of hearing words like that from the mouth of a barman, who worked all day in an environment where the name of the Lord was uttered only in blasphemy and where the raw material for conversation was supplied by the relations between men and women on the sex plane, everything that passed for wit, that evoked the response of laughter, being merely different (but never new) variations on the same theme. And here was a bartender talking of the Lord in the same way that a predikant would talk about him, with the same assurance, and possibly with a greater openness of heart. Perhaps it was that Hans Korf, being so deaf, did not hear all the things that were said in the public bar of the Northern Hotel, and so for that reason he had not been altogether contaminated.

But this was a question that Hannah Theron could not be bothered with. Those hints Hans Korf had dropped about some person being wrongfully slandered – it seemed a lot as though that person was herself. And it doesn't matter who you are: when you hear that people are saying things about you, there is something inside you of primitive curiosity that drives you on to trying to find out what it is that is being said of you. "They say. What say they? Let them say," may be all right for a man who invents aphorisms. No human being can resist the temptation of trying to find out what people really think of him. The Caliph Haroun Al-Rashid going about disguised as a beggar. You just can't help it. Hannah Theron felt that she would have to go about the matter very diplomatically, or Hans Korf would shut up.

"I have found that in this sort of thing women are worse than men," she announced, leaning forward and enunciating each syllable with the maximum of clarity, in the hope that Hans Korf would be able to understand without her having to shout. She had found, in the past, when she had still frequented the Northern Hotel lounge in the company of Bert Parsons and his mates, that Hans Korf could gather what she said if she spoke slowly and clearly and without raising her voice much, more easily than he could when she spoke fast and with her voice raised – as the others did invariably.

"Men?" Hans Korf repeated. "I don't call persons like that men. I am only an ordinary bartender. Six-ten a week and all found. That's all I get. And tips in the lounge. If you know what I get in tips you'd laugh. That's a small town like Kalvyn for you. Everybody knows everybody else and nobody gives you a tip. The only persons as still tips is the commercial travellers, the new ones, that is. They haven't learnt yet. But the others – I know you won't believe me. They all says, 'Hello, Hans, you still around?' And if I gets a sixpence in tips off them I'm lucky. I can only say that if that is what you call men, well then I don't know."

This seemed hopeless. She dared not put any more leading questions, Hannah Theron realised. If she seemed too anxious to learn what was said about her, and by whom, it would make Hans Korf suspicious, and he would dry up again. And here she was, all curiosity, dying to know what was being said about her. And no means of finding out. Her only hope, she saw, lay in keeping silent.

"Maybe I am only a bartender, even though I am a union man," Hans Korf continued. "But I says as a man that can talk about a girl in the way Bert Parsons does, well, that is the reason why for several days now I have been saying to myself as it is my duty to come round and cheer you up a bit, if you follows what I am trying to tell you, Miss Theron."

"Oh yes, indeed I do," Hannah Theron replied encouragingly, speaking slowly and very distinctly.

"And you a school-teacher and all," Hans Korf announced. "Now, what I says is that, if a man is in love with a girl and he turns that girl up, all right, maybe if he finds somebody he likes better he is entitled to turn her up, but what I says is that he has got no call to go blabbing out all over a bar counter the things he has done to that girl that he has turned up, like he says he has. If you understands me, Miss Theron."

"Yes," Hannah Theron answered, trusting that he would be able to read her words from the way she moved her lips. "Yes, quite."

"If the girl done turned him up in the first place," Hans Korf went on, "well, perhaps it might be different then. The man might get sore and call her a cow and a bitch – you will excuse me, Miss Theron: this is only my way of talking – "

"Oh yes, I understand," Hannah Theron said once more, wondering vaguely, as to how this language fitted in with his references to the dear Lord a little earlier on. "Please go on."

"But I say as a man has no call to going about saying as a girl, and a nice, respectable girl, too, and a school-teacher," Hans Korf insisted. "All the things that Bert Parsons says about you."

The cat was out of the bag now. It was not difficult for Hannah Theron, from then onwards, to elicit from Hans Korf some of the details of what Bert Parsons was in the habit of saying about her, over the bar counter, when he was in his cups. And she knew that Hans Korf was talking the truth. There were things he mentioned that had been known only to Bert Parsons and herself, incidents of which the outside world had known nothing and that Hans Korf could have learnt only from Bert Parsons himself.

By the time Hans Korf had taken his departure, Hannah Theron had obtained a very accurate insight into the way Bert Parsons was carrying on. Hans Korf had said that he would come round again some other evening when he worked an early shift, and there was nothing else for him to do in Kalvyn. He would come around again and while away an hour or so, and try and cheer her up some more.

But Hannah Theron conveyed to him – and she felt that she had left no doubt in his mind as to what she meant – that it would be an unnecessary sacrifice on Hans Korf's part to give up another evening, some time in the future, in order to come and visit her again. She appreciated his action in having come round on this one occasion. She was not sure whether she would be able to appreciate any further visits in the same way.

But the singular aspect of the information which Hans Korf had had to impart, insofar as its effect on Hannah Theron's mind was concerned, was that the feelings she had in respect of Bert Parsons's going around slandering her in public bars were only partly of anger. She was enraged; she was disgusted; yes, certainly. But somewhere inside her certain emotions got to work and obscured from her reason the realities of the situation.

The facts of the matter were, of course, that Bert Parsons was behaving like a brute; he was sticking out his chest, crowing like a cock on a dunghill, impressing the men around him with his rough maleness. In the rawness of sex there is a strong element of the sadistic. It was this element that Bert Parsons was exploiting in his obscene stories of his experiences with Hannah Theron. There was no more to it than that. But Hannah Theron was not able to see the situation entirely in that light.

Hannah Theron felt that there must be some reason for Bert Parsons finding it necessary to talk about her at all. Surely there were enough subjects one could discuss, leaning up against a bar counter, without having to bring in the name of a girl from the past. It must mean that Hannah Theron did not belong to the very remote past, as far as Bert Parsons was concerned. Otherwise he wouldn't want to talk about her. He would have forgotten about her by this time, forgetting her in his newfound love for Lettie van der Walt and in the ardour of his attachment to Dulcie Hartnell, who did not reciprocate his passion. The mere fact that he still spoke about her showed that Bert Parsons could not get Hannah Theron out of his mind.

And the fact that he spoke about her in the language of insult proved that he felt guilty about his relations with her. He felt guilty on account of the way he had treated her while they were still together. He was conscience stricken at the way he had deserted her. That was how one half of Hannah Theron's mind reasoned about the matter. And that was the stupid half, the sensitive half that was caked in dried blood: how easily that wound would start bleeding again.

But the other half of Hannah Theron's mind knew just what the truth of the position was, not in the bleak terms of having intimate knowledge of a man's psychological processes, but through the avenue of a woman's intuitions in these matters – something that is even more stark, even more nakedly divested of the idealism that is in a lost cause.

Hannah Theron had no real illusions in regard to Bert Parsons's true feelings for her. He had in no sense trapped her. For she knew, only too clearly, to what extent she was deliberately deceiving herself, deluding her mind in order that her body should live through another spring.

Chapter Nine

1

IT was not until the early part of the spring, when two more sets of school vacations had intervened, that Herklaas Huysmans once more showed up on Hannah Theron's horizon.

He had been spending the winter months – or so he told himself – in getting adapted to his new school. Not only was the routine of high school work different from the primary schools in which he had spent most of his years of service, but the atmosphere was also different. He liked high school work better. The scholars, he thought, had, on the whole, a brighter sort of intelligence, which more than made up for the fact that the minds of the masters had sunk into deeper ruts.

But during all this time he knew only too well to what an extent the memory of Hannah Theron had captivated his senses and his reason. He had heard at first only vague rumours of what had happened between Bert Parsons and herself. Then he got more authentic information. He knew that she was alone in Kalvyn, that Bert Parsons had deserted her.

And during all this time Herklaas Huysmans had made no attempt to come into contact with Hannah Theron. He had seen her on several occasions at a distance. Each time he had carefully avoided meeting her. Once he turned away quickly into the shabby little passage separating Kalvyn Modes from the printing works. At other times he had retraced his steps, going in a direction opposite to the one in which he had come. He studiously avoided Hannah Theron. It was almost as if Herklaas Huysmans, and not Bert Parsons, was the man who had jilted Hannah Theron, to judge from the extreme nature of the measures he adopted in order to avoid running into her. He carried on almost like a guilty lover living in fear of being forced into a shotgun marriage.

But the reason Herklaas Huysmans acted in this manner was simple enough. He had an inferiority complex in regard to Hannah Theron. He was afraid that if he ran into her he would not be able to conceal from her what he really felt about her. And he feared that she would misinterpret his reactions. There was no more to it than that. The thought of Hannah Theron was like wine to Herklaas Huysmans's senses, like the fumes of old port wine, warming your belly and creeping with mellow acridity into your nostrils. And he was afraid that if he came to her, now that Bert Parsons had deserted her, Hannah Theron would feel about him only that he was trying to sneak into a place that a person better than himself had vacated. That was all it was.

It was inevitable, therefore, that the time would come when Hannah Theron and Herklaas Huysmans would meet. If you have a feeling like that about a girl. When you gulp down a mouthful of night and her body exhales into your memory a fine, sharp perfume, which seems to curl from her in slow spirals. When it is disturbing to the senses, an unsweet fragrance, hesitant; breathing an infinity of unfulfilment. When it is a perfume that whispers of the underneath of life, but lightly, oh very subtly; and in your allowing it to lay a spell on you, but once you say that it is a heady thing, maddening. When you permit your thoughts to become wreathed in the swirls of an uneven drunkenness, forgetting how light this perfume really is; forgetting that, if its depths are those of the night, it is only that no night is much deeper or darker than any other night.

It is inevitable that when you start making mistakes like that about a girl, the sort of mistakes that Herklaas Huysmans made about Hannah Theron, all kinds of things are going to happen. And nobody, try how he may, is going to unravel the secret processes of your thoughts and emotions. It is also inevitable that life will start taking a hand in this affair, and that you will be forced to some sort of a showdown.

And maybe there was nothing more in Herklaas Huysmans's avoidance of Hannah Theron, during those months of the winter (even though he himself was convinced that it was his inferiority complex in regard to her that had kept him away), than the fear of that ultimate showdown.

It was in the early spring that they met again, Hannah Theron and Herklaas Huysmans. And it was a meeting which, this time, neither of them could avoid. The teachers of the district had been invited to meet the new Director of Education at a function arranged for him in the Kalvyn Town Hall.

The women teachers of Hannah Theron's school had been delegated to decorate the hall. School principals and teachers from many miles around attended the reception. The press had been invited, and also ministers of religion and members of the school boards and school committees from the surrounding countryside. And it so happened that in the allocation of seating Hannah Theron was placed next to Herklaas Huysmans.

So they fell to talking. At first only about trivialities. Later on Herklaas Huysmans found himself discussing matters that were of importance to him. They whispered to each other during the speeches. While the new Director of Education was talking. While Sybrand van Aswegen was talking. While the predikant of one of the Dutch Reformed churches was talking. While the Junior School Kinderkoor was singing. While the wife of the principal of one of the Potgietersrust schools was reciting one of Guido Gezelle's poems.

They heard one of the speakers making a pun. "Ons moet lei," the speaker was saying, and then he explained that the word was spelt 'lei' and not 'ly', and there was an outburst of polite laughter.

And during all this while, Hannah Theron and Herklaas Huysmans were making whispered observations to each other. And their conversation did not have more than the remotest kind of reference to the proceedings that were being conducted in the Kalvyn Town Hall, where the new Director of Education was being accorded a reception.

At the termination of this village function Hannah Theron, at Herklaas Huysmans's insistence, accompanied him to his flat. She made coffee. He produced a bottle of brandy from a wardrobe, and they had a couple of spots. And all the while they kept on talking.

And Hannah Theron found, to her surprise, that what Herklaas Huysmans had to say was not altogether without interest to her. She had always imagined him to be a peculiarly stodgy sort of a person, who tried to conceal his ordinariness under the cloak of a forced sort of originality. She was surprised to find that he was in many respects very human.

She also had the feeling that in her company he shed many of those painful artificialities which he brought to light in the society of other people. The way he used to talk in the teachers' staff room, for instance, in the old days. About his conversation now there was none of that nervous affectation. For the first time, after many long months of misery, Hannah Theron felt that she was warming up again to the sweeter things of life.

There was a singing inside Herklaas Huysmans late that night, when he walked back with Hannah Theron to her room. They walked together under the stars that were bright in only odd patches. They walked through the night, talking in the darkness, to Hannah Theron's room in the wing of a building that had once been a boarding-house. And through their hair, the black, straight hair of Herklaas Huysmans and the dark brown hair of Hannah Theron, with a slight wave in it, near the end, there blew one of the first cool winds of the early spring that had a pale sort of fragrance in it, a wind that was cool and soft and yielding, and yet had in it all the gentle insistence of a pastel spring and a florid summer, whose coming into the southern hemisphere would not be denied.

Before the door of Hannah Theron's room they parted, Herklaas Huysmans and Hannah Theron. Herklaas Huysmans seized hold of Hannah Theron's hand and kissed it, and let it fall again to her side after that. Herklaas Huysmans turned away quickly.

He walked back to his flat through the silent country roads alone, crossing the deserted main street, and thinking in terms of singing of Hannah Theron and in terms of practical realities of setting up, after all, as a barrister. He had the qualifications. He had his desk. His law books were all still there. They were dusty, but they were unsold.

And he felt now that he had the confidence, also.

2

But Herklaas Huysmans did not pursue very actively whatever plans he had with reference to setting up practice as a lawyer. He was too much in Hannah Theron's company during the months that followed. There were so many things he had to say to her. There was never much spare time left him after work and in between meeting Hannah. He could think of law and an office in Pretoria or Johannesburg only in the most vague terms.

Then Hannah Theron moved again, into a flat on the first floor of a rather modern looking commercial building. Almost every evening they were together, Hannah Theron in Herklaas Huysmans's flat or he in hers. And Herklaas Huysmans informed Hannah Theron after a while that he was in love with her, and he spoke of marriage. She did not accept him quite definitely: he said he could understand her reasons. Nor did she turn down his proposal. There was between them a tacit understanding that they would wait a while longer. To Herklaas Huysmans, Hannah Theron's answer was as good as a promise that she would marry him.

The process of Hannah Theron's melting to Herklaas Huysmans was slow. One day she found herself telling him about her life with Bert Parsons. And she said that in talking about these things she felt the pain getting healed. After that she told him a great deal of the things that had happened between Bert Parsons and herself.

Man-like, Herklaas Huysmans thought that she had told him everything. He did not know that there must of necessity be things that she would for ever conceal from him. And Herklaas Huysmans welcomed these confidences. It opened a window for him on to a life of which he knew nothing, this talk of Hannah Theron's.

At the same time, because he loved her, everything that she had to communicate to him had significance. And there was for him the external quality of a florid sort of romance in these stories that Hannah Theron related to him, laying bare the intimacies of her life with a man whom she now could feel about and talk of only as a brute.

"When I think of the things he did to me," Hannah Theron said to Herklaas Huysmans on more than one occasion, "then I can only feel that I must have been mad to have put up with that sort of treatment. It was just because I was lonely here. I don't need to explain to you what than means. You know what it is like to be lonely in a small town. And then he took advantage of the fact that I loved him to distraction. He didn't love me at all. He only wanted me for what he could get out of me. And when he found that I would give myself to him unquestioningly, he turned sour. Only a brute would act like that. And so, night after night, he flung the name of Dulcie Hartnell at me. Only now that I am free of the obsession that Bert Parsons was in my life can I see that Dulcie Hartnell is just a simple sort of girl and stupid and cheap even. She hasn't got any of that diabolical sort of cunning that I used to think she had. Of all these distorted views you have freed me, Herklaas."

In these terms Hannah Theron talked to Herklaas Huysmans night after night, in his flat or hers. They very rarely went out, and then it was mostly to a show at the local bioscope.

Once they went to a dance, but neither of them enjoyed it. Strangely enough, neither Lettie van der Walt nor Bert Parsons was at that dance. Dulcie Hartnell was not there either. Hannah Theron had gone to the dance without any feelings of trepidation in regard to coming across Bert Parsons there. She was satisfied that she was cured of him. She said as much to Herklaas Huysmans afterwards.

"I wouldn't have minded if Bert Parsons had been at the dance," she said. "I am sure now that he means nothing to me any more. The hold he had had over me was an unclean hold, based on the fact that he had made me feel low and unworthy and unwanted. He had made me feel, after a while, that I was a cheap slut, a sinful woman. I know now that it was he who had made me feel like that. I had thought at one time that the reason I had felt like that about myself was because I was really a degraded and lost creature, a stinking thing who had to be proud because I could still be of some little use to men, the lowest possible kind of use. But I know now that Bert Parsons means nothing to me any more: no more than this chair here in front of me."

At a later stage of their friendship, Hannah Theron told Herklaas Huysmans that when she thought of Bert Parsons at all, which was very seldom, and then only when something happened from outside to remind her of him, then the only feelings she had for him were a mingled hatred and contempt. She said she felt sorry for Lettie van der Walt, whom she saw every day at school. It was dreadful to think that a nice girl like Lettie van der Walt should have fallen into the clutches of a brute.

3

Nevertheless, at school, although the days passed placidly enough, a queer sort of a restraint had crept into Lettie van der Walt's attitude towards Hannah Theron. It was a singular thing. You would imagine, now that Hannah Theron was no longer alone, no longer unattached, and therefore no longer a potential menace to Lettie van der Walt in her relations with Bert Parsons, that therefore Lettie van der Walt would welcome the fact that Herklaas Huysmans was taking all this notice of Hannah Theron.

Because the whole of Kalvyn was talking about it. They stayed in each other's flats until all hours of the night, people said. And they were regularly seen walking about the streets together, arm in arm, Hannah Theron and Herklaas Huysmans, and you could see how devoted Herklaas Huysmans was to her. It seemed almost as if his long, stooped figure enveloped her, the way Herklaas Huysmans walked next to her, bending his head and shoulders forward so as not to miss anything she said.

Well, the funny thing was that Lettie van der Walt didn't seem to like that. Perhaps she felt hurt at the thought that her having cut Hannah Theron out with Bert Parsons had no real significance any more; that her triumph had become a hollow thing. Perhaps she had the fear that if Hannah Theron had recovered sufficiently from the blow dealt her by Bert Parsons to be able to get a man interested in her again, then she might once more have the guts in her to try and set her cap for Bert Parsons all over again.

Anyway, whatever the reason for it was, Lettie van der Walt's attitude towards Hannah Theron underwent a noticeable change when the story first got bruited about of the attentions that Herklaas Huysmans was paying her. First Lettie van der Walt became reserved towards Hannah Theron in their meetings in the staff room. After that she became unfriendly in a feminine fashion.

But Hannah Theron was now not in the least degree disturbed at anything that Lettie van der Walt could do or say. In some queer way she felt that she was Lettie van der Walt's equal in any sphere of life, including the arena of female competitiveness. In an even more queer way, Hannah Theron felt that she was Lettie van der Walt's superior.

"Would you like to marry a man much older than yourself?" Lettie van der Walt once asked of Hannah Theron in the staff room. "I was saying to somebody only last night that I would feel awful if I had to get married to an old man. I said I would sooner be a young man's slave any time, rather than an old man's darling."

It was obvious that Lettie van der Walt's allusions were to the disparity in years between Hannah Theron and Herklaas Huysmans.

"I have never thought of it," Hannah Theron answered calmly. "If a man wanted to marry me, I don't think I should mind very much how old he was if I loved him. Even if he was an uncultured sort of a man, and he had a kind heart and he loved me and I loved him, I would marry him, I think. But tell me, why are you asking these questions?"

Lettie van der Walt replied at length, and Hannah Theron was surprised to find that none of Lettie van der Walt's barbed shafts struck home. She had recovered to an extent that, even a few weeks ago, would have seemed incredible to her.

4

Hannah Theron was only partially aware of that feeling of pity, of a motherliness that was in her spirit, running like a tight thread through her other, rawer emotions, on the night in which she first gave herself to Herklaas Huysmans.

But Herklaas Huysmans was not taken in. By God, no. He lay awake far into the night, thinking.

So these were the feelings that Hannah Theron had for him. Deep and sincere feelings. The purity of a sweet love and a warm gratitude. These feelings could go a long way towards stimulating the white fires of passion. In some respects they were greater even than the burning ecstasy of flesh calling flesh nakedly, across the barriers of the soul. They lasted longer, too, perhaps.

But Herklaas Huysmans realised also that he might as well be dead. That wasn't what he had wanted. He knew he had been silly. What was there about him that had ever been romantic? What was there in his appearance, or in his personality, that could call out of the depths of a woman's naked feelings, out of the blackness of a woman's blood, that response from the primitive sources of her being that would make him one with the impregnating wind of the late spring, and one with the heavy clods of earth crumbling in the slow rains?

He saw now where he stood. He had made a bid for the things that he had always missed in life, and he had failed. He had received from Hannah Theron all that she was capable of giving him. She had given freely what she had to give. In largesse, in abandon, in a great generosity of heart and spirit.

But there was a portal through which he could not pass. Never in this world. Or in any world that came after. What she had for Herklaas Huysmans, Hannah Theron had given. And she might never know what that was that she had withheld, simply because she would not be able to believe that she had kept back anything.

But Herklaas Huysmans knew. In the fulfilling of his desires there was opened up inside him a pain for which there would never be any healing. There was no balm in Gilead. He would rail at life for this. And sometimes he would rail also, stupidly, at Hannah Theron. But that wound would stay open. That was what Herklaas Huysmans said to himself in the black hours of the night when he lay awake listening to Hannah Theron's placid breathing.

Hannah Theron was grateful to him, Herklaas Huysmans reflected. He had come to bring her solace in a time when she was stricken. And that gratitude she felt for him went very deep.

But he had not awakened the inner springs of her being. In her giving herself to him, Hannah Theron had not been impelled by the primitive dynamism of her blood throbbing in its purple intensities. She loved him, but it was not with the white flame of the flesh.

5

A week later – a week during which Hannah Theron had seen Herklaas Huysmans every night, and he had conveyed something to her, but in guarded and broken terms, of what he had discovered about the nature of her response to him – there was a knock at Hannah Theron's door, just at dusk.

Hannah Theron knew that it was not Herklaas Huysmans knocking at her door. Herklaas would not be around for some time yet. There was some apparatus for a physics lesson that he had to prepare. But, in any case, Hannah Theron could sense that the person at the door was not Herklaas Huysmans. Even before the door opened she was certain who the caller was.

Bert Parsons turned the handle and walked in. He was slightly drunk. Hannah Theron looked at his red face that had grown slightly bloated under the eyes. He looked like a stranger. And yet it was as though they had never parted.

"You must get out, Bert," Hannah Theron exclaimed. "You must leave at once. It is all over between us. You haven't been to see me for the whole of this year. You are not going to start ruining my life all over again. And Herklaas might come in at any moment."

"To hell with Herklaas," Bert Parsons replied, an insolent look coming into his eyes that looked slightly puffy now.

"Herklaas Huysmans is kind to me," Hannah Theron replied. "I won't have him hurt for anything."

"I won't do anything to hurt him either, kiddie," Bert Parsons replied. "He'll never know."

Before Hannah Theron had realised what had happened, Bert Parsons had locked the door behind him, slipping on the catch of the Yale lock.

"If he comes unexpectedly, I'll get out of the window," Bert Parsons answered. "I don't want to make that poor prune miserable for nothing, neither."

"Remember we are on the first floor," Hannah Theron continued. "It's too far to jump."

Bert Parsons opened the window and looked down. "There's turf at the bottom," he said, "I'll jump out from here if I got to, and no bones broken. This ain't the first time I climbed into your bedroom window at night, or out neither, is it, kiddie? Remember the time I got stuck – "

"You must go," Hannah Theron insisted. "You must go. Oh, you don't know how unhappy you are making me. Please, please go."

But there was not the note of real urgency in her voice. Bert Parsons knew that there wouldn't be. He advanced towards her suddenly, and she smelt the whisky on his breath, and he bent his head forward in the act of taking her in his arms.

"Please go," Hannah Theron said again, her voice muffled because Bert Parsons's jacket was pressing against her mouth.

Even as she felt herself yielding, Hannah Theron despised herself. As her body relaxed in Bert Parsons's strong grasp, and she felt her flesh surrendering to his male nearness, Hannah Theron felt the rising up of feelings of intense bitterness against Bert Parsons. She knew that she hated Bert Parsons. And when she felt the hot blood sweeping across her body and beating into her temples, she knew there was nobody in the world whom she hated and despised as much as herself.

Bert Parsons had come striding back into her room, and she had given herself to him in hunger for his body. And that was after she had already given Herklaas Huysmans to understand, by all the tokens that the earth went by, that she loved him and that, some time in the future, when their affairs were straightened out more, she would marry him.

Hannah Theron did not hear Bert Parsons leave. She heard the door slam, but she did not connect it with his departure. Her mind was too full of other things.

Uppermost in her mind were these feelings of remorse. So that was what it meant, being a strumpet, a whore. Just that.

She had not been able to thrill to the love that Herklaas Huysmans had to offer her; a pure love, based on a sincere inwardness. Herklaas Huysmans worshipped her. He wanted to marry her and to look after her. But because the thought of his flesh did not burn her, did not lick at her limbs with white flames, she was able to give herself to Herklaas Huysmans only in compassion, in gratitude for his kindness. And all the time her heart had been lusting for Bert Parsons's rank flesh.

And all the time Herklaas Huysmans had known this. Any sensitive man would have detected it. And he had made mention of it indirectly. Herklaas Huysmans had hinted that in Hannah Theron's response to his embraces there was something lacking. There was no hell in it. There was not that finality of a sensual abandonment from which the soul could never return.

But what had happened now? All right, Bert Parsons had come back. He had come back in impudent confidence. He had taken her and had gone out again, slamming the door behind him.

But there was more to it than that. Would they never understand that there was so much more to it than that? It was inevitable that Bert Parsons, after having left her in the way that he had done, at the end of the last year, with her body still burning from usage and from memory – it was inevitable that in his coming back here, into her room, half an hour ago, that he should have been able to stride right over her prostrateness.

But there was that other side to it. In that one act also, he had freed her from the bonds that his body had placed on her. She no longer hated him, now that she was calm again. She no longer despised him even. She felt just nothing for him. He was not even a stranger from some past life. She doubted whether she would recognise him again very easily, if she encountered him in the street. She felt that she would have to look twice to make sure that it really was Bert Parsons. And then it would not interest her in the slightest degree. Could they not understand that?

Did they not know that she was now really freed from Bert Parsons? Liberty – liberty. Her soul was now again her own, and her body was again her own, and she could give her body now to Herklaas Huysmans without any feelings of reservation. Surely, that was not much of a sacrifice! She realised that in no other way would she ever have been freed from that unfinished business which had remained between herself and Bert Parsons, fettering her flesh to his in all her conscious moments, and in the hours when she slept also.

Well, that hold that Bert Parsons had had on her senses was broken. It was a pity she would not be able to tell Herklaas Huysmans about it right away. It would come as too much of a shock to him. But she would tell him some time in the future, of course. At the moment it would be too much to ask of him, in view of his inferiority complexes, to expect him to understand that in what seemed to be the hour of Bert Parsons's insolent triumph, Bert Parsons had gone out of her life altogether.

It would be painful for Herklaas Huysmans, of course, having to take this fact raw. But he would have to face up to it. And after she had told him this story, and Herklaas Huysmans had accepted all its implications – even the most painful of its implications – their love would be put on a new, clean basis. Theirs would be a sweet, strong love that no storms of life could ever shake again.

Hannah Theron was still sitting in that same position on the edge of the bed, thinking along these lines, thinking long thoughts that went deep into her life, when Herklaas Huysmans came into her room.

That was a good while later. Bert Parsons, in his coming around that evening, taking a chance on Herklaas Huysmans being away, had timed it well. He had not run any risk of Herklaas Huysmans arriving while he was still in the room. There had been no risk, either, of Herklaas Huysmans encountering him on the stairs.

Hannah Theron remained sitting on the edge of the bed. She looked full into Herklaas Huysmans's face as he approached. No, of course, she would not be able to tell him about what had happened between Bert Parsons and herself less than an hour ago. She would not be able to tell him now. But a little later she would. In a few days' time perhaps. She could sense the way Herklaas Huysmans would react when she told him. His face would go ashen and haggard. His long features would suddenly become pinched, the bones showing up even more prominently than now, and there would be a darkness of deep pain in his eyes. And he would be incredulous.

And it would hurt her indescribably, having to tell him that, because she knew now that she loved him with a depth of love that she could never have had for Bert Parsons. And yet she would have to hurt him. But it would do Herklaas Huysmans a lot of good, too, somehow, afterwards. When he had stood up to a blow like that, he would be more of a man. He would have been introduced in an intimate fashion to the realities of life as it is lived by men and women. His spirit would be richer afterwards for that pain.

And in the end he would be able to understand also, what she herself knew already, that only in what looked like a betrayal of Herklaas Huysmans, in her having given herself to Bert Parsons in the way she had done, at his confident summons, she had also made it possible for the last emotional obstacle that had stood in the way of her love for Herklaas Huysmans to be shattered into dust. Afterwards Herklaas Huysmans would get to understand that. It would inflict on him a sense of pain that would last with him possibly for always. But when he accepted that fact, taking it full on the chin, he would be a bigger man for it.

Pain was not such a very terrible thing after all. It was wonderful how much you could learn through pain. Herklaas Huysmans could even, if he chose, try to regard that thing that had happened that very afternoon between Hannah Theron and Bert Parsons as a test of the strength of his own love for Hannah Theron.

But all that would have to be in the near future. She could not go into any part of it now. She was too exhausted. She would have to go on sitting for a long while yet, alone and thinking, in order to recover her own strength. And after that she could help to give Herklaas Huysmans strength also.

Herklaas Huysmans came up to Hannah Theron. He sat beside her on the edge of the bed. Without speaking, he put his arm around her shoulder and drew her close to him. He bent down and kissed her lips. Then, very slowly, he started moving towards the centre of the bed, easing Hannah Theron's long, thin body away from the edge also.

Hannah Theron, gently also, but with decision, disengaged herself from Herklaas Huysmans's arms.

"Not tonight, Herklaas," Hannah Theron said. "I have had a very tiring day. I want to ask you to do me a favour. I feel I must go to bed soon and to sleep. I'll come round and see you tomorrow night. I'll come and meet you in your flat instead. Tomorrow."

It was easier than she thought it would be. Herklaas Huysmans did not ask too many questions. He didn't fuss either, suggesting that he would make her comfortable before he left, or anything like that. She had asked him not to stay. And so he left shortly afterwards.

For a moment Hannah Theron had felt impelled to call him back again, not so much because she wanted him to stay with her a little longer, but because she thought he would be lonely, sitting by himself in the living room of his flat, waiting for it to get late enough to go to bed. But she restrained that impulse.

She heard his footsteps growing fainter down the corridor, and once again composed her mind to thought.

6

Next day, when Hannah Theron again came across Lettie van der Walt in the staff room, she flung a quick glance at the other girl. The tight lines at the edges of Lettie van der Walt's small mouth seemed to have grown deeper. They seemed like two clefts, cut in deep below her skin, imparting a look of singular bitterness to Lettie van der Walt's doll-like features.

Or was Hannah Theron merely imagining all this? She couldn't say for sure. Perhaps that was how Lettie van der Walt always looked latterly, and she had not observed her face so closely before. But it was also possible that Hannah Theron did not merely imagine all this, and that that look of disillusioned bitterness, which seemed to strike Hannah Theron almost like a blow, had come into Lettie van der Walt's face just about overnight.

It was quite on the cards that Bert Parsons would have gone straight to Lettie van der Walt yesterday evening, straight out of Hannah Theron's room, and that he would have recounted to Lettie van der Walt all the details of their meeting. Hannah Theron did not put that past Bert Parsons at all. He wouldn't care a damn at the thought of how he must be outraging the feelings of his mistress, Lettie van der Walt.

The mere fact that she was his mistress, that she yielded herself to him always, without question and as a matter of course – that was enough to make Bert Parsons completely ruthless in his dealings with her. Hannah Theron knew that from her own experience. She had not lived with Bert Parsons during all that time for nothing, without knowing exactly what he was; without knowing that there was that brute side to him that made it a natural thing for him, when a girl's defences were down, to heap scorn on her, to treat her like rubbish under his feet.

What added fuel to the smouldering coals of this heavy maleness in Bert Parsons, that thing of dark sex that conferred on him the delight of power over a girl because she no longer had a veil to hang before his eyes or in front of her body, was of course the humiliation to his masculine pride that Dulcie Hartnell had encompassed through her having dropped him just before he could have got tired of her. Hannah Theron knew how this thing of Dulcie Hartnell rankled in Bert Parsons's flesh.

Because of the unfair way in which he regarded Dulcie Hartnell as having treated him, Bert Parsons could not resist the temptation – as a balm to his wounded vanity – to trample on the body of a girl who fell in love with him. Hannah Theron knew how she herself had suffered in that way. She didn't care any more now, of course. But it took some realising, this knowledge that she was at last free to go her ways, and that Bert Parsons could make no impression on her again for ever.

But she understood only too clearly what Lettie van der Walt must be going through. It was even possible that Bert Parsons was playing

Hannah Theron off against Lettie van der Walt, in same the way that he was undoubtedly playing Dulcie Hartnell off against her. And in that case he would almost certainly have gone straight to Lettie van der Walt's room on the previous night, with the still warm news that Hannah Theron had once more yielded to him. And that he had had no need to be importunate about it, even. He had simply gone into Hannah Theron's room, in contempt for her, in cool insolence, without a word of explanation for his long absence; and he had taken her just like that, and he had put his hat on and had walked out again.

Very likely Bert Parsons had told Lettie van der Walt all this, Hannah Theron reflected. Well, let him. Only, don't let him ever try and come round to Hannah Theron again. He'd get the shock of his life. He would then have two women to feel inferior for, two girls who would shut the portals against the stridings of his body in lust.

Hannah Theron could think of Bert Parsons now as only a pitiful and pitiable creature. Everything about him was so obvious. That yellow streak in him wasn't a thing even of real sadism. The torture he inflicted on the girl who was soft enough to fall in love with him wasn't even as painful as the torment that he was causing himself. Everything about Bert Parsons seemed so silly now. Pathetically trying to besmirch other girls, to heap contumely on them, to strut before them as a hundred per cent red-blooded he-man, merely because one girl had made a mockery of his maleness, corroding the brass outside of his manly vanity.

In the staff room Hannah Theron looked at her watch. The bell would be ringing in a few minutes' time. She wanted to get to her classroom before the bell rang and she would have to stand in the playground watching the children get into their lines. She went out of the door. She had gone a few yards down the passage when she heard footfalls behind her and her name called. She turned round.

There was Lettie van der Walt. Her blue eyes were blazing. But it was in a useless, impotent fury that had no real backbone to it. In that moment Hannah Theron realised that Lettie van der Walt had no backbone left to her own body, either. Her spine had melted.

"I have only this to say to you, Miss Theron," Lettie van der Walt said, and she lowered her voice as she spoke so that her words came out in a strained harshness, "and that is that I could never have believed that anybody in the world could be as filthy as you are."

Hannah Theron turned on her heel without a word and walked on to her classroom.

In a queer way she felt triumphant. She felt no anger. In spite of herself, she was aware of a warm sense of pleasure in the knowledge that in Bert Parsons having come to her room on the previous night, she had won. Bert Parsons had come into her room in scornful lust, and had taken her broken body, and she had been a thing for him, a squeezed out dish rag that he had cast aside the moment he had finished using it, and she had been a lost creature and had responded like a trollop.

And the upshot of it had been that it was not Bert Parsons who had triumphed, but Hannah Theron, who had not wanted to win.

And Hannah Theron realised now that she had won over Lettie van der Walt, also.

She knew in that moment that her spirit and body were one again, and whole.

Chapter Ten

1

THE days and the weeks passed. It was getting on towards the last weeks of the last school term of the year. The summer was hot again this year, but without the oppressive heat, the suffocating immurement of the blood caught in the veins, as the last summer had been. Or, at least, that was how Hannah Theron felt about it.

Hannah Theron and Herklaas Huysmans had made arrangements to go down to the coast together. They had booked rooms in the same hotel. It had been tentatively decided between them that Hannah Theron's next term at Kalvyn Primary School would be her last. She would resign from the Education Department at the end of that term, and she and Herklaas Huysmans would marry in April.

Everything seemed to be going very placidly now. There was a serenity about the future that Hannah Theron had not felt about the future at any time during the past ten years. But the present did not have about it that deep sense of peace that should have been there as the calm following the storm. The passage perilous had not made the port altogether pleasant. It was the way Herklaas Huysmans was still feeling about things. And this was all the more distressing to Hannah Theron because she knew that it was all so unnecessary, and that the things with which Herklaas Huymans was torturing his spirit did not exist in actual fact. And she could not get him to understand that.

Herklaas Huysmans accepted the fact that Hannah Theron loved him. In just the same measure in which Hannah Theron accepted the fact that Herklaas Huysmans loved her. But there was this psychological obstacle to Herklaas Huysmans's accepting Hannah Theron as his woman, as a matter of natural right and as a complete reality: Herklaas Huysmans knew that Bert Parsons had been an obsession with Hannah Theron; he knew that what had existed between Bert Parsons and Hannah Theron had had about it nothing of spiritual understanding, of a mutuality of the soul; in their minds they had not been mated, Bert Parsons and Hannah Theron.

It was because of this bond that had existed between Bert Parsons and Hannah Theron, and that had not been a bond of the soul, but an attraction that was frankly physical in its nature, that Herklaas Huysmans laboured under a perpetual sense of physical unworthiness in his capacity as Hannah Theron's lover. And Herklaas Huysmans had begun talking to Hannah Theron openly of these inner conflicts that were searing into his flesh.

Herklaas Huysmans felt that there was a deficiency in his physicality, insofar as the relations that existed between Hannah Theron and himself were concerned. He believed that Hannah Theron had been brought into his orbit as his woman through those secondary emotions of friendliness and trustful understanding. They had much in common intellectually. They had many of the same interests. There was not that difference of class between Herklaas Huysmans and Hannah Theron, as there had been between her and Bert Parsons.

Herklaas Huysmans felt that Hannah Theron had been drawn to Bert Parsons by the primitive qualities of the blood. She had met Bert Parsons and she had yielded to him, her blood answering to the call of his blood, her body cleaving to his in the twisted nakedness of its own dark understandings. Bert Parsons had come into Hannah Theron's life as a male. He was her man in raw actuality; he also held for her all the *primordial phallic* symbolisations of man as standing over and against woman. The man, relentless in his urgencies, imperious in his passions, demanding by the ancient rights of the blood, love, that thing of the flesh that belonged to him, and receiving from the woman that ancient response from her body, hers soft and yielding, his hard with an unrelentingness.

Hannah Theron and Bert Parsons. They knew each other in terms of something that was older than language. And the only response to a man that a woman could make, when she gave all of herself unresistingly, was when there entered into their relationships nothing of the spirit of tenderness, nothing of the ordinary humanities. It was only when a man took a woman in the hard certainty of his masculinity, his blood knowing that it was his flesh after which she lusted, as his flesh lusted after hers, that a woman respected a man. That she saw him starkly as a man.

And this, Herklaas Huysmans felt, was a world of warm passion and stark allure into which he could not enter.

He had felt for Hannah Theron all these things at his first falling in love with her, long before his first mating with her, and after Hannah Theron had given herself to him he was left with the sorrow of a knowledge that bit into the yellow sinews of his life. He wasn't a child. He wasn't a fool. He knew, immediately afterwards, that Hannah Theron had for him none of the strong undercurrent of emotion that he entertained for her.

But in one respect he was a child. In one respect he remained a fool. And that was in his wanting to reverse the order of the processes by which Hannah Theron had come to him. That was where Herklaas Huysmans stayed a fool. For Hannah Theron had accepted Herklaas Huysmans first as a human being. Only in a secondary fashion had she taken him as a man. And the processes that had been here involved would remain immutable for all time. Sooner would Herklaas Huysmans be able to overthrow the entire physical pattern of the universe, starting with the first and simplest of the laws of nature, and then destroying all of organic creation as it stood in his path, than he would be able to reverse the order of the processes by which Hannah Theron had ultimately accepted him as her man and as her lover.

It was so old and so devastating and so insoluble a problem, a conflict with such hopelessly irreconcilable elements. It was the fight between the spirit and the flesh. Herklaas Huysmans wanted to appear before Hannah Theron primarily as flesh, in the way that Bert Parsons had come to her and had vanquished her primarily as flesh. In the first place there had been his body.

And naturally, in jealousy, in male rivalry, Herklaas Huysmans wanted this thing: that for Hannah Theron he himself should represent also, in the first place, the heavy symbolism of the phallus; Herklaas Huysmans must exist for Hannah Theron also, no less but rather more than Bert Parsons, as one of the Lords of Old Time. If Hannah Theron loved him more than she had loved Bert Parsons, surely then Herklaas Huysmans must be for Hannah Theron more of a primitive male than Bert Parsons had been. He must be for her, more even than Bert Parsons had been, of the undressed masculine animal. A chap. A boyfriend. A fellow. A guy. In more timeworn parlance, a swain, a wight. And, of course, he was just being silly.

After all, in the first place, why Hannah Theron took any notice of him at all was because she was unhappy with Bert Parsons, for her feminine intuitions had told her that he was shortly going to turn her up. And you had only to look at Bert Parsons. At his body. At the easy way he strode into a pub or into a drawing room or into a girl's heart, carrying his great bulk with a crude grace and with an elastic ease. Surely it was ridiculous for Herklaas Huysmans to imagine that he could compete against that sort of thing. It was inevitable that Herklaas Huysmans must be floored time after time, and every time, a knight doomed to inevitable disaster each time he entered the lists. So that the only fair lady who would bestow on him her favours would have been a fair lady who had been through the mill so often that she no longer had any confidence in sinewy, well-knit virility, and had perforce to turn to the sort of knight who hid under his defeated buckler a warm, kind heart.

This was the realistic truth of the matter. And in Herklaas Huysmans's unwavering reluctance to accept this truth there was introduced into his and Hannah Theron's love story, during the latter part of the last school term of that year, an element of strain that was as unnecessary as it was, at times, distressing.

The trouble was that Hannah Theron knew that she could cure Herklaas Huysmans easily. She had the weapons for it. She had, in actual fact, to do nothing more than to relate to Herklaas Huysmans, in some measure of detail, the circumstances of Bert Parsons's last visit to her in her flat, while Herklaas Huysmans was preparing some physical science apparatus in the high school laboratory. She had merely to explain to Herklaas Huysmans exactly what had happened. She had simply to relate the manner of her having gone to bed with Bert Parsons.

All she would need to do after that would be to tell Herklaas Huysmans in simple terms that Bert Parsons meant just nothing to her any more, after that. And, of course, Herklaas Huysmans would accept it. He would believe it. It was so obvious and simple a truth. Even Lettie van der Walt would be able to believe that, as far as Hannah Theron was concerned, Bert Parsons had neither significance nor existence.

Whereas, as Hannah Theron knew only too well, she would never be able to forget Herklaas Huysmans. Not in this world. And not in this life or the next. What woman would ever be able to forget a defeated knight, valorous in his tarnished armour, licked at the first canter, at the first levelling of the lances in the joust? What real woman, that is, would ever be able to forget a knight with a cracked shield and a dolorous mien?

And Herklaas Huysmans would believe her. The whole world would believe her. It was so simple. So straightforward. Let people do anything they liked to Bert Parsons, and she would not raise an eyebrow. Especially not now. But just let anybody try, no matter how indirectly, to slight Herklaas Huysmans – whose whole inside she knew so well by now – and then you would see a thing or two!

And if Herklaas Huysmans tried to bluff himself that that was something he didn't want, that only showed you to what an extent it was possible for a man to bluff himself.

The whole point was that, no matter how desirable the things were, superficially, for which Bert Parsons stood, Hannah Theron knew that in the long run they were of small account. There was Dulcie Hartnell, for instance. What were Herklaas Huysmans's feelings of inferiority, even in a purely physical sense, compared with Bert Parsons's feelings of inferiority – and again in even a purely physical sense – when you tried to conceive of the thing that Dulcie Hartnell had worked on Bert Parsons?

It was all very simple. Hannah Theron knew that. But she also knew that there was no way, just at the present moment, whereby she could convince Herklaas Huysmans, very easily and without inflicting a deep wound, of the ultimate truths of life as she had learnt to know them.

Herklaas Huysmans wanted to be like Bert Parsons. There was really no more to it than that. Herklaas Huysmans also wanted to be in the position of a man who had the reputation of a rake and who could lay a strong physical hold on a girl. Herklaas Huysmans also wanted to be able to feel that he had ruined a girl, that he had ruined many girls, that he had been able to discard a girl and had been able, after that, many months later, to walk back into her life, entering her room with an easy stride, and to take her body as nonchalantly as he would a tot of whisky.

And Hannah Theron knew that Herklaas Huysmans could never be like that, of course. He was too soft for that, too human. And she loved him because he was soft and human. The only kind of man who would ever mean anything to her again, as long as she lived, was a man who was soft and human. She was through with the other kind. God, and how through she was with them! They were the real weaklings, these cowards who strutted in their hour of small triumph and squealed when they came across a Dulcie Hartnell.

Hannah Theron also knew that this was the thing she had to explain to Herklaas Huysmans. And she knew that the only way in which she would be able to drive that truth home, so that Herklaas Huysmans reeled under the impact of it, but, in recovering, would emerge for ever as a man, would be through relating to him the details of her last encounter with Bert Parsons, when she had lain on the bed with him; and when he had gone out of her room he had gone out of her life as well.

The truth as embodied in both these circumstances constituted Herklaas Huysmans's claim to her regard, and her love that would not deviate from him any more.

Hannah Theron knew that it was only in her giving Herklaas Huysmans this one explanation, and in his accepting it, that the pathway of their love and of their future life together would no longer be beset with the thorns of jealousy. Herklaas Huysmans's feelings were actuated by jealousy of Bert Parsons. By nothing else.

And if Herklaas Huysmans could be brought to understand that it was in the very fact of his not having the male qualities of Bert Parsons that he had found the key to Hannah Theron's heart, then his conflicts would automatically be resolved. He would no longer be tortured with those frustrations of the flesh. He would realise that, in not being as good a male animal as Bert Parsons, he was a better man.

Several times Hannah Theron tried to tell Herklaas these things, trying to make mention of Bert Parsons's last visit to her. But each time she was restrained. Out of a fear of that hurt which she would have to inflict on Herklaas Huysmans in acquainting him with the real truth – whereby alone he could be freed and would be able to find himself – Hannah Theron, each time, hesitated.

2

He who hesitates is lost.

There is no real truth in that statement, of course. Any kind of a generalisation is more or less half-baked, including this one. Truth of necessity requires the exposition of both of two opposing points of view.

Nevertheless, it did appear, superficially at all events, and arising out of immediate circumstances, that Hannah Theron had erred in not having acquainted Herklaas Huysmans earlier on with certain facts which she had proposed bringing to his notice. She had decided eventually to tell Herklaas Huysmans the whole story when they were on holiday together at the coast. But she was forestalled by the march of history. It happened in this wise.

On the face of it, this was a sordid little story. But its ultimate significance went deeper than the surface.

Just before the end of the last school term, a couple of days, in fact, before the Government schools broke up for the Christmas holidays – within a week of Dingaan's Day – Bert Parsons again took it into his head to call on Hannah Theron. This time he had not timed the hour of his visit very accurately. Indeed, he was in Hannah's flat less than five minutes before Herklaas Huysmans had been scheduled to arrive. Hannah Theron and Herklaas Huysmans had arranged to go to the bioscope that evening, with the result that when it was Bert Parsons who had entered Hannah Theron's flat by the front door, Hannah Theron had been genuinely surprised.

Bert Parsons was very drunk. He staggered through the door. He took several paces towards the living room, then he collapsed on to the settee. By his attitude he conveyed the impression that he was going to stay all night.

Hannah Theron wasn't having any. There were times in the past – many times in the past – when Bert Parsons had entered the place where she was staying, after dark, in just about the same condition in which he was now. And she had been flattered to think that, drunk as he was, he had found his way to her room and her bed. *In vino veritas.* But those times were over.

"Look here, Bert," Hannah Theron informed Bert Parsons, "I'll give you exactly half a minute to get out. I'm through with you and your swinishness. Go to Dulcie or to Lettie. I've got a man who loves me and with whom I'm in love. Take your stinking carcass and your stinking drunkenness to some prostitute. Get out of here, you rat!"

Bleary eyed, Bert Parsons looked up at Hannah Theron in amazement.

"Say, kiddie," he remarked, "this is only Bert. You know, Bert – "
He rose to his feet unsteadily.

"And I'm not getting out of here, kiddie," he continued, "at least not for quite a good while yet."

He lunged towards Hannah Theron, who was now in a state of fury. Hannah Theron stepped aside, easily evading his drunken attempt at embracing her, and Bert Parsons came to a full stop against a wall of the living room.

He found the back of a chair, against which he leant for support. If his hand had not encountered the chair, he would probably have landed face down on the carpet. That was also a condition of his that Hannah Theron was used to. The next stage would have been, in the past, that she would have started undressing him and getting him to bed.

But it was very different now. She could think and feel about him only in terms of his being the vilest sort of scum, and his presence in her flat seemed to her like an outrage. If she had still been a virgin and a drunken coal-heaver had had the temerity to make indecent approaches to her, she could not have felt more outraged.

She felt in that moment that the only thing that would give her any sort of satisfaction would be to visit physical violence on him personally. She would disengage his hand from the back of the chair (that seemed to be his only support): and as he lay on the floor she would kick him on his posterior.

Hannah Theron wrenched at Bert Parsons's hand, seeking to disengage his hold on the chair. She succeeded and quite easily.

But in the moment of falling, Bert Parsons flung both his arms around her body. Drunk as he was, his grip was like steel. Hannah Theron felt terrified. In spite of his intoxication, Bert Parsons could still master her, and without much effort.

That was the moment in which Herklaas Huysmans walked in at the door. Bert Parsons had not timed his visit so well on this occasion.

The singular circumstance of the whole thing, as far as Herklaas Huysmans was concerned, was that he saw in the posture assumed jointly by Hannah Theron and Bert Parsons – their arms about each other in that fashion – nothing more than some sort of a clandestine embrace.

And acting on the spur of the moment, Herklaas Huysmans picked up a milk bottle that was standing on a table and that still contained about two fingers of milk, and brought it down, with a terrific impact, on Bert Parsons's temple.

Actually, Herklaas Huysmans had aimed at random for the top of Bert Parsons's head, somewhere, and it was just by chance that the blow, on account of Bert Parsons having moved his head slightly at that same moment, made contact with the victim's left temple. It was a shattering impact.

Stunned, Bert Parsons fell against the open window, the back of his shoulders coming to rest on the window-sill.

Before he could recover, Herklaas Huysmans struck him again, this time on top of his head. The milk bottle shattered into fragments, the two inches of milk flowing down Bert Parsons's round and full features – which had gone very white suddenly, almost the colour of the milk – to mingle with the stream of red blood that gushed from the top of his blond head.

What Herklaas Huysmans had done so far was, perhaps, more or less in order. But it was his next move to which the jury, some months later, appeared to take exception. He had knocked Bert Parsons unconscious. Very well. Bert Parsons was lying back against the window-sill, with his head and the top part of his shoulders protruding outwards through the open window. That was how he had fallen, first stunned by a blow on his temple from the milk bottle, and then coshed on top of the head once more, with the same implement. That much one could, perhaps, understand – and forgive even, taking into account the fact that Herklaas Huysmans and Hannah Theron were, by that time, betrothed.

But where Herklaas Huysmans exceeded the mark was in the next step he took. He seized hold of Bert Parsons by the legs and brushed aside the frenzied efforts of Hannah Theron, who sought to restrain him in his own interests, because she did not want him to get into trouble on account of somebody as worthless as Bert Parsons.

Herklaas Huysmans put every ounce of his strength into one fierce upward and outward heave. The result was that Bert Parsons went right through the window and landed, head foremost, on the turf fifteen feet below. (The exact height was ascertained later through measurements made by the prosecution. To the end, counsel for the defence contended that Bert Parsons had fallen no further than fourteen feet and eight inches.)

Herklaas Huysmans was breathless. The effort of lifting Bert Parsons by the feet and balancing his huge bulk against the window-sill, and then bundling him out with that last hysterical shove, was an exertion that lay far outside of his normal strength. Only the blindness of his rage had made it possible for him to have acted in the way he had.

Now he was exhausted and trembling. He was finished. He wanted to cry. He sat down clumsily on the edge of the couch and surveyed the floor. He saw the broken glass fragments on the carpet and the splashes of spilt milk, and the bloodstains.

Hannah Theron rushed to him with a mug of water.

"Oh, you poor Herklaas," she cried, kneeling on the carpet with a hand on his knee. "I hope they don't make any trouble about this."

Up to this moment it had not occurred to either of them to worry about what had happened to Bert Parsons as a result of the fall. It had all taken place with such devastating suddenness.

Herklaas Huysmans pushed her hand aside. "You whore," he said.

"I have been called that so often," Hannah Theron replied, but the tone in her voice was not as cold as her words, "that I don't care any more. You and your jealousies. You and your fear of Bert Parsons coming back into my life, or staying, all the time, at the back of my thoughts somewhere. Can't you see how little I care for him now? Can't you see now, that he means nothing at all to me? I wouldn't even mind if he were lying dead outside on the grass there. I wouldn't bother even to look out of the window to see. That's how little he means to me. I can think only of you."

Herklaas Huysmans jumped to his feet.

"Good God!" he exclaimed. "I chucked him out of the window, didn't I? What if he broke his neck? God, they'll hang me!"

But the next moment he sat down again on the bed, abject, and with a feeling that he was going to get sick.

"Anyway, I'm glad I did it," Herklaas Huysmans said. "I attacked a man who was hopelessly incapacitated through drink, and I have probably killed him. And I am glad. You and your Bert Parsons."

Once again he thrust her aside.

3

The rest happened very neatly and efficiently. The police came, also the ambulance. The scene of the assault was tidied up by officialdom in record time.

By the time Herklaas Huysmans got downstairs, in the custody of Detective-Sergeant Malan, Bert Parsons had already been removed to hospital by ambulance. Herklaas Huysmans was escorted into a waiting police car. The small crowd that collected on the pavement watched Herklaas Huysmans's departure in silence. Only when the car was already turning the corner did a woman in the crowd shout out, "Murderer!"

At the police station Herklaas Huysmans, forgetting everything he had learnt about law, accepted the detective's advice that it would go easier with him if he pleaded guilty and made a statement.

Herklaas Huysmans's statement took up several pages of writing. When he had signed the affidavit, he was conducted to the cells and locked up for the night, the authorities having first taken the precaution of removing his handkerchief, tie and braces, in case he thought of strangling himself.

So little confidence, also, did Herklaas Huysmans have in his forensic ability that he rejected the idea of trying to conduct his own defence. He engaged a lawyer from Pretoria to defend him at the circuit court – which sat in Kalvyn a month later – Herklaas Huysmans having before that appeared for preparatory examination in the local magistrate's court. The magistrate committed him for trial.

Bert Parsons died three days after Herklaas Huysmans had thrown him out of the window. He died of a fractured skull and multiple internal injuries.

He recovered consciousness only once in those three days. During the brief period in which he was conscious, the prosecutor and the detective gathered at Bert Parsons's bedside. They explained to him that he was in a grave condition, and they invited him to make a statement implicating the person who had attacked him.

Bert Pasons turned his face aside in disdain.

"I'm not a police nark," he answered, his voice only a little above a whisper, but the words coming out very distinctly. "I'm going to deal with the bastard Huysmans myself when I get out of here. You cops make me sick."

After Bert Parsons had died, a formal charge of murder was brought against Herklaas Huysmans. The charge was subsequently reduced by the Attorney General to manslaughter. On this charge Herklaas Huysmans faced the jury.

What went a lot in his favour was the fact that he had acted without premeditation. It was all on the impulse of the moment. He had struck the deceased with the milk bottle to protect his fiancée. And there was no direct evidence, apart from his own statement – for Hannah Theron said that her back was turned at the moment when that happened – to prove that Herklaas Huysmans had actually pushed Bert Parsons out of the window, or whether the deceased, drunk, and stunned from the blows on his head, had fallen out. It was on the suspicion that he had actually thrown the deceased out of the window that Herklaas Huysmans was convicted.

Defence counsel made great play of the deceased's condition at the time of the assault. The post-mortem had revealed that there was still a large quantity of alcohol inside him. And the fact that the implement the accused had employed was a comparatively harmless milk bottle – and not a whisky bottle or a gin bottle – also made a very favourable impression on the Court. The defence counsel made Herklaas Huysmans's character look as pure and white as the milk in the bottle.

Herklaas Huysmans was sentenced to twelve months' imprisonment with hard labour, the judge having apparently amply taken into consideration the local jury's strong recommendation to mercy.

On the termination of the circuit court's session in Kalvyn, Herklaas Huysmans – in prison garb and handcuffed to another convicted man – was taken by train and by two warders to Pretoria, where he was lodged in the Central Prison to serve out his sentence.

All the way to Pretoria Herklaas Huysmans cursed himself for having made that statement in the first place. Even if a man couldn't be convicted on his own statement, without corroborative evidence, he nevertheless felt that he had been. If he had kept quiet the whole thing might have been regarded just as an ordinary brawl, in the course of which one of the branglers had fallen out of the window. And here was he calling himself a lawyer. Still, he might have got off worse...

Hannah Theron resigned from the Education Department and left Kalvyn for Johannesburg to look for work.

She got a job, after a little while, in a private college in the centre of town. This educational institution was run for gain by a gentleman who undertook, by a process of concentrated cramming, to get backward and refractory and moronic scholars through the matriculation examination. The job that Hannah Theron got was to teach the different matric classes Afrikaans. The principal engaged her only with considerable reluctance.

"I don't believe in women for a job like this," he said. "It takes a man to keep discipline in this sort of an academy."

That was the attitude of the principal right through. It wasn't easy for Hannah Theron, this job of teaching a lot of misfits, who were, naturally, very cheeky on top of it. But she got by. She stuck it out.

And after a month or two the principal seemed to have become reconciled also, to the idea of having a woman teacher on his staff, "even though she didn't know how to keep discipline."

During all the time that Herklaas Huysmans was incarcerated in the Pretoria Central Prison, Hannah Theron remained on the teaching staff of this college.

Chapter Eleven

1

AFTER a while Herklaas Huysmans got accustomed to the routine of the Pretoria Central Prison. It wasn't that the Pretoria Central Prison was an easy sort of place to get accommodated to. Why Herklaas Huysmans got to that stage in which he found that, even in a prison cell, life was still tolerable, was due to the simple fact that there is nothing in this world, incredible though it may seem, to which the human body, and with it the human soul, cannot in time learn to adapt itself.

Because Herklaas Huysmans was a man of education and refinement, and also to a certain degree cultured, it was natural to assume that the prison authorities would allocate him to some sort of a job in which his educational attainments could be put to practical use. A job in the prison library would have suited him, perhaps. Or a job in the general issue stores. At all events, something in which a fair degree of clerical knowledge would not come amiss.

But those officials concerned with the running of a prison knew better, of course. Herklaas Huysmans was put into the stone-yard. He became No. 3/78 of the stone-pile gang, which did him a lot of good. He sat all day long in the open air on a stone, his corduroy prison jacket folded under his backside as a cushion, in front of what they termed a banker, with a crudely constructed metal scoop in one hand, and in the other hand a flat-headed hammer, with which implement he carried out the task for ten hours a day of making largish stones smaller.

It was a healthy sort of a job, in the course of which Herklaas Huysmans – now known officially as Three-Stroke-Seven-Eight, Stone-Pile – was brought into contact with a rough type of character with which life had not hitherto enabled him to make intimate acquaintance.

Towards the end of the first couple of weeks of his desultory activities on the stone-pile, Herklaas Huysmans found that there had sprung up between himself and the convict on his left, an illicit liquor-seller named Mop Jooste, a friendship that had a good deal of sincerity in it.

Mop Jooste had been in prison a number of times, with the result that he had in the course of time acquired, through observation and through personal experience, a large number of stories of the more seamy side of life – which was, incidentally, the only kind of life he had ever been used to.

After Mop Jooste had told Herklaas Huysmans very many stories, Herklaas Huysmans found himself, one day, on the stone-pile, telling Mop Jooste his own story. Such is loneliness in a prison and the lust for unburdening oneself to a fellow human being. Herklaas Huysmans had only one story. Mop Jooste had many.

Herklaas Huysmans related his story to Mop Jooste during the early part of a winter morning, when the convicts in their brown jerseys were cowering behind their stone bankers to get out of the wind, and the warder, known as Snake-Eye, stood in the shelter of the prison wall, more concerned about trying to keep warm than about whether the convicts were getting through more talk than stone-breaking that morning. So, because Snake-Eye was some distance away, standing on the lee side of the wall, Herklaas Huysmans could talk to Mop without much danger of being observed. He could move his lower jaw and his lips normally as he conversed. He did not have to try to talk sideways, as most of the other convicts did, out of a corner of the mouth that was furthest away from the warder.

Mop Jooste listened attentively to the story Herklaas Huysmans told him of his last year in Kalvyn, of the manner of his having fallen in love with a girl, Hannah Theron, and of the manner in which that girl had betrayed his love. Whether or not his interest in Herklaas Huysmans's story was simulated, Mop Jooste listened to it right through the morning, keeping his hammer and stone scoop moving merely as a gesture of respect to the official authority with which Snake-Eye was invested.

When the siren blew at midday, and the convicts lined up to march back to their cells for their midday meal of bean soup, Herklaas Huysmans was still talking.

"Shut up there, Three-Stroke-Seven-Eight, you bastard," Snake-Eye roared.

Herklaas Huysmans shut up. He also winced. He had not yet got accustomed to being addressed in orthodox prison language. He did not know either as to whether he was more resentful at being called by the figures painted in red on his hat and jacket, or at being termed a bastard. But he had just about got to the end of his story, by then.

The convicts filed into the various wings of the prison. As he came up the stairs to the section in which his cell was located, Herklaas Huysmans observed idly that it was again mail day. A number of convicts were lined up at the section-warder's desk to receive their letters: you could get a letter a week if you didn't lose any good conduct marks.

Herklaas Huysmans glanced casually at the list of numbers on the slate stuck against the wall. He read his own number, Three-Stroke-Seven-Eight. His heart missed a beat. The outside world. Somebody who remembered him. And yet – and yet. . . What the hell did he want with the outside world, anyway? It was much less painful simply to forget that there was such a thing as life outside of the prison.

He went up to the desk and signed for his letter. The handwriting on the envelope told him the letter was from Hannah Theron. It was a bulky letter. Herklaas Huysmans's first impulse was to hand back the letter to the warder, with the request that it should be returned to the sender, marked as unread by the recipient. But he didn't act on that impulse.

Instead, the moment that the tin dish of bean soup had been thrust into his cell by the cleaner, and the section-warder had locked the steel door on him, Herklaas Huysmans tore through the strip of gum paper with which the letter had been re-sealed by the prison censor, and commenced to read the closely written pages by the watery light that filtered into his cell through the steel meshing overhead. His hand shook as he turned over the pages.

"My dearest Herklaas" – Hannah Theron's letter read – " I have no doubt that you hate me. When I was standing at the side door of the court, after you were sentenced, and you came past with the two policemen, you pretended not to see me. Also, when I obtained special permission from the magistrate to visit you in the gaol at Kalvyn before you went to Pretoria, you sent a message with a gaoler to say that you weren't receiving any visitors.

"I want to tell you only how very sorry I am for you. And I can quite understand your hating me. I can also understand that you feel that it was through me that your whole life has been ruined. Well, I accept all that. All I can say is that I love you, and that you are the only man I shall ever be able to love again. And I shall do everything I possibly can to help you when you come out of prison. And it will make no difference to me whether or not you hate me. I shall go on loving you just the same, knowing that you have every right to hate me.

"I know what you think, too. You feel that during all the time when you and I were together that Bert Parsons was still an obsession with me. And that you hadn't taken his place really, and that he would always be able to rouse those feelings in me that he always did. Well, you were right about that, Herklaas. And I can see that it was in that way that I was sinful. I should have said to you right at the beginning that my heart was not free.

"But that wouldn't have been quite true either. Because from the moment in which I had first fallen in love with you, I knew that it was a true love and a deep love, and I knew that I would never be able to love any other man but you for the rest of my life. But there remained in my feelings an unhealthy attachment to Bert Parsons. You won't understand that. It was because he had hurt me and had humiliated me that he had that unhealthy hold over me, for which I despised myself much more even than I despised him.

"Now I want to tell you something that is going to hurt you very much, Herklaas. That is, if you feel anything for me at all any more. If you have forgotten me altogether, it won't hurt you, of course. You will then just be able to say that this proves that you are right and that I am nothing more than an ordinary immoral woman.

"What I want to say to you is that Bert Parsons did come and see me again, some time before that last night when you came into my flat unexpectedly, and all that happened. And that other time when he came to visit me, that time before, when you were still at school in the evening fixing up some science apparatus, and you and I had already made plans for our marriage in April, then when he came in I gave myself to Bert Parsons.

"I have been waiting to tell you about it ever since, because what I wanted to tell you was that after that evening (you remember, you came in and I told you I was tired and I asked you to go back and to leave me alone for that night), when I thought of Bert it was with no feelings at all. He was out of my system for ever. I know that that was the only way in which I could ever have got freed of him. But I can understand why you can't feel like that about it. And so I kept on postponing telling you: I thought, in the end, that I would tell you while we were on holiday together. And then it was too late. I didn't want to tell you because I knew how hurt you would feel. But I also believed that our love for each other would make it possible for you to get over that hurt, and that afterwards you would also realise that that was the only way in which I would have been able to get free of Bert Parsons.

"I should like to remind you of only one thing. And that is that you yourself were witness to the fact that after that thing that had overtaken Bert Parsons, I was quite unmoved. I was worried only for your sake. And when I heard that Bert Parsons had died I didn't feel anything at all. I wasn't even glad. My only concern was for you. And I also knew all the time that nothing very serious would happen to you.

"I have now told you what I wanted to. There is nothing more that you have to learn. I shall always think of you with a most sincere and intense gratitude. When I was a lost and forlorn creature you came into my life and loved me and comforted me and made me whole. Whatever you choose to think about me or feel about me, Herklaas, I shall always love you. – Hannah."

Herklaas Huysmans read the letter through to the end and then, with great deliberation, tore it into many fragments.

2

After lunch, with the weather having got slightly warmer, Herklaas Huysmans resumed his seat beside Mop Jooste. Somehow Herklaas Huysmans felt ashamed of himself for having allowed himself to lose control over his emotions to the extent of having disclosed all his inner conflicts to a fellow convict. For that reason he told Mop Jooste nothing about the letter he had received from Hannah Theron. Mop Jooste did most of the talking.

"What you told me," Mop Jooste declared to Herklaas Hermans, "is only what I known all my life. You can't never trust no moll. This moll of yours what you told me about" – and Herklaas Huysmans felt a strange sort of pride at hearing Hannah Theron described as his 'moll', when all the time he had known that she had in reality belonged to Bert Parsons – "she acted no different from any other moll as what I have ever knowed. All she was after was to get two men to get into a barney over her. And hell, look at what the two of you done. Here's that other fellow dead and you sitting here breaking stones. Don't never trust no moll. That's what I been saying all my life. A moll can't even keep you in bed warm properly. Not even as good as a hot water bottle what costs you only eight and eleven."

Herklaas Huysmans listened with grave attention to Mop Jooste's profound words. He felt that somehow this gaol-bird who had made regular visits to the Pretoria Central Prison had absorbed certain truths about life that he himself had failed to learn until now. But they were truths about life that Hannah Theron knew very intimately apparently, and that Bert Parsons had also known, but of which he himself, until quite recently, had been ignorant.

Seated on a pile of stones, with his folded up prison jacket underneath him, Herklaas Huysmans took what was almost a sense of pride in his condition. He was a man who was doing time because of some moll who had made a goat out of him. Hell, that made a man out of him all right. Or didn't it? His sitting here on the stone-pile, with the warder Snake-Eye watching him. What was he? Well, as they would say, he was a goat. That was the term they used for a person like him in prison. But he also felt, in some way that he had not understood before, that he was now also a man. And he realised that Hannah Theron, in having got him a stretch of time, had also made a man out of him.

There was some poem he had read many years ago. He didn't care very much for poetry. But he had got hold of an anthology of English verse and he had paged through the book on the off chance of striking something that he would be able to teach his class. And he had come across a poem – he had forgotten the name of the author – about a man who had been a galley slave. He described the bitterness of his life as a galley slave, but he had ended the poem with words to the effect that he "had served his time with men."

That was what Herklaas Huysmans now felt about himself also. Never mind about all the blah that got talked about being a gaol-bird, a convict, a criminal, a murderer. You could say anything you liked about him. You could smear him as much as you liked. When he came out of prison he would be a ticket-of-leave man: he would have to report to the probation officer every month that he got off from his twelve months on the grounds of being a first offender and on the score of good conduct in prison. You could call him a hoodlum, a delinquent, an outcast, the scum of the earth, a monster, a butcher, a garrotter, a thug, and you could say that he had no right to associate with decent people. You could brand him as Cain, even. But you could no longer call him a school-teacher. . .

Herklaas Huysmans realised now that he belonged with Lucifer, with the fallen angels. And the queer thing about it was that it wasn't so bad. For the first time in his life he felt a man. He was as good a man as any habitual criminal doing the indeterminate sentence. He was a better man than Bert Parsons. He knew that he had taken a mean and low advantage of Bert Parsons. He knew that he had acted in a despicable fashion with regard to Bert Parsons, striking him down with a bottle when Bert Parsons was just about incapacitated with drink – and then chucking him out of the window.

But in the most secret part of his soul Herklaas Huysmans felt that what he had done, in all its villainy and cowardice, was a part also of life. Take it or leave it, life was like that. Life was like it was, and if you squealed about it you got nowhere.

"I can see you got let down very bad by that moll," Mop Jooste said to Herklaas Huysmans. "You take my tip and cut her out. No good never ever come to no man as has fallen in love with the kind of woman as is in love with somebody else. With a different sort of man, if you understands what I mean."

Herklaas Huysmans agreed with Mop Jooste. Nevertheless, he was pleased when Mop Jooste started relating another story of his own, thereby consigning Herklaas Huysmans's story to the oblivion of a half remembered prison tale.

It was significant also that Herklaas Huysmans did not make any attempt, after that one surrender to human weakness, to acquaint Mop Jooste or any of his fellow convicts with the true facts of the situation that had landed him in prison. More, he told Mop Jooste nothing of that letter which he had received from Hannah Theron at lunch-time, and which he had destroyed and cast into the urine container that formed part of the simple furnishings of his cell.

3

Shortly after Herklaas Huysmans had completed about six months of his prison sentence, a head-warder of the discipline staff, with red tabs on his shoulders to indicate his rank, called round at the stone-yard. He had a sheet of paper in his hand.

"Three-Stroke-Seven-Eight-Huysmans," the head-warder called out.

Herklaas Huysmans rose to attention.

"Put on your jacket and come with me," the head-warder said curtly.

Herklaas Huysmans stooped down and picked up his yellow corduroy jacket, which he had been using as a cushion, and enveloped himself in its clumsy folds.

"He's just fetching you for a special discharge," one of the convicts announced facetiously. "Tell my old woman in Ferreirastown I'll be out of this cold stone jug in fifteen years' time."

Herklaas Huysmans followed the discipline head-warder with mixed feelings. Could it be that the Minister of Justice had gone into his case and had decided that he had served long enough?

The head-warder and Herklaas Huysmans walked through the carpenters' shop yard and through the mortuary gate – so called because it was the gate in front of which the mortuary van stopped when it called to collect the corpses of such men and women as had been judicially hanged – and through the hall into the front offices.

They came to a narrow passage on one side of which was wire-netting. Herklaas Huysmans had never been there before. And he dared not ask the head-warder what it was all about. If it had been an ordinary warder, or even a trades-warder like Snake-Eye, Herklaas Huysmans might have had the temerity to question him. But it was different with a head-warder...

"It's a visit for you," the head-warder announced suddenly. "Put your hat on straight."

So that was it.

"Who is the visitor?" Herklaas Huysmans enquired. "May I be told, sir?"

"Young piece by the name of Theron," the head-warder answered, consulting the paper in his hand. "A Miss Hannah Theron."

"I decline the visit, sir," Herklaas Huysmans answered. "May I go back to the stone-pile, please?"

So that was it.

Ten minutes later Herklaas Huysmans was back in his place next to Mop Jooste, breaking stones.

4

One evening, lying awake in his cell in B2 – the section reserved for first offenders – Herklaas Huysmans remembered something he had once read in *Jane Eyre* by Charlotte Brontë, a novel which had been prescribed as a setwork while he was still studying for matric. He remembered a certain passage.

He didn't know why it had come back into his mind suddenly after all those years. But that was prison for you. The most incredible kind of memories seemed to come back to you in prison, during those long nights when you lay on a straw mat on the concrete floor in the darkness, and the only sounds you heard were the half hours being knelled by the warder at the front gate.

The passage Herklaas Huysmans remembered was about Jane Eyre leaving that man – Rochester, his name was, yes, that was right, Rochester – and Rochester took Jane Eyre in his arms and he said to her (or words to that effect), "Jane Eyre, I can break you in my hands; you are so fragile; but your spirit will still be free."

And Herklaas Huysmans thought about Hannah Theron. And he felt that her spirit could not be free, as far as he was concerned. Always there would be something in her soul that would call to something in his own soul. And Herklaas Huysmans's soul would answer hers. And Hannah Theron's soul would respond to his.

And that was the reason why he hated her, the reason why she would destroy him for ever, also. The reason why she could throw him into prison in this way, easily, carelessly, and still have the impudence to write to him, and to come and visit him even, arrogantly certain that he would see her. (But she miscalculated there, all right. God! She didn't know very much about him really.)

And the reason for all that was simply that Hannah Theron was a cow. She belonged to him, in some way he couldn't quite comprehend, in spirit. But her body would for ever be free. Her flesh would for ever evade him.

For always Hannah Theron's blood would dream of a man other than the kind of man Herklaas Huysmans was. And all that time Hannah Theron's spirit would accept a man such as Herklaas Huysmans was.

Making out of Herklaas Huysmans a mug. A sucker. As they said in the Pretoria Central Prison, a goat.

No thanks. He would have none of that. All right, he had been through a lot during the past half year. But that was all over now. It was a relief almost, this change of being in prison. He felt that the grey walls were protecting him from that life into which he had deliberately plunged himself when he had first seen Hannah Theron as a woman.

And it wasn't only his fingers that got seared at the flame. He had sensed, when he first met Hannah Theron, that she represented the invitingness of the life of men and women which he had not had, and for which his flesh had yearned through dark nights. And in that sort of life the flesh and the spirit were one. And he only got to realise then, also, when he first met Hannah Theron as a man meets a woman, what it was for which his spirit had really hungered during the years in which he was studying law, and during the years after he had completed his studies, and he had gone on being a school-teacher because he had lacked the confidence to set up in the profession for which he had qualified.

But he had found out, oh, quite soon, that in that life of men and women, in that underneath of life, with its burning of the blood and its strong black currents – he didn't belong there. The prison was protecting him. He was safe. He could not be trapped again.

Hannah Theron could not help being what she was, perhaps. But she was a menace to him. She awoke in him desires which she could not satisfy, because it was only in her spirit that she could accept him. They could not be mated in the flesh, Hannah Theron and he. Her body would always go free. Hannah Theron was made that way. Her body could respond only to the strong lusts of men who were close to the raw things of life. When a man like Herklaas Huysmans came into Hannah Theron's orbit, her body had for him only a secret contempt. And so she would eat him alive, like the female spider ate the male.

Only a man like Bert Parsons could come into Hannah Theron's life as a lover and bring dreams and warmth to her flesh. For a man like Herklaas Huysmans, Hannah Theron would for ever have only pity and compassion.

The prison had been a protection for him. Through having gone to prison, and having lain through the long nights thinking, Herklaas Huysmans had learnt. No matter what Hannah Theron felt about Herklaas Huysmans with her heart, her body would always make a fool of him.

At the portals of her body he would always stand in stoop shouldered inferiority.

He was lucky to have escaped her, even though it had to be through the main gate of the Pretoria Central Prison. The gates of the Central Prison did not make as much of a clown out of Herklaas Huysmans as did the gates of Hannah Theron's body.

Chapter Twelve

It was again midsummer.

Herklaas Huysmans had been discharged from prison and had been in Johannesburg for several months. He was working as a clerk for an Afrikaner firm. A predikant of one of Johannesburg's Dutch Reformed churches had got him the job.

One evening Herklaas Huysmans went into a café that was just off Eloff Street, near the Y. W. C. A., for a grill. The tables in the café were separated from each other by narrow partitions.

And that was where he saw Hannah Theron again. She had not seen him. She was sitting alone.

He saw her mostly in profile. She seemed thinner than ever. And the sight of her long thin features had the effect on him, once more, of heavy perfume that comes out of the night. He saw her raise the cup to her lips. He knew it so well, that movement of her hands and head.

His first impulse was to seize his hat and walk out of the café quickly before she could see him. But he did not act on that impulse.

Instead, he took up his hat and walked across to Hannah Theron's table. He hung his hat on a peg on the partition beside her. Then he came and stood before her.

"Hannah," Herklaas Huysmans said.

Hannah Theron looked up slowly, full into Herklaas Huysmans's face.

It seemed as though something was going to start up all over again. Smokily.

Notes on the Text

The present edition of *Jacaranda in the Night* follows the first printing– published by APB Bookstore in Johannesburg as the 360-page first edition launched in early 1947 – completely and without omissions.

Of all Bosman's works, this one presents the least editorial problems. We may suppose that he corrected the proofs himself, carefully and at leisure, for the text is almost entirely without error. Only once did the minor character Lionel Andrews become Adams; the condition of Hans Korf's handicap varied from totally stone deaf to only partially so (but must have been the latter throughout or otherwise he would not have been able to overhear the bar room gossip in the later scenes); the full name of the school has to be the Kalvyn Afrikaans-medium Primary School (as at the end it appears that there is also a matching English-language one in town).

Leading of the spaces between lines was sometimes unsystematic (as it tended to be in all APB books of the time), to the extent occasionally of its not being clear whether spaces between paragraphs were meant to be chapter breaks or not. Here, by beginning text after a break flush left, the distinction is made clear. By contrast, in Chapter Four the text became so jammed up that obvious section breaks seem to have been omitted; here they have been restored, and some page-long paragraphs have been broken down.

To avoid going an extra 8 pages, the final Chapter Twelve was run on under the previous one, but here achieves its correct pagination. In *Cold Stone Jug* and elsewhere Bosman rendered the possessive of Huysmans as Huysmans's; for the sake of consistency that has been adjusted here (together with Parsons's). Rather beguilingly, expletives continue to be represented by long dashes; where swearwords were cut in the 1980 edition, they have been reinstated here. Nor did Bosman italicise Afrikaans within his English-language text; and so here. The final word of the novel, set apart, is in place once again.